ARROWS *of* DARKNESS

World of Arcas

by
B. I. Woolet

ARCASARTS

For permission requests, bulk discounts, or other information, contact ArcasArts at the following address:
ArcasArts
P.O. Box 731
Notre Dame, IN 46556

www.arcasarts.com

Appendix star charts and pronunciations were adapted with the courtesy and written permission of IAU and *Sky and Telescope Magazine*.

Cover designed by Regina Wamba of www.maeidesign.com
Copyediting and Interior Design by Amy Eye of www.theeyesforediting.com

Printed in the United States of America

ISBN: 978-0-9898735-2-9 (paperback)
978-0-9898735-3-6 (eBook)

Visit us on the web: www.worldofarcas.com

First Edition

For our parents and grandparents who held to their vows and held to their faith, believing firmly that death was merely a journey out of this broken world into the eternally glorious one. Thank you for guiding us to the brightest and most powerful light in the universe, the Son of God.

TABLE OF CONTENTS

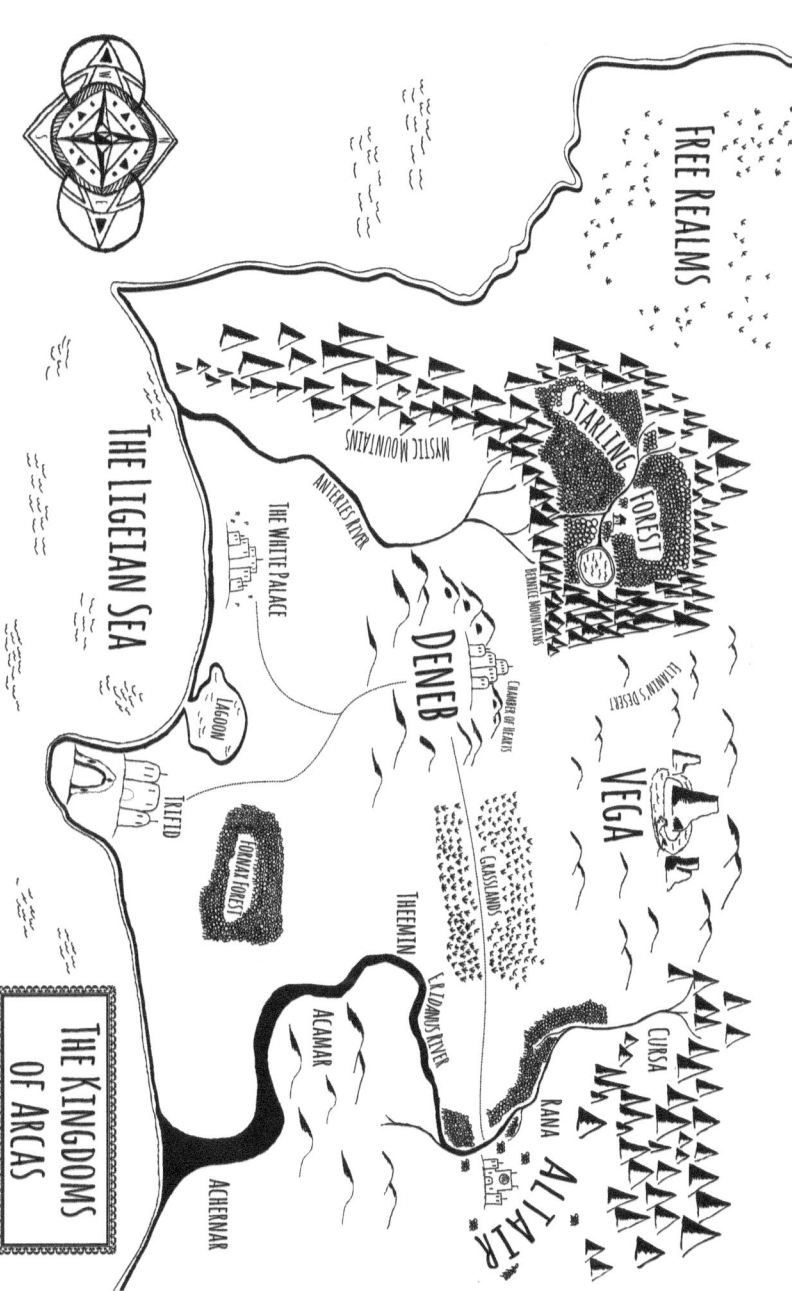

[They are] raging waves of the sea, foaming out their own shame; wandering stars, to whom is reserved the blackness of darkness for ever.

—Jude 1:13

Prologue

Orlund Johannes looked out at the tumultuous waters swirling twenty feet below the falls. Taking one last breath, he pushed against the rocks to his right with the blade of his paddle. Plunging down, down, down through the liquid vector splashing violently around him, he held his paddle straight alongside the cockpit and tucked his body as close to the deck as he could bend. The riotous waves were deafening, but his mind remained clear and focused. He dove straight down, beneath the rapids. Battle raged against the orange hull of his kayak, flipping him instantly. His paddle's blade crashed into a hidden rock pile underneath the plunge pool. It broke, sending the half in his left hand flying violently backward into his lip and nose. He was still holding his breath but now tasting blood.

Watery vortexes continued pushing Orlund under. Like the gates of Hell, merciless rapids above barred him from reentering the world of the living while the waters below beckoned him like an open portal to enter a new realm. Terror and adrenaline flooded him, but Orlund was used to these sensations. Each time he developed a new method of cellular manipulation within his field of biomedical nanotechnology, he felt the same. One wrong digit could cost him his hold on a groundbreaking experiment; one wrong twist below the rapids could cost him his hold on the breath of life.

Orlund felt both powerful and powerless releasing the useless, broken paddle from his right hand. Then, instinct took over. As his chest constricted from the lack of oxygen, he tightened his abdominal muscles and rolled. Orlund's head and body fought up through the current in the plunge pool. His mouth gasped open, pulling in the taste of moist air and blood as he balanced himself above the water. The rapids pushed him downstream as his friend Zach paddled out to him.

"That was a monster!" Orlund yelled out as his friend approached.

"Yeah, you look like you got in a fight with a monster." Zach shook his head, pointing at the blood and bruising.

"Dude, I told you to chuck and duck!" Jeff lightly smirked as he threw a rope from the bank, grateful his friend was safe. Orlund grabbed the rope through his gray gloves as Jeff pulled him to the bank.

The three buddies set up a quick camp to rest and eat before they continued down the river.

The weather this fall was unseasonably warm out west, allowing them to kayak much later than usual. Occasional clusters of trees in this rocky, desert terrain still held the majority of their yellow, red, and orange leaves. Colorful leaves along with tan-and-red-striped rock, and the bright yellow sunlight surrounding them, created a deep sensation of visual and physical warmth.

This quick, early-November weekend trip to the wilds of Utah was Orlund's "last hoorah" before winter's cold took over. Orlund, a man of action and an innovative genius, typically surrounded himself with sterile environments, precise equipment, top technology, and statistics. The wild outdoors was his mind's retreat, and adrenaline was his preferred drug. Kayaking every free moment supplied Orlund with a frequent dose.

Orlund pulled the rubber wetsuit off his arms and shoulders near the chosen campsite. After sitting to remove his shoes and tugging the suit's legs off, he rested for a moment and admired the amazing bluffs. Out of nowhere, a silvery, white image appeared in the distance, blazing with a striking contrast to the red-rock landscape.

"Guys, look at that!" Orlund anxiously pointed toward a natural rock arch in the distance where the brilliant image was standing.

"What's it this time?" Zach asked, uninterested.

Orlund's antics and jokes wore thin after a while. He wouldn't fall for his friend's convincing emotional hype this time.

"Dude, quit playing around and help get the fire started," Jeff added.

"No, I'm dead serious. I couldn't make this up! There is a man with huge white wings up that hill by the arch. He just appeared dragging a kid along with him."

"Your paddle hit you good, huh?" Zach wasn't buying it and wasn't looking up. "A man wearing wings. Poor guy just missed trick-or-treating in the desert."

"Ha! Funny, Zach. Let's see, the storyteller has threatened us with tales of bears and water snakes and cave dragons before, but a drag queen in the desert might be his scariest tale yet!"

Rather than laugh or reply with a sly remark, Orlund continued to stare at the arch. Faint voices echoed off the canyon lands until Jeff and Zach casually looked up to see where the noises were coming from.

"What the!" Jeff exclaimed.

"I told you. That man has wings." Orlund scrambled to his feet and grabbed his dry pack concealing his pistol and phone. "I'm going up there. I think the kid is injured."

The arch faded out of sight as they climbed the steep bank. When the huge, curved landmark came back into view, no one was there.

"Where are they?" Zach scanned the uneven terrain.

"Maybe it was just a large bird?" Jeff reasoned.

"No. That man definitely had hands and legs. Feathers, yes, but no beak." Orlund continued, unraveling his black .44 Magnum and phone from the waterproof layers.

"Dude, seriously?" Jeff looked at his armed friend, preparing to fight the vanished villain.

"It could have been a Native American ritual costume! Maybe the boy was starting a coming-of-age ceremony. There's a reservation up north." Zach would often bring up Native American culture. He claimed to be some sort of expert because his great-great grandfather was supposedly a full-blooded Cherokee.

"No way, that bird man was even whiter than you are," Orlund teased.

"Hey, I'm not totally white," Zach protested.

"Believe what you want, man, but one-sixteenth Native American wasn't enough to get you a scholarship, and it really isn't enough to claim you're a minority," Jeff jumped in.

"Whatever. You'd both claim me as a Native American in a second if it got us another research grant."

"That's right, Tonto," Orlund agreed with a smile.

The three reached the base of the huge arch towering before them. The canyons lay quiet. A few birds flew high in the distance and several rodents scurried in the valleys below, but no humans moved within sight.

"There's nothing here. We're just hungry." Jeff turned to walk back to the river. "Let's go eat."

"Wait! We walked all this way. Let's at least get a picture under the arch."

"I'll take one of you guys first." Orlund replaced his pistol in the dry pack and grabbed his phone. "Step back a little so you're right under it." The young scientist took several rapid shots with the tap of his finger.

Suddenly, Jeff and Zach disappeared from the frame on his phone. When he looked up, the arch appeared empty, though strange, colorful heat waves seemed to be dancing within it.

"Did you guys find something?" Orlund walked under the arch expecting to see his friends on the other side of the natural rock columns, but he saw much more.

Orlund joined his paralyzed companions as they witnessed a black horse and rider gallop, then dive off a cliff to their left into the ocean below. A bear, woman, and man ran from the scene and climbed up and over the white fortress walls.

"Someone is hurt!" Jeff alerted. As a former battlefield surgeon, he instinctively ran forward followed by the other two.

Nothing could prepare them to see the dead body in front of them. Blood pooled around and on top of the corpse with a severed stump at the end of his arm and a large hole through his chest. A second lifeless body was lying nearby.

"What is this place?" Orlund grabbed his .44. White-winged flags waved in the sunlight on top of the fortress while the sound of horns and shouting echoed beyond the walls. Suddenly, soldiers, wearing red tunics with white wings and three suns, streamed into the large courtyard in front of the seaside peninsula.

"There! At The Bridge!" Soldiers shouted. "Those Earthians killed Sulafat! Find White Wings!" Threats, commands, and accusations exploded through the air as otherworldly troops stampeded toward the confused travelers.

Orlund dropped his gun in alarm, terrified they would arrest him for murder. Dead bodies, angry allegations, and sword-wielding soldiers devoured the three friends with panic. They bolted frantically back through The Bridge. In moments, they were in the familiar canyons just past the arch. They raced over rocky mounds and down steep valleys. Stopping to breathe or look behind weren't luxuries they couldn't afford. Frenzied upon reaching the campsite, they threw together only essential gear, grabbed their kayaks, and slid back into the safety of the white rapids.

The vivid visions of the dead, the strange creatures, and the great white fortress haunted their well-educated minds while riding away on the river. For their safety and sanity, the friends swore each other to secrecy. Once safely back in the company's private jet, they headed to the Pacific Coast. A quick medical-tech innovations seminar and then a day of calm ocean kayaking would clear their troubled thoughts. But the extraordinary world they had wandered into was going to collide again with them soon, for the ocean tides were slowly pushing a creature to shore, a creature that didn't belong to Earth.

Chapter 1

The Split and the Stone

Jackson held his sword firmly with both hands. *Chop! Chop! Swing! Hack!* With speed, precision, and strength, he cut his way through the jungle using only the princess's voice to guide him. As soon as he heard Andi was captured, Jackson grabbed a sword and took off in pursuit.

> *Queen Cassiopeia,*
> *The princess for the crown jewels.*
> *Yours Dually - The Gemini*

Though the queen and her men stood paralyzed by the surprise abduction note left on Andi's vanity, Jackson ignited into action. He refused to let the wretched thieves get away, especially when he'd traveled so far to see her again. The thick jungle and menacing Gemini were no match for his courage and resolve to rescue the princess.

The Gemini were twin brothers, a notorious bandit duo who hid out in the eastern wastelands past the Eridanus

River. Legend told that the Gemini moved so quickly they could enter and exit a dwelling before the front door ever creaked on its hinge.

"Don't worry, little princess." One of the men suddenly appeared next to Andi's face on the right.

"Yeah, little princess," the other agreed, appearing on the left. "If dear Mommy doesn't pay today…"

"I'm sure dear Daddy will pay tomorrow," he finished as both twins erupted into rumbling laughter.

"Oh, you'll get your pay alright," Andromeda threatened, proudly looking straight ahead as if she weren't bothered by the criminals breathing down each side of her neck. "When you're swinging at the end of a rope!"

"Dear Mommy and Daddy can't swing us if they can't…"

"Can't catch us!" the twin echoed.

Jackson crouched low behind a large fern, watching the Gemini laugh, taunt, and show-off their unique skills to the princess by rocketing from tree to tree. Distracted by their hubris, it was the perfect time for Jackson to act. He slid behind the tree Andi was tied to and softly squeezed her hand.

"I'm getting you out of here," Jackson whispered, sawing away at her binds.

"Jackson, is that really you?" Andi sighed with relief and excitement. "Watch out behind you!"

Jackson spun around, swinging the sword in defense as

one twin zoomed at him. In an instant, the other Gemini appeared. Without a moment for thought, the Son of Earth clashed his sword back and forth against each attack.

"Ahhh-a-ahhh!" A Tarzan holler flew through the jungle as a giant, camouflaged Ursa swung down from the trees and shoved his clawed feet into both of the twins. The thieving thugs fell down into each other. Jackson crouched over the twins and placed his long blade across both identical necks.

"You have two choices, boys." Jackson bargained as Otava joined him, bearing his teeth. "Get eaten by this bear today, or run far, far away and live to see tomorrow."

"We'll run fast!"

"Yeah, we'll run fast, fast away." They agreed with fearful, wide eyes.

"Then go." Jackson removed the sword. "Now!" The Gemini ran and ran and ran like they'd never run before as the giant bear roared loudly, shaking the jungle around them.

Jackson quickly cut the rope that bound Andromeda. She ran into his arms and they embraced.

"I didn't know if anyone would come, Jackson. I thought you returned to Earth."

"I couldn't stay there—not when *you* were here." Jackson brushed a wisp of hair away from her eyes.

And just as before in the cool caves of Deneb, the two teens gazed into each other's eyes and...

Chush. Chush. Chush. Snap!

Jackson immediately stopped looking at Andi and turned toward the approaching noise in the woods.

"I thought I'd find you here," Matthew interrupted the daydream. Trying to sound upbeat, the younger brother pried a half smile from his mouth. Forty acres of woods filled the world behind their house and Farmer John's next door, but Matthew knew Jackson would most likely be sitting here on a bench in the clearing.

"Yeah. I just had to get out of the house for a bit." Jackson put down his pencil, took one last glance at the beautiful Andromeda, then quickly closed the sketch book. He didn't want to explain to his younger brother why the girl he drew was tied to a tree. Such old-fashioned romance scenes may be enjoyable alone but feel embarrassing, or slightly creepy, when discovered by others.

"You done packing?" Jackson asked solemnly, looking up to assess his brother's condition.

Matt nodded while slowly walking up and sitting on the adjacent bench angled toward the large rock fire pit. Since Jackson had been working for Farmer John a few days a week, it wasn't hard convincing his parents to let him stay. But his brother had no such voice in the matter. Jackson felt guilty that he had a choice as he watched Matt pick up a twig and methodically snap it in half. He continued to break the two halves in half until he had sixteen little pieces of almost-equal parts. Water began welling up in his eyes again, so the eleven-year-old boy silently focused on the twig pile in front of him. He arranged the first layer in a square with parallel pieces overlapping those underneath to create a tiny log cabin effect. When all sixteen parts were used and the little square cabin was still standing, he bent down to grab another twig, cracking it in halves again to build the structure higher.

"I'm sorry, man" was all Jackson could manage to release through the knots in his throat.

Matt nodded a small recognition of the sentiment, but he couldn't talk. If he opened his mouth, the bubbling magma of emotion he kept swallowing down would erupt into a sobbing mess of destruction across his face. Matt didn't want to lose his cool in front of his older brother. And he didn't want his mom or dad or little sister to see the evidence of him crying.

As the oldest in the family, Jackson wanted to say, "Everything's going to be okay. You'll be back before you know it! Mom and Dad will work things out." He wanted to say those things. He wanted to breathe hope into the situation, but he couldn't get the words to come out. Each wishful phrase felt somehow false. Like saying at a funeral, "Don't be sad, they're at peace now," or "Don't worry, you will see them again some day." Such words are meant to lighten the pain, but some pain is too heavy to lift. Some pain is meant to be felt. And nothing you say changes the fact that death still sucks. Death sucks. Divorce sucks.

Oh, sorry, Mom! Did I say that wrong? Jackson sarcastically asked himself the questions that he would never verbalize out loud. *It's just a little separation for the summer, right?*

"Jackson! Matthew!" their dad called from the back porch.

Both boys froze, staring at the ground. The smooth seventy-degree weather with clear skies and a soft breeze should be the type of early summer weather to fill the hearts of the young with energy and adventure, but in their hearts, it was thirty-five degrees and raining. For the brothers, it was neither cold enough to see the beauty of the snow nor warm enough to dance in the rain. Outside, all was green and life and warmth, but in the depths of their souls, it was damp and cold and ugly.

Matt flung the back of his hand into the tiny stick cabin as he stood, sending it flying to the grass below in scattered, separate pieces. Jackson stood as well and silently followed his brother toward the house. Mom was already in the driveway, trying to coax the littlest in the family, Maddie, to give up the treasure in her hands.

"That sketchbook belongs to Jackson, Maddie," she reasoned, bending down to the kindergartener's level. "You can't take that with you to Grandma's house, okay?"

Lori didn't want to cause a scene. Over the last uncomfortable weeks waiting for school to end for the children, she worked hard to convince the family that traveling back to her parents' house for the summer with the two youngest was the confident and rational choice. The last thing she wanted was for a well of emotions to overflow on the way out of the driveway. She wasn't going to give her husband an opportunity to say, "I told you. Look at what you're doing to our family, our children. What are you thinking?" Nothing was going to guilt her, and nothing was going to change her mind. She felt empty and cold. She needed time away from her husband, away from the stale routine. And now was the best time to withdraw.

Matt shuffled his feet through the grass, watching his tennis shoes move painfully forward. His muscles walked in conflict with his bones that wanted to run back far into the woods and hide until this whole mess blew over. When he reached his dad, Tim put his firm arms around his son and hugged him. Matt stood limp in the moment like a puppet who had given up trying to walk on his own because he knows other forces are controlling the strings. His dad finished the embrace and ruffled the top of Matt's brown hair.

"Take care of your mom and sister, okay? You're going to be the man of the house over there. Help Grandpa out, okay?"

"Okay," Matt agreed, then walked straight for the car, sat on the passenger seat, and shoved headphones into his ears. He closed his eyes and rested his head against the seat, wishing he could sit in the back. Matt didn't want to talk to his mom during the forty-five-minute drive. The front was too close to her, but the back was covered with bags and suitcases next to his sister's booster seat.

"What's wrong, Maddie?" Jackson kneeled down on the grass near the driveway.

"Mom doesn't want me to take your book, but I want to!" Maddie wasn't loosening her grip.

"You can take it with you. Tell Matt to read it to you, okay?" Jackson smiled warmly. Maddie kept hold of the sketchbook as she jumped full force into Jackson's arms, nearly causing him to lose his balance. Dad was right behind, waiting for a hug from his little girl.

"I'll see you soon, baby, okay?" Tim lifted her up in his arms.

Okay—it was the one word we all could agree upon and the one lie that nobody believed.

"Bye, Jackson." His mom walked over and hugged him. "I love you." Now taller and broader than his mother, Jackson stood stiff and gave a half-hearted pat on her back in return. She turned swiftly and slid into the driver's seat while her husband buckled Maddie in.

While over half of his family drove away, Jackson turned and walked briskly back into the woods. Well hidden by the thick, growing greenery around him, the tears finally streamed down uncontrollably. The liquid sorrow continued to fall as he picked up a stick and whacked it furiously against a tree over and over again until it broke.

He was angry. Angry at his dad for not fighting harder to keep the family together. Angry at his mom for leaving. Over and over again, he blamed the stress of his autumn disappearance on the split. If he caused it, perhaps he could fix it again, right? But deep down, Jackson knew his parents were barely functioning together even before he was thrown into Arcas. Exhausted, he cast the tattered stick to the side and collapsed to his knees.

"Ow! Aag!" Jackson grunted in startled pain. His knees had not landed on the soft, rich soil as he expected. Something stiff and hard sent painful shocks through his bones instead. Normally, he wouldn't pay much attention to a rock underneath him. But this rock felt oddly large and flat, so he pushed aside the grass and weeds smashed on top to examine it. Jackson then peeled up a thin layer of decomposed leaves and dirt. *Stars?* Jackson wondered at seeing the familiar shape carved into the homemade stepping-stone. His eyes grew wide and his heart began to pound. Quickly, he scraped the rest of the debris off the rock until it revealed a crescent moon, sun, star cluster, and gem shape.

"A pillar stone?" Jackson breathed out, staring at the flat rock and rubbing his hand over each carved object. As he stood to make sure that his dad didn't follow him, he noticed a small "X" carved into the tree directly behind the stone and knew exactly who left the clue. "Oh, Grandpa, you're still looking out for me."

For the last six months, Jackson had often been tempted to use the transport gem he found in the attic after his return home. He longed to visit the quiet cabin surrounded by mountains in the Starling Forest. He wanted to feel the warmth of the crimson, coral, and golden suns. He wanted to gaze in Andi's purple eyes and learn more about her, learn everything about her. Until now, the safety of transporting was a gamble at best. But now, he knew where Rigel and Merope had entered to bring him home. If his assumptions were correct, transporting from here would lead him safely to the front step of the cozy cabin in the Starling Forest. In an instant, the weariness of this world melted under the promise of another. Summer was here, and it was time to plan his vacation.

Chapter 2

Summer Vacation

"I'm going to meet a friend in Chicago this weekend." Jackson's father announced as he stared at the corner kitchen wall to escape any possible eye contact with his son. "I'm leaving right after work tonight. You can come with me and hang out with your cousin if you don't want to stay here by yourself." He smiled warmly and glanced over, hoping Jackson wouldn't see past the casual façade to the truth about what type of "friend" he was pursuing in Chicago.

But Jackson already knew. He'd seen the profile of the brunette thirty-something, divorced mom of two from the online matchmaking site. His parents never thought to cover their digital tracks, and it only took seconds for Jackson to figure it out—Dad was giving up on his sixteen-year marriage and moving on.

"Nah. I'm doing the chores Saturday morning while Farmer John is out at the auction. I'll be fine by myself."

Jackson shrugged as if he didn't care and stroked his finger down the front of his phone as if reading something of importance. He sat still, wearing a poker face, continuing to crunch rhythmically on his slightly sweetened cereal though he really wanted to smile widely, jump up, and run for joy. The large ring box with the red-and-yellow gem was beckoning him.

"Alright. I know you'll be fine." His dad walked to the door and then paused. "I'm sorry things worked out this way, son."

Before, Jackson would have kept a composed, disinterested stare while screaming from within at such a remark. *Worked out? What do you mean worked out! You didn't WORK to keep our family together. You didn't even try! You LET Mom walk out. You LET our family fall apart.* Before, Jackson would have burned with anger, hurt, and pain simultaneously gripping his head and stomach, all while suppressing it to perfection. But now, Jackson knew the location of the pillar stone. Now, he was only burning with eager anticipation.

"Yeah, I know, Dad. It's okay." Jackson easily flashed a reassuring smile across his face.

"I should be back by Sunday afternoon." His dad stood, placed his empty coffee cup in the sink, and grabbed his over-night duffle bag. "The keys to the old car are hanging on the hook in the cupboard if you need to go somewhere. Just give me a call if you need anything."

"Yep, sounds good."

"And I don't care if you have a friend over but no wild parties, alright?"

"Oh, you know me, Dad," Jackson added sarcastically, "wild parties every night!" They chuckled as he walked out the kitchen door, threw his bag into his truck, and drove away.

As soon as his dad's truck was out of sight, Jackson bolted out of the house and into the woods. He had to find the pillar stone. He followed the tiny X-marks he had carved into each tree along the way a few weeks earlier. As Jackson reached the last tree, he breathed deeply and scraped off the pile of leaves that he used to hide the stone. Rubbing his hand over the familiar, flat rock again, Jackson felt both excitement and terror boil within him. It was like the feeling before stepping up to bat. The bases are loaded, his buddy strikes out, and it's up to Jackson to make the hit and get everyone home. Swinging a bat at a flying ball in front of a crowd can be thrilling and fun, but it can also be riddled with mishaps and danger of failure. Jackson stood on the pillar stone of Earth, knowing his turn was coming soon. Like a final practice swing, he pretended to have the gem between his fingers, drew a door, and walked through empty air imagining triumph and glory awaiting him on the other side.

The rest of the day was full of preparations. Jackson set aside jeans, a T-shirt, pocketknife, and his hiking boots. He emptied the last of his school papers still lingering in his backpack, and filled it with bottled water and snacks. Last thing before he went to bed, Jackson went to the fridge to prepare a few sandwiches. He didn't think he'd have time for hunting and cooking while in Arcas, and he was still uncertain about what he could eat there without The Hunter's knowledgeable guidance. Jackson set out the bread and opened the meat drawer in the fridge.

"Go figure!" He laughed fondly as he looked into the last plastic pouch of lunchmeat. "Turkey sandwiches it is!" Of course, it wasn't so much the turkey that Jackson was fond of but the memory of Arcas. Finding only turkey left in their sparse two-bachelor fridge felt poetic, like this little trip was meant to be.

Jackson needed to leave the brokenness and pain on Earth and escape to Arcas, even if it was just for one day. True, the alien world had often been a place of danger and monsters, but those threats seemed small now compared to the turmoil of his family breaking apart. At least Cygnus, the dragon, and the scorpion had already been defeated. What remained in Arcas now were his friends who fought and bled with him and never abandoned him. It had been too cloudy lately for him to enjoy the light of the stars and feel close to his Arcasian family. In fact, everything felt shadowy and gloomy for too long. What Jackson's soul needed most at this moment was a land with no darkness.

With everything prepared for the next day's adventure, Jackson lay on his bed in an empty house, grabbed a mostly-empty notebook, and began drawing the eyes, nose, hair, and mouth of a certain princess. Since his sister took the completed sketchbook filled with his many Arcasian adventures, he had redrawn several of the pictures of Andi in this newer book. In the first pages, Andi was climbing a tree, then riding a horse, then standing in front of the portal with her fingers playing in the dancing lights, then sitting on a ledge near the ocean cliff, then climbing over the fallen rock pile, and—most importantly—walking straight into Jackson's lips in the cave. When his hand grew tired and his eyes weighed heavy, he fell asleep with Andi's freshly sketched face next to his.

Jackson's eyes suddenly shot open, and he ran to the window. "Oh, come on!" he complained, watching the steady rain pour down around him. He grabbed the ring box from under his mattress and opened it. Jackson looked outside and then gazed at the red-and-yellow transport gem. "Oh, well. Rain or shine!" He changed his clothes, tied his hiking boots, shoved the gem in his pocket, and grabbed the backpack. Before he headed to Farmer John's, Jackson snatched his two turkey sandwiches from the fridge.

He sprinted through the soft, constant rain until he made it to the farmer's first barn. There were three barns total, but none were very far from each other. After a half hour of throwing feed and hay and filling up water troughs with the hose, Jackson was done. He picked up his bag, felt his pocket, and took a deep breath while watching the rain shimmer against the yellow barn light. The clouds darkened the sky enough that the barn lights hadn't yet turned off from the morning sunshine.

It was time. Jackson threw the hood of his windbreaker over his head and sprinted until he made it to the cover of the forest. Though he was still getting rained on, the thick green leaves helped to shelter him. Little spots of soaking moisture were wetting his skin through his sleeves when he reached the pillar stone. Jackson stood on the stone and grabbed the transport gem. For a moment, he just stared at it, deciding whether he should really be entering the other world. But when the teen looked back toward his house, everything looked empty, damp, and dark.

With confident precision, Jackson pressed his wet fingers firmly against each point on the gem. Light and vibrations shot out from between his fingers. He drew a large arched door with the light and walked through. Jackson expected to be surrounded by the peaceful breezes and soft warmth of the Arcasian suns permeating through the green hills and forest. Instead, he felt the harsh heat of flames radiating against his face as fire consumed the little cabin in front of him.

Chapter 3

Smoke in Starling

Jackson immediately jumped back from the heat and flames flushing his cheeks a warm red. The quaint little cabin that was supposed to be his vacation spot melted, warped, and crumbled in front of him. But the cabin wasn't the only thing burning. The entire forest blazed behind the cabin and flames rolled along the forest floor like a surging tsunami of red.

"Otava!" Jackson shouted out as his eyes wandered to the hilled area by the mountain stream. There was no time to think or plan. Jackson simply began to run.

Faster.

Faster.

Faster.

The last time Jackson ran to Otava's cave on this same path, he fled from danger to save his own life; now he sprinted toward the danger to save a friend. The beauty of the Starling Forest slowly melted behind him into thick, black ashes of smoke. Little creatures darted before him, fleeing their singed homes for the parallel woods still glowing green in the sunlight.

Jackson stopped to catch his breath and looked behind him. Elevated a little higher on the hill, he could see much farther. The sea of fire surged on. Though he had placed some distance now between himself and the waves of flame flowing over the forest, little time remained to warn his friend of the danger.

There! He could finally see it. Otava's cave rested quietly upon the flat, rocky clearing just a little up the hill. Reminiscent of the past, a large pot was bubbling over a small fire. He had to be close by.

"Otava! Otava!" Jackson yelled out as he reached the campsite. *Rustle. Rustle. Snap!* Noises alerted the Son of Earth to scan the woods for his friend. Instead, a lone Monoceros colt sprung through the thick brush and bounded past him to safety.

Perhaps he's at his cabin. If he remembered correctly, Otava's home rested up higher, just beyond this cave where the ground leveled out again. Adrenaline surged through his veins as Jackson looked behind at the coming fire, determined to climb around and up the hill. But before he rounded the mouth of the cavern, he heard a low growl and stopped.

"Otava! It's Jackson! There's a fire coming toward your

home!" He called out the explanation as he smiled at a familiar, brown furry beast moving out of the darkness of the cave. The circumstances were dire, but he could not deny the warmth and happiness he felt to finally reunite with his friend.

As he eagerly waited for Otava to bumble out of the cave, trees and brush shivered around him in several different directions.

"Hurry, Otava! The fire is coming quick. We've got to get out of here now!" As the furry creature finally reached the light, it was as if the eyes of the devil himself were gazing at Jackson, waiting to consume his soul. This was not a bear but a wolf.

"Aww, but if you leave now, you and your friend will miss dinner," replied the beast with bright orange eyes.

Five other wolves slowly tread out of the woods toward Jackson in unison.

"Hey, Lupus, isn't this a Son of Dirt?" one snarled out to the apparent leader who had been in the cave.

"Yeah! Yeah! What is a Son of Dirt doing on Arcas?" asked another as saliva dripped from his large teeth.

"I'm just here to warn my friend about the fire," Jackson tried to remain calm while the pack approached him. "Have you seen him?" Jackson stood firm.

"Who is this Otava, Son of Dirt?" Lupus asked as the other five wolves circled Jackson.

These wolves were not the majestic kind with blue eyes and streaks of gray and white. These beasts were dark brown and black, shadowy like the smoke consuming the sky above and blocking the light of two suns.

Jackson knew he couldn't depend on his typical adrenalin-powered flight defense. There was nowhere to run with the fire raging behind, and the six wolves circling around him with their dripping fangs, hot breath, and orange eyes.

"What are you doing in these parts?" Jackson tried to distract them with casual small talk.

"Lord Sephdar sent us here. It's our forest now."

"I see." He nodded casually. "Have you seen a big bear around? Met the seven sisters?"

"Ha! The shrieks of the Ilmatar left a long time ago! Those tree dwellers kept us confined to the cold, barren mountains but now we will feast freely on the bounty of Starling." Lupus released a growl bursting with power, anger, revenge, and blood-lust.

"Yeah! We were just makin' dinner! Wanna join us?" Another wolf's black tongue licked his black lips.

"We have a little wood, a little fire, now we just need a little meat to smoke!" Several of the wolves chuckled with a slow rumble from the back of the throat that morphed into synchronized howls all around him. The sound was loud and resonated painfully, bursting into Jackson's ears. He quickly covered them with his hands. The unison howls rose to the sky with the sound waves glowing as if they were beams of light. The radiating waves swirled in the air like an orange tornado. The top of the funnel expanded larger and larger in the sky until the rotating light burst into flame and exploded downward like rain. Drops of fire poured down from the sky around them.

There was only one route of escape. Jackson reached in his pocket and pressed on the transport gem with three fingers. His forth finger hovered over the tip of the red-and-yellow gem, ready to escape back to Earth.

"You see, Dirt, the fire doesn't burn us because we are the fire," Lupus explained through his smiling, bared teeth. "But I'm sure you'll roast up just fine."

"How 'bout we start with his leg," a wolf snapped out and grazed Jackson's leg with his teeth.

"I fancy that idea! Nothing's better than a smooth, straight bone covered in flesh!"

"Let's cook 'im first! I like mine a little burnt!"

The wolves moved into a half circle and slowly edged Jackson backward toward the forest fire.

He could feel the heat pressing against his back like an iron slowly melting the hot fabric into his skin. Smoke billowed around Jackson's nose and eyes, stinging the senses. It was time. Though dangerous to transport into uncharted areas, nothing could be more hazardous than the fire and fangs surrounding and threatening him this very moment. Jackson pressed his last finger onto the gem then flung his arm out in front of his body between him and the beasts.

The wolves stopped their advance, staring in wonder at the light shooting out of the human's fingers.

"What are you doing, Son of Dirt?" Lupus growled as Jackson drew a shimmering doorway in the air.

But there was no time to respond to the demon dog or walk through the blue and orange dancing lights.

"Rhaaa!" a shout flew through the air.

Jackson whipped his head around toward the noise and flames just as a shadowy body rammed into his back with thick boots extended out. Breath ceased as his body flew forward through the portal.

Down.

Down.

Splash! Thud! The pain of intense heat and smoke were instantly drowned by a cold, damp darkness. Only a dim circle of smoky light entered from the open portal providing slight visibility. Jackson knelt in a shallow pool of clear water, rubbing his jolted hands that were still vibrating from the shock of impact.

The other body released the rope he was swinging from and landed steadily on dry rock. *Shiiing!* The dark figure drew his sword and jumped into the water next to Jackson.

"What are you doing?" Jackson yelled in terror, thinking at first that the blade was coming after him.

Devilish, orange eyes soared through portal amid the billowing smoke. A demon was pursuing them down to

Earth. The black wolf opened his mouth, baring gray teeth and a fiery tongue as it lunged toward Jackson's face. Horrifying shrieks bounced continually off the walls as the sword pierced the creature's chest. The sword flared yellow as it submerged into the wolf. The man immediately turned to Jackson, who had sprang backward but was still sitting in the shallow water, holding tightly to the gem.

"Shut the door!" he scolded angrily.

Embarrassed that he had not closed the portal sooner, Jackson obeyed and released his grip on the gem. For a moment, the water near them glowed and steamed as the dead wolf sizzled like a pile of hot coals into the coldness of death. As the fiery creature cooled, its dim light disappeared into utter darkness. Slightly sore and disoriented, Jackson took a moment to breathe. He couldn't even see his hand, but he felt moist and cold rocks around him. The thick smell of musk entered his nose and lungs as he consciously slowed his breathing.

At least I'm alive, Jackson thought optimistically. *I guess Cygnus was right about one thing. It's risky to randomly transport between the worlds. Risky, but totally worth it this time.*

"Is your world really this dark?" The stranger's face was not visible through the black air, but he sounded disgusted. Jackson didn't know why this voice spewed hostility toward him, but knowing they'd just survived a traumatic event and this person saved his face from being bit off, he tried to keep the conversation civil.

"No, it's not always this dark. We're just in a cave." Once this realization left his lips, Jackson knew there was no easy path to sunshine. He'd escaped the flaming forest and the ravenous wolves, but was now facing a disorienting darkness, possible starvation, and an endless maze of tunnels.

"What were you doing in the Starling Forest? I thought you agreed to never return to Arcas."

"Agreed?" Jackson asked, obviously confused. "What are you talking about?"

"Rigel and Regulus made a pact that no charges or harm would come to you for stealing the gems and opening The Bridge *if* you immediately returned Earth. You were sent home peacefully while Rigel, the Ilmatar, and the Ursa were granted entrance into the Free Realms."

"I don't know what you're talking about."

"Then how did you steal that gem back from Regulus?" he accused angrily.

"I didn't steal anything!" Jackson stood up, offended at the charges and protecting himself from a possible hostile attack. He held a cold wall with one hand and the gem with the other. "I found this transport gem in my home on Earth." Jackson clenched the gem on the flat sides and lifted it up in the dark as if to show it to the stranger. Immediately, the gem glowed. Light did not shoot out of it this time, but it illuminated like a glow stick, providing visibility to a small area surrounding it.

"Don't try anything, Son of Earth!" The soldier put his hand threateningly on his sword.

"Chill out, dude. I haven't done anything to you. I was just bringing a little light into the room." Jackson pretended he knew the gem would light up. "Seriously. What am I going to do?" Jackson retorted, slightly irritated by the barrage of verbal attacks against him. "Jump back into the flames on Arcas?"

"I don't know yet what you're capable of." His hand remained on the sword. "The last time you were here, you took half of Arcas into battle!"

"I didn't take anyone to battle," Jackson defended himself. "Cygnus threw me into your world and lied to me about why I was there!"

"Sure, I see. So, last time you destroyed our people by ignorance. And this time, you willingly came back and just happened to show up around the same time that my company got attacked?"

"Now you're going to blame me for the wild wolves?" Jackson scoffed. "That's me, wolf-man. You might as well add world hunger and earthquakes to my list of calamities."

"Not the wolves," his tone turned somber, "a regiment attacked us. We were riding peacefully through Starling when we were ambushed out of nowhere. Then the forest was set on fire. My horse fell with an arrow through his neck, so I climbed a tree to find my men. I didn't find them through the flames, but I found you."

Jackson was beginning to understand why the stranger was on edge.

"Do you think any of your men are still out there?"

"I don't know." He paused abruptly then quietly added, "It's doubtful any made it past the flames alive."

"I'm sorry. I had nothing to do with it though. The forest was already burning when I arrived."

Peering through the dark space between them, Jackson could now see the stranger wasn't any older than himself. The young man looked tattered from battle, singed by flame, famished, and worn from long travels. His skin was a deep brown like many from the Free Realms. And though he was confrontational, he didn't appear to be malicious, so Jackson tried to once again ease the tension.

"Are you hungry? I have some food in my bag, but I'd appreciate it if you don't stab me while I grab it." Jackson smiled and motioned to his backpack while the stranger nodded his head in agreement.

As he pulled the bag off his shoulders, Jackson was relieved that only the bottom was wet from the standing cave waters he'd landed in. *Zriiip!* The Arcasian teen cautiously watched him unzip the top and reach in to grab the two turkey sandwiches. Jackson sat on a large rock and tossed a sandwich over.

"My name is Jackson."

The boy was studying the food and the plastic bag around it as if it might be something dangerous.

"They call me Nekkar."

"Good to meet you, Nekkar. Thanks for killing that fire wolf." Jackson smiled warmly, opened his bag, and took a hearty bite.

"What is this?" Nekkar held the white bread sandwich by the middle, watching the edges sag over his fingers.

"It's a turkey sandwich."

"That doesn't look anything like turkey or bread. Do your people look thin, flimsy, and sickly like this meat they eat?"

"No." Jackson chuckled, remembering his feelings when first looking at and tasting the food on Arcas. "Where I live, most of us have plenty of meat—and other cushioning—on our bones."

Since the Son of Earth didn't die from the strange food, Nekkar followed suit and consumed the sandwich rapidly as if he hadn't eaten in days. They ate and sat in silence for quite a while, studying each other and trying to peer through the consuming darkness around them to find a path or a glimpse of light. Thirsty, Jackson felt around his bag for two water bottles and threw one over to Nekkar.

"Thanks for letting me escape with you," Nekkar quietly announced. Jackson nodded his head in acceptance though they both knew he didn't have much of a choice when Nekkar rammed into him. "Perhaps you were meant to return to Arcas."

"Do you know who attacked you?" Jackson asked with

concern and curiosity. "I figured Arcas would be at peace with Cygnus gone."

"Cygnus may be gone, but not his army and not his second-in-command. Sephdar is more ruthless than his predecessor. If he maintains control of the White Palace, his gaze will likely shift to regaining The Bridge that YOU opened to Earth."

"I didn't mean to open The Bridge. I told you Cygnus lied to me."

"Yes." Nekkar stood with confident resolution. "But now it's your duty to fix it."

"No, no, no." Jackson stood to match Nekkar's resolve. "I'm really sorry, man, but I don't have time to go back to Trifid!"

"We are not going to Trifid, Jackson. We must go to the Free Realms, and you must present yourself to our leader, Regulus."

"You don't understand! I have to get back home before…"

"No, you don't understand, Son of Earth," Nekkar interrupted. "All the gems—including the one you carry—belong to Regulus, and we must seek his will before we do anything else. I may not know much about cave lands, but I can tell we aren't getting out of this one unless we first return to Arcas. Besides, Regulus will know how to get you back home better than anyone. Since the fire and the wolves have taken over the forest, we will simply head south through these caves then use the gem to go back." Nekkar confidently pronounced their mission as if Jackson was under his command. "It's not a long journey. Once we reach Deneb, there's a narrow path we can take directly to the Free Realms."

Jackson didn't understand why all the gems supposedly belonged to some leader in the Free Realms. As far as he was concerned, the transport gem was found in his house with his grandpa's stuff and labeled with his name. Jackson had way more claim to it than anyone on Arcas. And the other gems had clearly belonged to the ancient kingdoms of Vega, Altair, and Deneb. None of this made sense, and he was prepared to protest further, but once "Deneb" was mentioned, everything changed. A journey to Deneb was something that Jackson couldn't refuse—not when there was a chance that he could gaze again at the purple-eyed princess who danced through his dreams every night.

But this pitch-black cave would not deliver them back peacefully. They were going to have to fight their way back to the light of the three suns.

Chapter 4

Unexpected Rescue

A Few Weeks before Jackson's Return to Arcas

"Do you hear that?" Alcyone walked over to the window and scanned the Ligeian Sea.

"A harp?" Asterope rolled her eyes. "Great. It's probably that wretched Sulafat returning. I've immensely enjoyed his absence from this place."

"No," Taygeta blurted out from the corner of the room.

Shocked by the outburst, her two sisters turned their heads toward her. Taygeta had been silently sitting in that corner for hours, slowly tracing her finger up and down the seam lines where the palace bricks met.

Ever since the six sisters were abducted from their home, her mind had been less than functional. Like a broken record, each day Taygeta would become fixated on one task and repeat it over and over again. First, it was the horribly continuous song about flying darkness, then the rocking back and forth, now it manifested itself in tracing the same two square feet of wall over and over again.

"Who do you think it is?" Alcyone crouched down beside her, gently touching her troubled sister's shoulder.

"Don't bother, Alcyone. We haven't gotten a straight answer out of her since the ravens carried us from the Starling Forest. You aren't going to get one now." Asterope didn't want to be discouraging, but she was worn out over trying to fix Taygeta or get any meaningful conversation out of her.

"That song is not from the darkness." Taygeta started rocking back and forth, continuing to trace her finger along the wall. "That song is from Merope."

Not far from the White Palace, Rigel quietly rowed toward shore while Merope softly strummed the powerful turtle-shell harp, creating a dense cloud that disguised their large canoe as it circled around. Their borrowed ship from the Free Realms rested beyond the cliffs, hidden from sight of the White Palace, and waiting for them to return with Merope's six sisters. As the front of the canoe lightly scraped against sand and pebbles, Merope grabbed the side and hopped out of the small boat. The music stopped as she moved, causing the cloud around them to slowly dissolve and blow away on the ocean breezes. She hovered briefly over the water, sank her feet into the sand, and pulled just behind the bow deck until the front was steady against the beach. Rigel leapt out behind her, submerging his feet up to the ankle.

The skilled, masculine hunter took over the canoe. Rigel gripped the handhold with strong precision, lifted the bow from the beach, and ran up the soft sand. As he heaved the vessel out of the water, thousands of dry grains clung to the sides of his wet boots. Merope floated behind him, strumming the harp. A small whirlwind danced under her feet, covering their footprints and fading the long groove in the sand created by the canoe. When the boat was concealed against the white, rocky wall that rose from the beach straight up to the towers of the castle, they began searching the cliff walls with their eyes and hands.

"What does it look like?" Merope whispered.

"It's grayish-white, short, and narrow. It just looks like a deep crevice in the wall."

The two worked swiftly and methodically, rubbing their hands around the jagged rocks in search of the concealed entrance. They didn't have much time to sneak their way into the palace. Though many in the White Winged army perished at the Battle of Fornax Forest, others had fled back to the palace in search of their leader. The siege at Trifid just ended in victory for the Free Realms, but another powerful legion led by Sephdar—Cygnus's second-in-command—was rumored to be returning soon from the Starling Forest.

After a lengthy battle through the wilds of Starling, Regulus pulled his men back to the safety of the Free Realms. Sephdar chased them over the mountains to the border, but he knew better than to enter. Considering the retreat a clear victory, Sephdar gathered his men to return to the White Palace. These soldiers hadn't heard yet of the outcome at Trifid or the demise of their fallen, white-winged leader, Cygnus. But Rigel and Merope knew they needed to get the Ilmatar sisters out of the White Palace before the large army returned and found out.

"Here it is!" Rigel pointed. "But it's a little different than when I walked out of it."

Merope ran over to him. Though she had never seen the secret door to the White Palace, she immediately knew the change he was talking about. Six boards crisscrossed over the opening, blocking the narrow entrance. Rigel pulled out his sword. One by one he dug the sharp edge in between the ocean-weathered nails and the boards. *Creak. Creak. Creak. Creak.* The nails fought, bent, and complained their way out of the rock. When only the tip of each nail held the first board in place, Rigel gave his sword to Merope. With a swift grunt, he yanked on the loose lumber. The rock wall released the barrier with an echo of cracking wood and jolted stone throughout the dark tunnel, but outside, the ocean waves drowned out the sound.

"That wasn't too hard. Apparently, Cygnus didn't make this barricade to keep out The Most Skillful Hunter." Merope lightly teased Rigel using the very words of the flattering, but deceptive, winged man. "He didn't even put a guard out here for you to humble."

Rigel smiled as he worked on ripping out the next nails with his sword, but then he stopped and looked at Merope with grave sincerity.

"Meri, they didn't put these boards up to keep us out of the palace." He paused. "They put them up to keep your sisters in."

Thunk! Rigel ripped out the last board. He then sheathed his sword and scanned the beach for approaching threats.

"Hurry, Merope, give me the lyre." Rigel quickly set the turtle-shell harp against the wall inside the tunnel. Then reached his hand out to her. "Get in here before we are discovered."

Merope grabbed his hand as he gently pulled her inside the dark tunnel and held her tightly against his chest in the darkness. She breathed against him quietly, trying to contain her anxieties. Merope's well-tuned ears heard nothing outside except the waves and sea birds. She lifted her body above the ground so her soft cheek glided against his rough stubbles.

"What is it?" she whispered, trying to figure out if their plans were about to be altered. "I thought we were going to wait for Otava's signal before entering the palace."

Rigel kept one hand around her waist and moved the other into her thick, dark hair behind her head.

"We *are* waiting for Otava." He breathed out into her ear then kissed her cheek, slowly moving forward until he reached her mouth. "It's just better to wait in here." The soft warmth of their lips interlocked with a deep passion built over a thousand lifetimes of being pulled apart. Rigel had tried to run from it. Merope had tried to bury it. But at last they were together, alone, and all other troubles in the world vanished for a moment.

"Yes, it's much better to wait in here," Merope agreed with a smile and squeezed her arms around his back.

"And, you know Otava." Rigel raised an eyebrow and caressed his fingers against her cheek, curving a thick wave of hair behind her ear. "He may take a while."

Bong! Bong! Bong!

"Not nearly long enough." He sighed. "That's our dinner bell," Rigel confirmed as he lightly squeezed his arms around Merope. Blinded by the dark passageway, he traced his hand from Merope's back up to her shoulder then down to grasp her hand. The two climbed silently up, up, up on the carved rock stairs. Cold and dark, the secret passage felt like a stairway to death. But the sound of their breath and the warmth of their clasped hands comforted the couple.

They had entered the enemy's house together, and together, they were the most powerful.

"Stop," Rigel whispered. "We're here." They stood silently underneath the floor door, listening.

Knock. Knock.

"Dinner, my ladies!" Sadr announced from the hall. A eunuch from birth, Sadr was the chosen servant for the Ilmatar. No other man—save for Cygnus himself—was allowed to enter the sisters' rooms.

The servant had arrived with dinner quicker than Rigel predicted. *Otava truly is both a skilled warrior and a skilled chef,* he thought with an inner chuckle. Still, if the sisters ate before Rigel and Merope stopped them, it would complicate the escape and put them all in danger of being caught. They continued listening as Electra opened the door, grabbed the platter full of bread and soup for two, and thanked the servant. Merope didn't waste any time once the hallway door shut again. She placed her palm flat against the wooden door over their heads, and gently sang, beckoning her sisters to find her.

"Celaeno, Celaeno. Electra, Electra."

"Did you hear that?" Celaeno looked at her closest sister with urgency and concern.

"Merope?" Electra quickly set the food down, opened the bedroom door again, and looked down the empty hallway. The White Palace servant rounded the corner at the end of the hall, heading to deliver the next meal.

Tap. Tap. Tap. Merope lightly knocked her fingernail against the floor board.

"Shut the door, Electra!" Celaeno commanded in a hushed voice. "She's not out there." Celaeno moved the platter of food from the table to the bed. "She's underneath us!" Electra joined her in pulling two padded stools off the rug and then moving the small square table.

They lifted the heavy rug decorated with lavender and white flowers and folded it over. Rigel pushed up on the floorboard as he and Merope walked up the last stairs leading into the room.

"Rigel! Merope!" Celaeno and Electra exchanged hugs with their youngest sister and long-time friend.

"I was hoping that when you returned, it would be through the front door with Cygnus." Electra tensed her eyebrows with concern, realizing that sneaking into the palace meant danger lurked nearby. "For then we would have celebrated with a grand party full of music and dancing." Electra grinned, swaying her hands back and forth with Merope's. Even the threat of immediate danger couldn't dampen her zeal for a good party.

"I know, but things are not well in the kingdoms," Merope explained. "Cygnus is dead, there's an army in the

Starling Forest, and The Bridge at Trifid is open again between Arcas and Earth."

"What?" Electra and Celaeno asked in unison, completely baffled.

The sisters had long been secluded from any kingdom news, but it was even more surprising to hear of war and an open portal after living quietly guarded in Cygnus's palace for many weeks. Cygnus had precisely controlled all information that reached the Ilmatar. Though they felt uneasy at times, they were always assured of their safety. The sisters had been treated as honored guests since their arrival. They were led to believe the White Palace was the best and safest place for them to stay. Cygnus assured them that he would defeat the enemy dwelling in Trifid quickly— Gurges Ater—the lone nemesis who was to blame for the sisters' abduction and the looming war. With no home to return to, they tried to be grateful, but more and more the sisters felt like prisoners.

"Merope, what in the light of the three suns is going on out there?" Celaeno probed, looking out the window at the world beyond the palace. Merope grabbed each sister by the hand and spoke in hushed tones, so they would grasp the severity of her words.

"All I can say right now is that Cygnus brought you here and kept you here as part of some secret scheme. He's not coming back though. We're getting you all out of here and away from the kingdoms before the palace erupts into chaos. His armies are returning right now and will soon discover they have no leader. I can fill in all the details later. Where are the others?"

"I'll show you," Celaeno volunteered, understanding the gravity and necessary haste of the situation. "Electra, stay here and guard our room."

Celaeno opened the door, peered into the empty hallway and then motioned Merope and Rigel forward. Rigel lightened his step as if he were hunting sensitive game. Merope and Celaeno raised their feet above the ground and hovered just over the white marble floors. Asterope, Alcyone, and Taygeta resided just around the corner to the left and three doors down. Maia lived at the end of the hall to the right.

"I do hope you feel better after eating, My Lady," Sadr encouraged Maia as he opened her door and set down dinner. Merope and Rigel stiffened as the servant entered the hall again, but Celaeno continued down confidently.

"Hello, My Lady. You finished your dinner quite quickly. Do you need help with something?"

"No, if you'll excuse us, Sadr, we are just visiting my sisters."

"Hey! Aren't you The Hunter?" he asked excitedly. "Yeah! You're him!" Rigel put his hand on his sword. Sadr continued, animating each phrase as if he were quoting from a play, "the height of a centaur, the strength of a minotaur, the stealth of a leopard, and the cunning of a wolf."

"Hahahaha!" Rigel played along and patted the guy's back like they were instant pals. "Yeah, I guess that's me. Though I do think I'm a little shorter in the flesh."

"Ha! Well, even if you are shorter than a centaur, you're still a lucky man! Cygnus must favor you deeply as no other man in the palace is allowed to enter the ladies' rooms, save for me. When did this Ilmatar join us?" Sadr pointed toward Merope, trying to place her face with a memory. "Ah, you must be the famous seventh sister! We've been waiting for you, but I haven't had time to prepare your room!"

"No worries! That all can wait." Celaeno broke into the conversation with peppy energy. "Aren't you hungry, Sadr? You work so hard for everyone else. You must be famished by now!" She moved next to him, placed her hand on his back, and started humming. The servant's attentions turned away from Rigel and Merope as he rubbed his belly, reacting to her musical influences.

"I think I am hungry, My Lady." Celaeno nodded her head in agreement and lightly sang as if she were reciting a well-known childhood ditty.

You're hungry; you're hungry
Go walk down the hall
You must eat this moment
Can't you hear dinner call?

Rigel and Merope opened the door while Celaeno led the servant to the kitchen.

"Good, that's very good, Taygeta." Alcyone sat patiently beside her fragile sister, coaxing her to eat another bite as if Taygeta was a reluctant toddler.

"Merope? Rigel? I can't believe you're finally here! Honestly, if you waited one more day, you would have had at least two crazy sisters on your hands!" Asterope welcomed them as warmly as she could while sarcastically rolling her eyes, making sure they knew how distressful it had been for her to deal with Taygeta's madness.

"Don't eat the soup," Rigel warned Alcyone.

"Of course not, Rigel! I'm coming to embrace you both!" Alcyone jumped up, smiling, and hugged them tightly. "I knew you would bring my Merope back with you." She turned her eyes toward Rigel and winked.

Thump. Taygeta, who was being hand-fed while sitting in front of her favorite wall, slumped over headfirst to the side.

"Great," Asterope huffed. "We are finally getting out of this loony prison, and she blacks out again!"

"It wasn't Taygeta's fault," Rigel explained. "The soup was made with volantis. But you girls can wake her, right?"

"No!" Asterope burst out emphatically. "I mean, yes. We can. But if you've come to get us out of here, it's better that we don't."

"She's right. It'll be better to wake her once we are long gone from the palace," Alcyone agreed.

Caw! Caw! Caw! echoed through the window from outside.

Celaeno anxiously ran into the room from the hall. "They're coming!" she warned in a hushed, anxious tone. "The black corvus are here. They are flying in ahead of Cygnus's army!"

"We need to get out before the army reaches the palace," Rigel urged. "They'll know something is wrong when they aren't greeted past the outer guards."

"Please. Get my sisters out of here," Merope pleaded with Rigel. "I'll get Maia. I haven't been trapped here, so she will believe me quicker than any other when I explain all that's happened."

Rigel agreed, but he was still deeply concerned about leaving Merope. Ever helpful, Alcyone insisted she would stay to guard the room with the secret passage until Merope and Maia arrived safely. With plans settled, Rigel lifted Taygeta's limp body and carried her out. He would lead the sisters down to the boat hiding on the white sand beach near the palace. They all entered the hall at the same time, but Merope quietly moved in the opposite direction. As Rigel rounded the corner carrying Taygeta, he locked eyes with Merope. A hundred emotions poured out of his soul through that one glance. *I love you. I trust you. Be safe. I will take this entire kingdom down if anything happens to you.*

Merope's beloved sisters vanished as she reached Maia's door alone. She tapped on the thick, whitewashed wooden door that blended seamlessly with the white stone walls. No reply. She knocked again. Silence. The entire palace slept quietly under the influence of Otava's powerful concoction that flowed freely from the infiltrated palace kitchen. The only sounds came from distant horns and the shrill *Caw! Caw!* of the corvus leading the army back to a leaderless home. Merope turned the knob and entered.

"Oh, Maia. I thought we were safe coming to you last. You never eat while your soup is piping hot." Merope looked compassionately at her oldest sister. She hadn't even made it to the table to eat. Maia was slumped over on her bed with the tray of food in front of her and a damp spoon lying next to her. Merope sat down on the bed and stroked her sister's cornflower blue hair highlighted with silver and purple. She grabbed Maia's hand and hummed softly but deeply from her innermost being. As she continued to hum and hold her sister's hand, Maia's fingers began to twinge and her eyes fluttered.

"Merope?" She stirred, lifting her head and stretching her arms.

"Yes, it's me. Don't sit up too quickly. You'll get dizzy."

"Nonsense!" Maia rose up, slightly drowsy, and wrapped her arms around her sister. "I'm so glad you're safe. I'm so glad that you're here. The palace has been good to us, but now I know why Cygnus has been absent so long. He found you at last." She moved back to look at Merope's face, which was unable to conceal concern behind the happy embrace. "I know the capture was scary for all of us, but we have a new home here. Thanks to Cygnus, we have a new purpose. I have so much to tell you. I'm just glad that you've joined us at last!"

Merope's smile dropped under a solemn weight in her spirit. Unlike her other sisters, Maia was still completely deceived by the winged lord of the White Palace.

"I'm glad to be with you, too. But we can't stay here, Maia. We have to leave now. It's not safe anymore."

"What are you talking about?" Maia felt that Merope was the confused one. Obviously, her little sister hadn't heard the good news. "Cygnus told me himself that he defeated Gurges Ater. He's raising a new kingdom in Arcas, one far better than any of the kingdoms today and any of the kingdoms of old." She squeezed her sister's shoulders. "Don't you see, Merope? This is our home now. We are going to be like mothers over all of Arcas and healers between the two worlds." Maia's face lit up with excited radiance, earnestly trying to explain the grandeur of their new life.

"Oh, Maia, Cygnus lied to you. He lied to us all. There was no Gurges Ater. He created an enemy so he could use us and the kingdoms to do his bidding. The Bridge is opened between Earth and Arcas because he wanted it to be open. *He* ordered the corvus to capture us and the raiders to cut down our home."

Maia released Merope's hand and turned her face away.

"You are so wrong," she argued coldly. "Even if he did lie about a few things," she explained, "it was out of love. It was for our protection."

"Do you hear yourself? Love doesn't lie. It always reveals the truth, even when it's painful."

"And what do you know of love, Merope?" Maia stood, turning away from her sister then flashed her eyes back at her in direct confrontation. "Is love some hunter who wanders all over the Free Realms and only calls upon you when the game moves north?"

"Rigel has nothing to do with this!" Merope stood up, angry her sister was missing the point.

"Really? I'd say he has everything to do with this. Cygnus wanted us all to be a family. He was trying to bring you and Rigel together. He was giving Rigel a position of honor. And The Hunter did what he always has done. He ran away. And now he's filling your head with nonsense and trying to make you run away as well. What if Cygnus lied a little? What if he stole us away? It was all for our good. What Rigel does is for himself and himself alone!"

"You are deceived! Rigel left me because he didn't want to break up our family. He didn't want to separate us. Cygnus separated us by force when he sent the corvus to steal us. He paid criminals to destroy our home! Everything he did was for his own power. Do you know he threatened to kill me at Trifid? He would have killed all of us if we got in his way. But thank goodness Rigel fixed that problem for our family, for all of Arcas. Thanks to him, we are free from White Wings forever."

"What do you mean?" Maia grew angrier, and her feet rose off the ground as a blue, translucent hue swirled around her. Merope stood her ground with compassionate confidence realizing she may have revealed too much too soon.

"I'm sorry, Maia." She breathed in deeply, anticipating the consequences of the truth about to be unleashed. "Cygnus is dead. He fell through a portal to Earth with an injured wing. Cygnus is not coming back. His armies have no leader. It's over. It's time to leave all this and start a new life."

"Aaaaaaahhhhh!" Maia shrieked from the depths of her soul, resonating the palace with piercing vibrations. The force of the sound propelled Merope back into the wall. Merope shook off the shock of impact and rose in the air, meeting her sister as a violet hue swirled around her like a ribbon. The white around Maia's silver eyes grew red as the veins enlarged.

"Maia, calm down," Merope pleaded. "You are going to wake everyone up. We need to get out of here. We can talk this through later."

"How could I go anywhere with you?" Maia spewed the question from her gut with distain and disbelief. "You killed the man I love!" Merope gasped at the alarming revelation. She hadn't noticed the change in her sister before, but now she clearly recognized a slightly rounded bulge on Maia's lower stomach. Wrapping her hand around the bump, Maia screamed, "You killed the father of my child!"

Chapter 5

The Escape

Merope sprinted around the hall's corner as a mournful song echoed throughout the White Palace walls. Her feet moved swiftly and softly while tears ran heavily down her cheeks. Between Maia's lamenting and the outer horns blowing to welcome in the army returning from the north, it wouldn't be long before the slumbering guards and servants were alerted to the intrusion and attempted escape.

"I am sorry, Arkab, that the rest of the servants and guards have not come to greet the commander," Sadr apologized as he led a soldier up the stairway. The eunuch of the Ilmatar never made it to dinner. Since the slumbering doorman hadn't returned from his meal to open the palace to the high-ranking warriors pounding outside, Sadr took over the responsibility. "Most are eating dinner at the moment. It must be an enjoyable meal today as none have returned to their posts yet." He reasoned nervously.

"No harm done. Let them enjoy their meal. We've all been busy during this time of war and transition. In truth, the only ones Commander Sephdar cares to greet him are the seven Ilmatar."

"Yes, indeed. Cygnus instructed us to gather them together upon the commander's arrival. In fact, I believe we finally have all seven sisters here."

Merope closed the door behind her just as the two shadows reached the top of the stairs at the end of the same hallway.

"We have to leave," she anxiously breathed out as she moved the table and chairs in front of the door. "The soldiers are coming now to fetch us."

"Wait! Where's Maia? What's wrong?" Alcyone asked with concern, noticing the wet tear streaks down Merope's olive-toned cheeks.

Knock. Knock. Knock.

"Let's go!" Merope grabbed Celaeno's hand to lead the way down the steep stairs into the dark tunnel underneath.

"My ladies? We've come to introduce you to the commander returning from victory in the north," Sadr called out. "My ladies?"

Though perplexed, Alycone understood the urgency. She grabbed the edge of the escape door, closing it over the top of their heads just as the table and chairs screeched against the hardwood while Arkab shoved them out of the way and entered the empty room.

Otava grabbed the windowsill and nervously scanned the water below around the ship. The slumbering servants and guards were starting to moan and writhe in the dining quarters. It was time to get back to the boat, but Otava wanted to make sure his companions made it out first. There! A ring of fog swirled around the cliff, steadily hovering over the water and moving toward the ship. Otava sniffed and slurped the simmering soup one last time then saluted his groggily waking audience with his damp ladle as if to say, "It was a pleasure being your chef today." He clipped his belt on to the zip-line and slowly lowered his body down from the window onto the strong rope. Otava's heavy stomach teetered and tensed as the rope bowed and throbbed under his weight.

"The honorable work is done, and it's back to the wretched monkey business!" He fretfully consoled himself while twisting his body to hang underneath the line. Otava used his claws to grab the rope and inch himself onward to the ship. Before, he swiftly slid down to the palace. This time, the line was a slightly inclined climb back to the top of the mast.

The cloud around the sisters lifted as Rigel grabbed two hanging ropes and reattached the smaller boat to a pulley that would soon lift it off the water to the ship's side. One-by-one the sisters climbed up the ladder, which extended down to the keel of the ship and was gently rolling at the bottom with the foamy sea swells.

"Merope, the bear's in danger!" Asterope motioned to the kitchen window.

Merope turned around three quarters up the climb. At the end of the zip-line, the palace cook was pointing at the furry intruder with a soldier next to him. The man wore the emblem of Lord Cygnus with the three suns surrounding white wings. Immediately, he raised his sword and started hacking away at Otava's rope.

Thunk! Thunk!

"Ursa Major!" Otava yelled. "They're going to feed me to the water beasts!"

"Play the lyre!" Merope handed it up so she could finish climbing into the sea-faring craft.

Asterope clutched the curved wooden neck that attached to the hollow turtle shell at the bottom. She timidly began strumming the notes, afraid to mishandle such a powerful instrument. A cloud of blue, yellow, and orange floated around the deck.

"You can do it," Merope encouraged. "Just focus on where you want the cloud to go." She pushed up on the last step and flung her legs over the top of the boat.

Pop! Otava's rope severed from the grappling hook holding to the kitchen window. The once-suspended zip-line dropped. Growling and howling, the bear's nails and paws frantically gripped at the rope. His body finally jolted to a halt when one nail snagged a loose cord. Barely holding on, he swung rapidly toward the ship like a wildly thrown pendulum. With immense velocity and weight propelling him onward while bending the mainmast, either the vessel or Otava was bound to be damaged soon. At worst, the large, warm-blooded wrecking ball threatened to sink them all.

"Ahhhh!" The swinging bear scraped at the rope with his free arm to get a better hold. *Crack!* His thick, dark nail broke in half.

Just in time, a cloud hovered underneath him. Below, hungry ghost sharks jumped, snapped, and circled to score the first bite of this falling hunk of meat from the palace. To the beasts' disappointment, the dense fog cushioned Otava's fall and lifted him away from the water's surface.

The frazzled bear was safely caught, but he remained stiff. With eyes sealed tightly shut, he was convinced that the slightest movement would wiggle him out of the thick cloud and into the ravenous teeth below. Otava landed safely in the ship and several Ilmatar surrounded him instantly. Petting his soft head and paws, they comforted him, trying to get the bear to open his eyes and stand up.

Rigel cranked up the heavy anchor as Merope took over the lyre. Hundreds of soldiers appeared on the beach, cliffs, and palace towers. Some shot arrows at the ship while others prepared the palace cannons already aimed at the water. Soldiers hauled small boats out to the water's edge and men jumped inside, paddling vigorously toward the ship. Just as flaming torches arrived for the archers to burn down the sails, the power of the Ilmatar took over.

The six sisters formed a circle around the mainmast. While they grasped hands, a harmonized song rose in the air. The swirling cloud of sound and wind filled the sails and rapidly pushed them out of range toward the open sea and the Free Realms. The power of their combined voices was separating them from both the enemy and their one remaining sister. Though the sisters looked forward to building their lives anew, all worried that their family might never be whole again. The rescued sisters might arrive safely in the Free Realms, but they didn't know yet that Rigel, Merope, and Otava were leaving them again soon to fulfill one last oath to Regulus.

Merope watched the White Palace fade behind a distant cloud. With tears swelling around her silver eyes, she sincerely hoped that Maia would forgive and somehow join them again. But in her oldest sister's mind, such hope was futile. Maia had completely accepted the White Palace as her home. To her, the palace represented a place of love and safety and importance. Her family may have been brought there as captives, but Maia freely chose to stay. She may have chosen differently if only she knew her freedom and favored welcome in the White Palace were coming to an abrupt end.

Chapter 6

Cancer in the Cave

Jackson and Nekkar on Earth

Deafening shrieks filled the pitch-black air. Shoulder to shoulder, Jackson and Nekkar raced from the pursuing horrors. With only a dim glow illuminating the next step, it was extremely dangerous to run in this underground labyrinth. But as an army of a hundred thousand bats swarmed toward them, they couldn't control the panicked urge to escape.

What first echoed from the distance as a small hum grew into the clamor of beating wings and a dreadful symphony of guttural chirps. The boys hollered, covering their heads as the bats rammed into their backs, squealed around their ears, and fluttered leathery wings against their cheeks. Like a slow-motion nightmare, they were stuck in the vortex, surrounded by a whirlwind of shrieking winged rodents.

"Enough, already! Get us out of here!" Nekkar cried through the chaos.

"Ow!" Jackson yelped as his knee rammed into something hard. He aimed the glowing gem down at the object and noticed a rock ledge sticking out. Dropping to the floor, Jackson rolled underneath it. *Screech!* A small bat that had landed on his back scurried from behind his shoulder and flew away. Jackson shuddered as he lay on the cold ground, breathing heavily. The creatures continued to zoom past beside him in hoards.

"Jackson!" Nekkar panicked that his ticket out of this place was either unconscious, having the blood sucked out of him, or worse yet, returning to Arcas and leaving him behind as bat bait. "Are you alright? Where are you?"

"I'm fine!" he called out remembering that Nekkar was still out there. "Drop to the floor and roll to the left."

Nekkar couldn't see anything, but he fell to the ground and rolled left until Jackson let out a grunt as their shoulders collided.

"Alright," Jackson finished drawing the arch. "There's your door back to Arcas." They both stared up at the lights hovering above their heads. Deciding to test the door first, they moved their heads out of the way, and Nekkar threw a rock—wrapped in a plastic sandwich bag—straight up through the portal. They waited. *Clunk! Kist!* The small stone let off steam as it landed on the cool, damp floor next to their arms. After a few seconds, Jackson lifted the rock up toward the portal lights to examine it. The plastic sandwich bag now curved tightly around the rock, infused by an intense heat. The smooth plastic now displayed blackened edges, random holes, and melted ripples. Nekkar's face fell.

"I'm sorry, man. Like I said, the forest could burn for days."

"We're not staying in this hellish pit for days!"

"Wait!" Jackson remembered. "I think I know how to find which way is south," Jackson wiggled his backpack off and laid it in the small space between his stomach and the rock ledge above them.

"Great!" Nekkar exclaimed sarcastically. "And which sun in here are we going to follow?"

"This one." Jackson finally recalled his most valuable asset, pulled his phone out of the inner zipper pocket in his bag, and pushed the power button. Nekkar watched suspiciously. "No Wi-Fi, but the compass should work." He held up the lit screen and moved it around, so Nekkar could see it working.

"No!" The Arcasian rolled away, back toward the bats. But they both realized quickly that the freaky creatures were finally gone. Jackson followed him out and lifted up both his phone and the gem for added light. Nekkar's hand flew to his sword once again. "I have taken a vow, Son of Earth. I will not use sorcery or witchcraft no matter what dangers I face."

"Dude, it's not witchcraft." Jackson laughed, throwing his bag over one shoulder. "It's technology. Science?" Nekkar stared at him blankly as if he were speaking gibberish. "This transport gem is more like sorcery than my phone."

"The gem is not sorcery! The Creator designed all the gems for a purpose. It was man who corrupted them and used them for evil."

"Well, my phone had a designer and it was created for a purpose as well. Right now, its good purpose is to help us get out of this cave and back to Arcas." Jackson glanced at Nekkar, who obviously wasn't convinced. "Stay here if you want"—he shrugged, throwing up his hands,—"but I'm walking south down this tunnel."

One drip. Two drips. Three drips. Jackson counted the steady rhythmic patterns of water falling from a crevice in the rock ceiling down to the cave floor. The constant drip-drip filled the void of conversation between them as Nekkar reluctantly followed Jackson.

"Stop!" Nekkar was growing tense in the shadows. He didn't like following others, especially someone using a strange device to guide him, especially an alien Son of Earth.

"What's wrong?"

"Let's try again. We must be out of the forest by now. I honestly can't stand being in this damp stench a moment more."

"Sure, why not?" Jackson climbed as high as he could then pressed his fingers on the gem and began to draw the arched door in the black cavern air above their heads. "Throw another rock up." Nekkar nodded and tossed another plastic-covered stone up through the door, but this time, more than the rock fell back in.

"What's that noise?"

"I don't know, but something's different with the portal. It doesn't look right." The swirling lights seemed to thicken and swell like a weighted cloud about to release a torrent of rain. Suddenly, water burst through the portal like an exploded dam.

"Run!" Just as the word left Jackson's mouth, a raging flood of water swept the boys away and carried them down through the murky cave.

"AHHH!" they screamed as the water pushed through the tunnel and smashed them into walls on each side and rocks underneath.

Shut the door! Shut the door! Jackson commanded himself while being carried by the current. A stone column of stalagmite rose in the distance like a lone tree dividing a trail in the woods. With his phone lifted high in one hand, and the gem in the other, he pushed his heals against the rocks underneath him to edge closer to the column ahead as the water carried him onward. Jackson first thought of letting the water push his open legs into the column to catch it, but memories of falling onto his bike at the age of ten quickly nixed that idea. Instead, he lifted his arms high and wide, still clasping to the valued items in each hand.

Thud! Jackson's shoulder and hip crashed into the pillar. He threw his forearm tightly around the thick growth of rock. The raging flood dragged his body down, down, but his grip held firm. Jackson focused his thoughts on the gem, slowly squeezing his fingers to the side until the pressure points released and the gem's power fell to a light glow once again.

"Jackson, where are you?" Nekkar called nervously, his arms only slightly visible like branches sticking out of a river at night.

"I'm right ahead of you. Follow the light and grab on the rock sticking out in the middle of the water." Jackson waved his phone towards the right side of the cavern while cold water rushed around his chest.

"I see it!"

Nekkar reached to grab the protruding rock. Just as his fingers brushed against the rock, a large fish rammed into Nekkar's neck. He was confused and blinded by the rushing waters, but he gripped tightly. As the rapids slowed slightly from the portal source being cut off, Nekkar noticed how smooth this large rock felt. It wasn't rough and grimy like most of the salt-covered calcium growths in this cavern. His curiosity turned to concern when the rock started to sway.

"This rock is moving!" Nekkar screeched.

"Is it loose?"

"I don't know, but I can't hold on much longer!" All Jackson could see through the dim lights were shadows.

Nekkar's shadowy body was getting closer as it floated back and forth in the air like a phantom. Jackson knew he couldn't let go of the pillar. The current was still too strong to stand. The only way to help his companion required a sacrifice. Holding his breath, he tossed his phone to the side, hoping it could survive the rocks and the water. Jackson then reached for Nekkar.

"Grab my hand!"

Nekkar's body flew through the air and plunged back into the water. Jackson's hand dove under the wet darkness and caught Nekkar's. The Arcasian teen spit and coughed water out of his mouth as he surfaced. He continued fighting to grip the ground with his feet and keep his head above water.

"What happened?" Jackson asked once Nekkar caught his breath and grabbed to the same pillar.

"That rock, or whatever I was holding, started to move against the current."

Finally, the waters calmed enough for the two to stand. Still holding to the stalagmite column for safety, Jackson aimed the gem at the strange moving rock. The mysterious figure grew wider, taller, and stranger as they watched. When black eyes and reddish-orange pinchers emerged from a round shelled body, both boys gasped.

"Holy giant crab!" Jackson exclaimed in a whisper.

"Acubens! It must have been sucked in from the bottom of the river in Starling."

Ankle-high in water, both slowly backed away from

the beast. Jackson turned slightly and noticed his phone sitting in a tiny puddle on a raised ledge nearby. As he lifted the dripping, dead device, Nekkar bellowed in shock and pain.

"Help!" Nekkar gasped.

Cold, wet, pincers clamped around his abdomen and lifted him in the air. With Nekkar in its grasp, the crab quickly shuffled directly to the right of the open path, away from the gem's light.

"It's gonna snap me in half!" Nekkar cried as the pinchers squeezed his insides together.

Can you reach your sword?" Jackson suggested in panic. *At least scorpions inject their pray with poison before eating them*, he thought feeling helpless. *This is pure torture!*

The crab didn't intend to eat. It was attacking out of pure, meaningless fear. Nekkar reached over the pinchers, grabbed his sword, and proceeded to hack away at the creature.

"You try! Its armor is too thick here!" Nekkar cried, throwing his sword at Jackson while sweating and wheezing. Jackson picked up the sword and ran toward the crab. But every time, he came toward the crab, it scurried the opposite direction. From right to left, right to left, it moved away, Nekkar's body swinging in the air.

"It's running from the light!" Jackson realized out loud.

Sprinting to the creature's blindside, Jackson drew a portal underneath the water. It was difficult to see clearly through the waving liquid and colors, so Jackson prayed he was making the right choice. Otherwise, he would never see Nekkar again.

The portal below started sucking down the remaining water. Jackson ran to the other side, holding the gem in one hand and the sword in the other. Yelling with both hands above his head, he chased the beast.

"Jackson, what are you doing? Don't send me through the portal now! He'll kill me!"

Just as the crab's right four legs slipped and fell down the portal, Jackson released the gem. *Crack!* The door instantly closed, severing off the pincher holding Nekkar. The body and head were gone to Arcas, but the pincher and Nekkar remained on Earth.

"You could have cut my legs off!" Nekkar reacted as he pried open the morbid claw. Jackson just smiled and raised his eyebrow as if to say, *Really? You're going to yell at me for just saving your life?* Nekkar saw the look and quickly swallowed his angst.

"Thank you." He spoke quietly and humbly, giving a quick nod of gratitude.

"No problem," Jackson warmly accepted the recognition. "Looks like we can't go much farther."

Jackson peered just past the pillar they had held to during the flood and saw a huge drop down. Like a petrified lava lamp, random growths of tan and white calcium filled the world beneath them. The Arcasian water swirled and mixed below with a natural standing pool of underground water, overflowing dried trenches below and causing small creatures of the dark to scurry toward higher ground.

"Should we be going back to where we started and wait out the fire?"

"No, let me try my weapon of sorcery first," Jackson teased as he held up the gem to his phone. He wiped the liquid bubbles off the screen with his shirt. A thin row of scratches covered the glass screen on the upper left corner. "Of course…" Jackson shook his head in disgust. The display underneath flickered rapidly like tiny volts were shocking it. "Maybe you're right. It melts just like a witch when water hits it."

"Water melts witches?" Nekkar asked, baffled.

"Never mind." Jackson smiled, knowing it could take hours to explain the joke to someone far removed from a world of movies and touch screens. With no other options, Jackson reluctantly powered off his phone and shoved it in his pocket. Who knew that of all the things he brought in his bag to Arcas, rice would be the food he would most regret leaving behind. "Let's just try again over here." Jackson shrugged his shoulders and held up the gem. "I'll draw a tiny door right next to this drop." He pointed at the dark death trap that would have claimed them even before the crab if they hadn't grabbed onto this lone pillar. "If we hit water again, it will just fall down there rather than on us."

Nekkar agreed but moved back from the area and casually grabbed on the column of stalagmite as if it were a

71

resting post rather than a safety net. Jackson cautiously drew a small door, just large enough to stick a hand through. They quietly waited, staring at the small open gate between the worlds. Nothing happened.

"No water. Fire?"

"I'll try it." Nekkar ripped off a piece of his sleeve that was already badly tattered. He then pulled out his sword and tied the thin cloth around the pointed end. The blade that had glowed yellow after piercing the fiery wolf now glistened next to the portal as water droplets reflected off of the smooth steel. The sword slowly disappeared into the hole. They waited. After a few minutes, Nekkar pulled the sword back into the dark cave. The blade was not glowing yellow with heat, and the cloth bore no signs of soot or singe. Nekkar felt the fabric all around and breathed deeply into it.

"It's dry. And warm!" he announced excitedly, then plunged his hand through the door. Nekkar sighed in relief and smiled the first real smile that Jackson had seen since meeting him. "Nothing feels like the warmth of the three suns!"

Jackson closed the small door then moved slightly away from the cave's drop to draw the larger entrance. While he sidestepped over, his foot landed on something slippery. He stumbled but quickly regained his footing on the solid floor.

"What is that?" Nekkar asked.

"I think it's a fish!" They both examined the scaly creature about the length of a shoebox. Its head was caught under a crevice of rock while it still flapped up and down rhythmically, heaving for breath. "It must have come in like the crab."

"Quick! Open your bag," Nekkar commanded while picking up the fish by its fin. Jackson unzipped his backpack thinking Nekkar wanted some water or another item of use. Instead, Nekkar dropped the slightly wet, heavy fish into the bag.

"Yuck! What are we going to do with that?" Jackson stared inside his bag at the flapping, slightly smelly creature.

"Um, eat it." Nekkar curved his eyebrows and answered as if this alien had just missed the most obvious use for any fish.

"You can." Jackson zipped up his bag and shook his head. "I'm not eating anything from Arcas unless I know what it is."

"It's. A. Fish. You know, has scales and a fin, swims in water?"

"Yeah. I know," Jackson rolled his eyes. "Is it volantis or pisces?"

"Pisces!" Nekkar once again acted like Jackson had asked the most obvious question ever. "Everyone knows not to eat volantis."

"Alright. Whatever. Let's get back to Arcas and have a fish fry then." A second nature to him now, Jackson effortlessly awakened the gem and drew a larger doorway.

"You saved my life, so I'll go in first." Nekkar pulled out his sword in case any wolves or dismembered crabs were waiting on the other end, and walked out of the dark caverns into the bright lights of Arcas.

For a long time, all the boys could do was lie in the flat field of warm grasses growing between the forest and the mountains. Behind them, thick smoke was still rising from Starling. Before them, the Bernice Cliffs towered high, blocking their way. The warmth of the Arcasian suns comforted their cold, wet, and tired bodies as they cooked the backpack pisces, ate, and fell asleep.

Nekkar was already sitting up on the other side of the campfire, staring at the cliffs when Jackson awoke. There was no easy path around this mountain range that separated the Starling Forest from the rolling hollow hills in the Kingdom of Deneb. Though Nekkar and Jackson had survived fire and flood together, the vertical climb up the Bernice Cliffs promised new danger. This treacherous climb wasn't Jackson's biggest problem, however. As he reached for his injured phone resting in the grass above his head, dread took hold of him. Jackson anxiously crawled around, combing through the grass. He stood, patting his pockets, then reached for his backpack.

"What's wrong? What are you looking for?" Nekkar asked with curious concern.

"The gem!" Jackson dumped his backpack and frantically pealed open every zipper. "It's gone!"

Chapter 7

The Lord of the White Palace

Sephdar stood near the pearl-white table in Cygnus's formal dining hall. His black hooves were shined and polished in the village preceding the White Palace. A clean cloak branded with white wings surrounded by three suns flowed from his neck past his navel. From the back down, it lightly blanketed his red-rust-colored fur and dark brown tail but stopped just above his hocks. Different from most centaurs who delighted in their long, flowing tails, Sephdar kept his short. Like a buzz, the bristly hair barely rose past the flesh and was wound over tightly with cloth to protect the skin from sun and battle. His red-rust fur blended near perfectly with the smooth but hairy human skin layered over his torso, arms, and face. Sephdar's rusty brown hair and beard were trimmed short, a rare indulgence for warriors during the long travels and consuming battles. But it was time for the battles to end. He fought for Lord Cygnus, and patiently readied himself in the village before entering the perfection of the palace. Sephdar was prepared to meet Cygnus and prepared for his reward.

Wobbly servants—still waking from Otava's soup—nervously scurried around the room, setting the table with breads, cheeses, and fruit for the commander and his summoned guests. Though he would not let a morsel of food touch his mouth before the Ilmatar joined him, he slowly and methodically drank his tea. As the smooth chestnut-flavored liquid flowed down his throat, the fiery, throbbing pangs in his gut weakened to a slow ache. Alone in the room while the servants hurried to the kitchen, Sephdar smiled. It was a rare occasion for true contentment to cross his lips, but today, his suffering would end.

Like most centaurs, Sephdar grew up in the Free Realms. He became a skilled archer and hired himself out to King Algieba from the Altair Kingdom during The Pillar Wars. His unique equestrian speed and steady aim helped bring the mighty dragon Thuban to the ground. By the end of the last battle, however, the kings of Altair, Deneb, and Vega had all fallen. Sephdar had no ruling authority over him to control his spiteful, proud, and greedy nature. As the last Sons of Earth walked through the open portal at Vega to their death, he sneered and cheered their demise.

Not only was Sephdar uncompassionate to the living, but he also left no honor for the dead. While others gathered bodies of the fallen, Sephdar gathered their valuables. When he could carry no more, he left the dead lying in the blazing suns and returned to the Free Realms. Wealthy from the spoils of war, he believed he could live in his homeland, far from the tattered kingdoms he once served. But not everyone approved of his methods and news traveled fast. The leaders of the Free Realms banished the centaur, for it was forbidden at the time to profit from or participate in the kingdom wars.

The Kingdom of Vega remained abandoned and desolate, so Sephdar returned to Altair where King Algieba had hired him as an archer. He was familiar with the Eridanus and the people. But Cassiopeia and Alderamin threw him out of the kingdom realms when priceless gems and royal heirlooms, including Algieba's and Denebola's crowns, were found stashed in his new home. The dead kings should have been carried to their burial ceremonies in honor with shimmering crowns upon their heads, but Sephdar had robbed the departed kings of their last rights to the crown.

After a thousand years wandering the southeastern wilds past the Eridanus, those who still lived forgot about the treacherous centaur. His face and name vanished. But in time, Cygnus's eagle, Aquila, brought Cygnus news from the corvus. A centaur with a disabling black hole in his gut was living in Trifid. Curious about activity in the ancient ruins, Cygnus found Sephdar curled on the ground, suffering with a festering bite from Minaruja. Minaruja was the largest and most venomous hydra snake. His constant lust for flesh drove him to attack any moving creature on land or sea. Sephdar was wounded and alone, lying in the rubble of Trifid with only the dark ravens as his companions. An ebony circle filled with pus and scabs covered his stomach and spiraled out like swirling spider veins. Cygnus brought his personal healers to Trifid, and they nursed the centaur back to stable health.

Sephdar had worked faithfully for Cygnus since then, rebuilding Trifid and The Bridge that would soon be an open portal between Earth and Arcas. Trifid became an additional training ground for White Wings' soldiers. Over time, Sephdar was rewarded with rank and prestige, but one reward still waited to be fulfilled. The centaur pleaded many times with Cygnus to have the Ilmatar sisters heal him from his stomach pangs left by Minaruja's attack. A final pledge from the white winged leader would be realized once Sephdar fought back the Free Realms in the north, and a new kingdom around The Bridge was secured. Upon his victorious arrival to the White Palace, Sephdar would finally be awarded healing from the lingering venom that plagued him daily.

Eager anticipation overwhelmed Sephdar as the dining room door opened. To his surprise and disappointment, Albireo entered the room. Nervous, dirty, and sickly-thin, he informed Sephdar how their situation had drastically changed.

"Yes, The Bridge is indeed open, but Arcturus and the Free Realms have gained control of Trifid."

"What! How?" Sephdar spewed, perplexed by the news. "Where is Lord Cygnus?"

"No one has seen White Wings since the fighting began. Sulafat was found dead inside the fortress. I even sent a man through The Bridge, but it led to a desert wasteland with no trace of Cygnus. We held Trifid as long as we could, but we were starving. Our provisions ran out, and we had no choice but to hand over the city in exchange for a safe return to the White Palace."

Before the commander could reply to the shocking update, Sadr and Arkab joined them.

"They've escaped, Sephdar! We tried to stop them, but they sailed away on a ship from the Free Realms." As Arkab spoke, Sephdar's eyes went black and he grabbed his stomach.

"Who escaped?" He seethed the question through clenched teeth though he was certain he knew the answer.

"The Ilmatar." Sadr stepped forward and explained. "But one of them stayed behind. She is loyal to Cygnus, may His Lordship rest in peace where ever he is."

"Bring her in," Sephdar commanded as sweat moistened his forehead and his hands lightly clenched into fists.

"I don't think she'll do you much good. She's not feeling very well," Sadr attempted to excuse her.

"BRING HER IN NOW!" Sephdar yelled, throwing his empty teacup at Sadr. The fragile, pearly glass shattered against the wall as Sadr scurried out.

"If Cygnus is gone, then who is in charge of the palace? Who is giving orders to the men?"

He stood tall with his hand on his sword, testing Albireo and Arkab.

"I will follow you, *Lord* Sephdar," Arkab immediately spoke up.

"As will I," Albireo swiftly agreed.

"I would be honored to lead in place of Cygnus. Together, we will make sure his death was not in vain, and that his legacy will live on."

"Ahem." Sadr cleared his throat while entering. "May I present Maia, the oldest and most beautiful Ilmatar."

Sephdar slowly walked forward, circling her with each hoof clunking dramatically against the hard floor.

"They say you are loyal to the palace. And the rumor is that you are Cygnus's woman."

"I am," Maia replied with confidence and poise.

"Good. Cygnus promised me that the Ilmatar would heal my venomous wounds. Will you be loyal to him even in death and honor his request?" He raised the red tunic, showing the black, spidery swirl infused within his skin. The wound was no longer open, scabbed, or puss-filled. The venom had simply become a part of him.

Maia stretched out her hand and touched the large scar. She closed her eyes and hummed. The melody exited her body, flowing through her fingers into the black hole. Sephdar closed his eyes and breathed deeply, waiting for relief, waiting to be whole again.

"Ahhh!" he yelled, jumping back. Sephdar bent over,

holding his stomach in pain. When he lifted his hand from the scar, the black webs had grown even farther out. "It's worse! What are you doing to me?"

"I was trying to draw the venom out, but it has been there too long. I do not have enough power to do it alone."

Maia also felt a sting in her gut as she admitted defeat: the sting of being separated both physically and emotionally from the power of her sisters. At least she could still comfort herself in the palace with the smells and sights of her winged man. And she could comfort herself with Cygnus's heir slowly growing inside her.

"After all my troubles, I am welcomed by one pathetically weak Ilmatar." He turned to Arkab commanding, "Ready our men. We need to hunt down the other six while their tracks are still fresh. And you," he shifted his orders to Sadr, "take her to the dungeon. Palace security is apparently less than efficient, but we will at least keep *her* from escaping."

Maia placed her hand on Sadr's back, and the tiniest sound radiated through her.

"That won't be necessary," Sadr disobeyed under Maia's influence. "She will stay in her room, and I will watch over her."

"Who are you loyal to, eunuch? The master or the whore?" Sephdar reached both hands down, touching his weapons.

"I am loyal to Cygnus, but since he is gone, Lady Maia will take care of the palace. And I will take care of her!"

In an instant, Sephdar pulled out two long blades, each resting next to a front equestrian leg. The light of the crimson sun glared off of the shiny metal through the windows. With quick and merciless effort, Sephdar sliced the blades through Sadr's neck and removed his head from his body. Maia jumped back with a scream as Sadr's body crumbled to the ground in a pool of blood. Sephdar grabbed a napkin from the table and wiped off his swords one by one.

"Arkab, put a blade at her back and take her to the dungeon. Then send a regiment back to Starling to collect the sisters when they return to their little forest. If you don't find them, gather the wolves and let them flush the songbirds out."

"No!" Maia cried and lunged toward Sephdar at mention of the wolves. Arkab reacted instantly by pulling out his sword and pointing it at her chest.

"Do not pity her or trust her, Arkab," the centaur instructed coldly. "Maia betrayed us all by allowing the Free Realms to enter this very palace and steal away her sisters. She clearly desired to rule in place of Cygnus. If the Ilmatar releases even the slightest hum to influence you, cut her voice out."

"Yes, My Lord," Arkab affirmed in obedience.

"Albireo, lead them down. And tell the old man that the new lord of the palace says, 'Thank you for the tea.'" Sephdar smirked. "Apparently, it's going to remain my only remedy until we can hunt down the other six."

The confident songstress was now silenced as she walked down the familiar halls with a blade at her back. Shock, terror, and grief overwhelmed every muscle of her body. She really did try to heal Sephdar. She didn't mean to get Sadr killed. Maia trembled as she followed Albireo toward her new home, a cold room behind cold bars. The dungeon door creaked opened. Maia's trembling slowed as she listened to music traveling up the stairwell. An aged voice was singing heartily into the darkness.

Mira, Mira
loosen the reigns
your pride is a poison
it slays with great pains
fighting a battle
that no one can win
oh, sisters, beware
you kill from within.

The man continued to sing through occasional dry heaves and didn't even stop as he noticed the strangers, but finished the very end of the second verse as they reached the bottom of the stairs. The folklore was sung loudly and joyfully, but the message pierced Maia to her core.

"Still singing the same old songs, huh, Charles?" Albireo called out. "You and the old man at Altair have to got to be the only people in all of Arcas who know all the verses."

"That's right!" Charles piped up, taking advantage of the chance for human interaction. "Have you come to join me in these luxurious living quarters, Albireo?"

"No, no, Charles. As much I'd love to chat with you for old times' sake, I'm actually bringing you a lovely neighbor to keep you company." He opened the cell next the old man and motioned for Maia to enter.

"How nice of Cygnus to send a little grace and beauty down to the dungeon just for me." Charles smiled, trying to be compassionate and complimentary. There was an obvious heaviness to his spirit that this poor woman was joining him here in the darkness.

"Oh, Cygnus didn't send her down. We actually just acquired a new leader," Albireo explained to Charles as Arkab grabbed a stool outside and carried it into the cell for Maia to sit on.

We are not barbarians, Arkab thought, nodding his head at the new prisoner. He would give her what little comforts he could, but they were soldiers. Their duty was to follow orders and, now, those orders came from Lord Sephdar.

"So, who is this new leader?" Charles asked with curiosity and a little hope. "Perhaps he'd like to meet with an aged Son of Earth?"

"I don't think that will be necessary. He already knows you. And the new Lord of the White Palace wanted me to give you a message. 'Thank you for the tea.'"

Charles's playful demeanor changed in an instant. His eyebrows tightened, and his pupils widened. The old prisoner's face turned from pale white to ghost-like as he quietly and slowly prayed under his breath, "God save Arcas."

Chapter 8

Bernice's Hair

Wild, olive-green vines flowed down the gray cliffs like dreadlocks draped over the skull of the mountain. With an open palm, Jackson glided his fingers down several vines. Each leathery, smooth strand looked to be the size and strength of a good climbing rope, but he wasn't sure he trusted the plant with his life yet. At least there were no thorns to avoid, only the occasional leaf growing from the long tresses.

"See? No worries," Nekkar assured as he confidently tugged on vines. "Bernice may be a large stony woman, but she is a lady." He then playfully grabbed an armful of hanging cords, draped them front of his body, and raised an eyebrow. "She has most kindly clothed herself with her own hair, so we are safe from her more dangerous parts."

"Ha!" Jackson chuckled, shaking his head in amused disbelief. He tried to appear light-hearted though he couldn't stop thinking about the lost gem. The two boys spent hours looking every possible place near where they'd slept—in the field, in their bags, and in their clothes. Nekkar was sure that a small furry varmint or worse yet, a corvus, found and took the polished stone. Jackson never accused, but he couldn't stop the feelings of mistrust.

What if Nekkar took it? Could he have? Nekkar made it clear that he didn't think the gem belonged to me. There's no way he would take it then stick around, help me look for it, and lie right to my face, Jackson reasoned.

He was feeling paranoid, powerless. Jackson didn't want to start a fight, especially when Nekkar was the only weapon he had now—besides a small pocket knife and a dead phone—to survive this world. Above all else, Nekkar seemed to finally be warming up to him as a friend rather than treating him as an adversary. So, Jackson swallowed the paranoia, smiled, and pretended that he wasn't shaken to the core by the gem's disappearance.

"I've never imagined a *nice* lady being clothed *only* with green hair," Jackson joked back.

"Aw, don't listen to the Son of Jack, Bernice." Nekkar dramatically caressed the smooth strands still draped inside his arm. "Son of Jack" was Nekkar's new pet name for Jackson. He thought it was funny and strange that the Son of Earth had neither a father nor grandfather named Jack. Though not so important to a modern Midwestern family, those types of names always had literal history linked to them in Arcas. "I love a woman for much more than her hair color." Nekkar ended his romancing of the vines with a theatrical dip.

Jackson smiled and rolled his eyes as he grabbed another vine and raised his body over the ground to test its strength. They both knotted a thick olive-toned plant-rope around their waists. No helmets or climbing shoes, but at least the hanging vegetation could also serve as safety lines. With numerous strands surrounding him to grab and a cinch around the middle, Jackson felt somewhat secure while facing the vertical rock wall before them. Underneath the hanging vines, the cliffs were quite good for climbing. Instead of a flat, smooth surface of stone, the Bernice Cliffs were layered, cracked, and jagged. In some spots, it looked as if large, rectangular blocks were piled unevenly upon each other.

Jackson lifted his left foot onto a protruding edge as he reached up with his right hand, sliding four fingers into a large crack while steadying himself with a vine in his other hand. He smiled at how much he'd changed in the last year. The old Jackson would have remained firmly planted in the grass below until someone promised a harness, belayer, and helmet. Safety equipment was the one essential condition that convinced him to try the man-made, traveling wall at the county fair several years ago. His friends would have never coerced him effectively without an excess of equipment, trained spotters, and legally insured protocols.

Even with every available safety net, the old Jackson would currently be overwhelmed with nauseous anxiety, clammy hands, and a white face. But Jackson was a changed person.

His greatest inner fears were no longer ignited to life by unknown beasts or heights or pain or even death. As he paused to tighten the slack on the vine around his waist, Jackson almost scoffed at the now dangerous distance between him and the ground. There were things far greater to fear than falling to his death.

What if the Free Realms lock me up forever as an alien criminal? What if they banish me through The Bridge and I die in the desert wandering around to find civilization? Jackson worried. *Without the gem, I'm either trapped here or trapped there.* Jackson felt control slipping away from him. He could no longer choose to move between the worlds. He was now completely at the mercy of others. Just like at home.

Jackson was no longer just concerned about surviving an untamed Arcas. He was concerned that he couldn't survive being trapped on his own world, in his own home. Sure, this Regulus person in the Free Realms carried the other transport gem, but Jackson's worst fear was being forced to return home without the power of escape that the gem provided. His empty house still held traces of Grandpa's smell and his little sister's laughter. A place of joy and peace had gradually been replaced by death and inevitable divorce. The physical darkness of Earth that used to merely consume the night, now consumed the day. And not even the light of three suns could dispel that darkness.

"Jackson! Can you come up and grab my sword?" Nekkar yelled down—slightly frustrated—about three arms' lengths to the left.

"Sure." Jackson searched for good gripping grooves ahead of him. "What's wrong?"

"My arm and legs are caught." Sweat soaked through Nekkar's tunic in large patches and he seemed short of breath. "Stupid vines." The vine wrapped around his arm also seemed to have coiled around his chest.

"If you twist your body a bit, I think I can get the sword," Jackson recommended, edging nearer to the Arcasian.

"Try to lift it from the cross-guard," Nekkar suggested. Jackson thought back to his journey with Rigel, tracing his memories to recall where the cross-guard was. *That's right! The cross-guard!* He remembered that the horizontal bar that sticks out above the blade added a cross shape to the sword. It was closer to him than the handle sticking up in the middle.

Jackson fought through the spasms and growing numbness in his weary legs. Turning his hand palm up, he lifted the sword from its sheath. Sweat dripped from his hair and his muscles pulsed with fatigue as Jackson sawed back and forth, back and forth against the strong, leathery vine griping Nekkar's arm. *Creak! Rip! Snap!* Nekkar's forearm jerked down rapidly, falling free from the plant's hold. The coils loosened around his chest, bounced against rocks, and tumbled to the ground.

Both young men clung to the wall for a moment, looking at the stripes of white against Nekkar's brown skin like several tourniquets had been tied to his arm. Wiggling and stretching his fingers, the Arcasian attempted to regain full blood flow and the strength needed to finish the climb. A few more minutes up the mountain, and they could rest in a large cleft before the final trek to the top. But as Jackson started sawing at another vine caught around Nekkar's leg, someone had a different plan.

Whip!

"AHHH!"

THUNK!

Suddenly, Nekkar's body flipped backward, falling until his head cracked against the rocks. Blood dripped down the gray rocks below him as he hung upside down, held only by the vines still coiled around both his legs.

"Are you okay?" Jackson yelled in concern.

"I think so," Nekkar replied, stunned but conscious. "Somebody jerked up on the vines around my legs."

Before Jackson could use the sword again to cut his companion free, the vines steadily began pulling Nekkar's body upward. Nekkar winced and groaned as his back scraped and bounced against stony edges.

"Give me the sword," Nekkar whispered and reached out. Jackson carefully flipped it so the handle pointed upward and passed it to Nekkar. "You're free of the vines?" Jackson nodded in reply. "Good. They can't pull you up then. I will talk to whoever is up there and fight them if I have to."

"What should I do?" Jackson called out in a hushed voice.

"I come in peace!" Nekkar hollered up toward dark open cleft. Clearing his mind before battle, he rested his sword on his chest, waiting for foreign faces to appear above him.

Nekkar's legs soon arched over the top of the cleft. Once his back reached the flat rock, he sat up, pointing his sword in defense. His muscles were tense and sore but every nervous fiber pulsated electrified energy that only a trained warrior could control. Nekkar waved his sword from left to right, searching for those who dragged him up the cliff.

Nothing.

No one.

"Hello?" Nekkar lowered his sword to appear less threatening, hoping to invite someone to appear. "I'm not going to hurt anyone. Thank you for helping me up the cliff."

Again, no response. The vines were still pulled tightly against his legs, now dragging his seated body forward— deeper into the hollow. Once his feet slid onto a silky, pink rug, the tugging stopped. He smelled something sweet like fresh fruit. The smell intoxicated the tired and hungry traveler, and his taste buds reacted with saliva in his dry mouth and a strong desire to fill his empty stomach. Assuming the threat was over, Nekkar called out to Jackson.

"Come on up! I don't think they want to harm us." Then Nekkar returned his conversation to the cave. "I'm only going to use my sword to remove these vines from my legs. Then, I would be pleased to meet you and buy some food from your table if you are willing."

The natural line he'd tied around his waist was easily loosened and released. Though the end was now long, it didn't take much time to untie it. Unlike this limp strand he'd tied around his stomach, the vines constricting his legs seemed to have gained more strength. He placed his sword over each strand by his ankles and sawed until the tension broke and the circulation in his feet slowly returned. While examining and rubbing his legs, Nekkar assumed the severed vines merely fell still to the floor. Instead, they had snapped back like the injured tentacles of an octopus.

Jackson pushed his stomach up onto the cleft's landing to join Nekkar, then one-by-one heaved his heavy legs to the safety of the flat ledge. He lay there for a moment near the edge with his forehead resting on his arms. Jackson had no desire to move farther. His tense muscles slowly melted like cold butter placed in the sun. He desired nothing more than to lie in this puddle of relaxed muscles on the soothing, cool rock and sleep. But when he glanced up at Nekkar, the remarkable sight filling the cleft demanded all his senses awake.

Chapter 9

Sleeping Beauty

Nekkar stood not on the edge of a rug but on the threshold of an enormous, open flower. One silky petal curved around the entire teardrop-shaped opening. The reddish-pink petal adorned the top like a crown then flowed to the floor like the train of a royal robe. The hollow body grew to the back of the cleft like a pitcher plant. Only, this flower's body opened to the size of a large, round storm drain. The inside walls swirled with greens and yellows while a single purple circle adorned the top of the outer petal like a bruised, black eye. As Jackson stared at the giant flower, rays from the crimson sun streamed into the small cavern. Ten smaller, but identical flowers sprung from the back of the cleft like little ducks perfectly lining up behind their blossoming mother.

Thit. Thit. Pheep. Thit. Thit. Thump. Soft strange noises erupted from somewhere inside the deep cleft, shaking the boys from the calming view of the flowers into a tense alertness once again. Jackson sprung to his feet as a shadowy figure rapidly rolled left and right. The awful sounds continued with a high-pitched squealing. Then the figure rolled into sight.

"What is that?" Jackson blurted as soon as the shadow rolled into a beam of sunlight. Small strands of vine wove around white and gray figures like an enclosed hamster ball.

"It looks like mice," Nekkar replied while squinting to see the tiny raging creatures rolling around in their green cage. The strange sight caused them to forget all about whoever or whatever lured them up the cleft.

Neither boy could turn away from the natural yet carnal instincts of two squeaky males vying for the same seat of power. It was a silly thing really, the smallest of creatures biting, scratching, and pouncing on each other to prove who was strongest. Eventually, one would give up or die. But the triumphant victor would soon face the fact that he, too, was lost in the ultimate battle. His little gray body and white underside would also die if he could not defeat the larger battle to escape the vines caging them. Working together, perhaps both mice could survive, gnawing and scratching at the thick green cords instead of at each other, but for the moment, these tiny little alphas were blindly attacking and lessening their chances of continued existence.

"What say you, Son of Jack?" Nekkar asked with posh formality as if he had the power of a Roman emperor over two gladiators locked in an arena. "Should we cut the winner out of the vines when the battle is over or should we see if he can free himself?"

"I don't know." Jackson pondered the options. "I think we should cut him out if he lets the other mouse live, but if he kills him or eats him, leave him caged. I don't want a murdering mouse scurrying around freely while we sleep."

Nekkar smirked and chuckled in agreement as they continued watching. The mice swirled around a few more times inside the stationary sphere until the tail of one and feet of the other both seemed to get stuck to a petal below them. Still rabid, the mice pulled and scratched to attack again, but the more they struggled, the less they moved. The vined cage slowly released from around them, then slithered back like a hose being coiled up. Each mouse lie panting on the petal with feet, tail, and fur stuck to the flower.

"Look, Nekk, the petal is like a sticky trap! The more they move, the more they get caught."

"Yeah… I know."

"What?" Jackson asked, turning his focus to Nekkar, who hadn't responded with the expected juvenile enthusiasm about the bizarre plant vs. animal game.

"I'm stuck too," Nekkar announced with irritation. He wiggled and pulled and stretched, but his feet were firmly attached to the petal.

"Here, give me your sword." Jackson reached his arm out while keeping his feet off the petal that decorated the slab floor. "I'll try to pull you out." Nekkar handed the sword over and Jackson set it on the ground. They grasped one hand, and when that didn't work, Jackson crossed his arms and grabbed both of Nekkar's.

"Pull harder, I'm slipping!" Nekkar shrieked as sweat dripped down his forehead.

"I'm trying. I think the flower's moving you!" Jackson looked down in horror as the petal swelled like rolling waves, sliding Nekkar's feet and body farther into the depths of the flower.

"Can you get your shoes off?" he asked, but the idea came too late. Hundreds of tiny needles suddenly sprung out of the top petal floating above Nekkar's body.

"Watch out!" Jackson cried, but before Nekkar could react, the top petal collapsed into his backside. He bellowed, stiffened, then instantly fell under the weight of the beautiful, floral beast. The thick, reddish pink petal surrounded him like a cocoon, thinner around the head and feet while bulging over his thicker shoulders and chest.

"Nekk! Nekkar!" Jackson wailed, still pulling desperately on his friend's two brown, limp hands sticking out of the flower's closed lips. His eyes widened in terror and his face paled white as he yanked and tugged at the lifeless body. Finger by finger, the Arcasian hands slid out of the Earthian's hold. The creature that once rested still and beautiful had now swallowed Nekkar completely into the bowels of its stomach. Jackson fell to the ground.

"Ah! Ah! Ah!" Jackson breathed out in panic, then scurried back from the large flower. *What is happening? This can't be real!* His moment of denial fled rapidly when he spun around to look at the smaller blossom. The top petal lay softly over the two small, motionless bulges of mice.

Clink! Jackson's foot knocked into the sword. His pulse increased and the white in his face flushed to red as he lifted the sword from the ground. Anger flooded his body. He'd lost so many things in the past year. Things—not stuff you can buy, but the more intangible belongings like trust, security, people—were taken from him, and he had to sit by, watching as every good thing slid out of his grasp. He wasn't going to watch anymore. Today, he was going to fight.

Hack! Hack! Hack! Clank! Rip! Snap! Like a maddened warrior cutting each limb from his enemy's body, Jackson chopped, swung, and assaulted every living piece of fiber coming from the plant. The flower didn't moan or scream as it was punctured and torn, but the vines awakened from their slow, stealthy movements and sprung to attack. Following the vibrations of Jackson's body, large green tentacles lunged out, trying to grab him. One by one, Jackson swung through the flying appendages, amputating them from the body. When every last vine was finally severed, the mother plant's limbless frame appeared limp and lifeless like Nekkar's body. But Jackson wasn't about to stop. Each beautiful flower, though lovely to gaze at, was full of snares, poison, and death. He sliced through the belly of every single flower and cut through the main stems. A transparent, pink fluid oozed out of the largest belly. The blood of the beast could no longer bring life to itself and death to others.

When the battle had ended, the cliff-side cave was quiet and still. Stem particles, sliced petals, and slime covered the rock floor. Jackson's fury had exploded and shrapnel lie everywhere as proof. Panting and sweating, he stabbed again into the large petal lying over his companion. Sawing carefully, he cut around Nekkar's feet. Then he grabbed the sliced silky fabric and began ripping it. *There he is!* Jackson's felt a wave of relief wash over him as Nekkar's legs were uncovered. He continued to tear and pull, rolling the thick petal over, and Jackson tossed it to the side like a large comforter. Just as easily as the tiny needles pierced the Arcasian's flesh, they slid out. Small spots of blood filled the tiny puncture holes and stained his shirt when each needle exited. While Nekkar's back resembled a bloody pincushion, his limp front was still plastered to the sticky petal underneath him.

Jackson smeared the sweat from his palms onto his jeans before reaching for Nekkar's hands once more. Pulling, pulling, pulling, he grunted and yelled while fighting against the last power the plant held. Though Jackson's legs were bent and planted firmly against the ground, the watery slime that continued to flow from the gutted belly of the beast crept underneath him. In an instant, his feet slid on the slime until his heels thumped against Nekkar's side and his rear fell to the floor.

"I can't catch a freaking break!" Jackson shouted. Now he too was stuck. He sighed and shook his head in disbelief. How could he get Nekkar out now that half of his own body was also atop the infamous, sticky trap of death? His energy was gone; his hope was gone. So, Jackson turned to the last source of possible salvation. He didn't close his eyes or bow his head or utter an audible word from his mouth, but he prayed. He cried out from the innermost depths of his soul to a power he couldn't see or understand. *Well, God, Grandpa always said You see us and You hear us. If You can, please get Nekkar and me out of this mess.*

Jackson stretched his arms back until his fingers tipped against the sword. Perhaps the cool steel wouldn't adhere as easily, and he could cut himself out. He tapped against the handle until he was able to grab it. As he lifted the sword and twisted his body, something amazing happened. His feet moved! Jackson slid his shoes back and forth. Though his back pants pockets were secured to the flower, his feet were free. *What's different?* Jackson questioned. He examined his legs. Neither foot was stuck but each appeared dark and wet.

"The slime! The slime!" Jackson shouted excitedly with a giddy, exhausted laugh. He quickly scooped up the pinkish liquid and wiped it around his pants legs. Once the solution touched something, the stickiness immediately fell dormant. Splashing and throwing the goo around, he freed himself and then began working from Nekkar's feet up to arms and face.

"Will you quit trying to drown me?" A grumbling, drowsy voice huffed, coughed, and spat. "I'm awake already."

"Nekkar!" Jackson dove to the ground as his friend groggily sat up, wiping the slime from his mouth. The Son of Earth momentarily forgot the codes of teenage manhood and threw his arms around his friend. Of course, after a second of joyful triumph and reunion, he remembered the socially acceptable distance, jolted back, and turned his eyes away. "I didn't know if you were going to wake up."

"It would have been a poetic way to die, right?" Nekkar smiled while stretching every muscle out of its slumber then changed his voice to a deep, singsong declaration. "'He survived against warriors and wolves and waves but was consumed by a sleeping beauty.'"

"Yeah, that sounds more manly than 'killed by a flower.'"

The two sat next to each other on the edge of the cliff, rubbing and peeling off tacky residue from their clothes and bodies. They rested, exchanged stories of Earth and Arcas, and bantered until a deep warmth flowed through the cleft onto their heads and backs. Both boys turned around to witness the light of the coral sun peeking in behind them. When Jackson chopped down the flowers and vines to kill the beastly plant, he also uncovered an opening just large enough for a man. They walked over to it, squinted in the bright light, and looked below. Miles and miles of rolling rock hills covered the land before them.

"Is that Deneb?" Jackson asked, feeling both relieved and anxious.

"Yes," Nekkar replied with a solemn voice, turning away and retrieving his sword from the ground.

"What's wrong?"

"I want you to take this." Nekkar held his sword out with two hands as an offering. Confused, Jackson examined the Arcasian but did not move toward the weapon.

"Why? You know how to use it way better than I do."

"No. I want you to have it." Nekkar's eyes were both sad and serious. "This sword is called Lodestar. It was a gift from Regulus when I vowed my services to our people as a warrior. If you carry Lodestar, you take my place in the Free Realms. Then I will take your place in our courts for any crimes brought against you."

Nekkar placed the grip of the sword into Jackson's hand and then removed his belt and sheath, fastening it around Jackson's waist. Jackson immediately felt guilty for questioning his friend's loyalty and integrity when the gem disappeared. No one had ever offered him such a valuable and sacrificial gift.

"I don't understand."

"I was wrong," Nekkar explained. "You have been as steadfast and true as any warrior in the Free Realms, as any of my brothers fathered by noble Arcturus. From now on, you are my brother. I will face my father. I will face Regulus. And I will pay your debt to Arcas."

Jackson stood for a moment, gazing over the vast cave lands below. His hand brushed the top of the sheathed sword. Its weight still felt foreign and strange but invigorating. Lodestar helped him defeat the sleeping beauty and rescue Nekkar. The heavy weapon promised the strength of purpose, protection, and power. Finally, all shadows of mistrust between him and Nekkar vanished. Jackson was no longer afraid of journeying to the Free Realms.

"No," Jackson announced with confidence, knocking his fist against his chest as he had seen Arcasian warriors perform in agreement. "If we are brothers, we will face Regulus together. I know people died because I believed Cygnus and opened The Bridge. I will state my case, and if I'm found guilty, I'll pay my debt to Arcas in full."

Jackson understood that he had to make things right between himself and the Free Realms. After all, Arcturus was guarding The Bridge, and Regulus held the other transport gem. The only available paths back to Earth required their permission and good graces. Nekkar also seemed quite at peace with his friend's reply. The journey had bonded them as friends and as brothers. Though their souls—now bound by oaths of loyalty—had withstood threats of death, a force far more powerful was brewing in the lands before them, waiting to be wakened, waiting to tear them apart.

Chapter 10

Enemy on the Eridanus

The deep, brackish waters near the mouth of the Eridanus stirred unnaturally upward. A hundred oars circled up and down in unison on the sides of each war ship, rowing against the smooth flow of fresh water emptying into the Ligeian Sea. Brave fisherman, thrill seekers, and large-game hunters occasionally defied the common fears by flowing downstream on the mammoth river. If they returned alive, these adventurers possessed the right to boast heartily of the unusual sights and dangers survived along the infamous Eridanus River. But to row against the current, to stir the waters and invite the mystical wrath of Mira and other buried beasts to rise from underneath the veil of blue, required utter madness. Sephdar possessed this madness.

The poison ailing his mind and soul were more visible than the poison ailing his stomach. While Cygnus had lead with eloquently manipulated words, confidence, and a handsome face, Sephdar ruled with fear, force, and death.

He'd acquired fresh power and wealth by instantly succeeding Cygnus's rule of the White Palace and its armies, but none of this pleased him. No power, wealth, or pleasure could adequately dull the constant, burning pangs swirling inside of him. Nothing mattered except capturing the other six sisters and finally gaining relief from his torment. Only then could he relish in his new kingdom and enjoy his newly exalted state.

The acquired soldiers, still baring the white wings of Cygnus on their coat of arms, rowed onward. Their muscles were tight and their brows dripped with sweat, but they knew better than to slow or rest. The outcome of war or dangerous waters remained uncertain, but if one defied Sephdar's orders and rested for a moment, death would befall him in an instant. Like most supreme hierarchies, those who managed to please Lord Sephdar received the choice food, clothing, pleasures, women, and—of course— unchecked power over others. But those who displeased the new ruler now decorated the outer gates of the White Palace, an array of decapitated heads. Their sullen faces and drooping jaws surrounded by crawling and flying blood-sucking insects spoke louder than any rumors in the ranks. Terrified, it didn't take long for the common soldier to collapse into immediate submission and rote obedience.

Still, one heart beat defiantly in the midst of the flagship. Alone with her thoughts, Maia rubbed her growing stomach while peering through the small porthole in her cabin wall. The fresh, misty air fluttered in around rays of golden sunlight. Though she remained a prisoner, at the moment, Maia was rewarded with an officer's cabin. It wasn't a royal room by any means, but it was a more comfortable dwelling than the dungeon of the White Palace or the damp ship's brig. If she didn't find a way of escape, however, these small pleasures and cushioned chairs would soon be replaced—no doubt—by harsh consequences. It was only a matter of time before Sephdar found out the truth.

Maia lied.

She could still hear his badgering, desperate interrogation replaying in her mind.

"Where. Did. Your sisters. Go?" He bent down chanting each word only inches from her face. Maia could smell the herbal tea steaming from his breath. But worse, she could smell the poison clashing against the hot brew inside of him. Sephdar's mind and heart had been consumed long ago, but his body still warred with the venom.

"To the Free Realms? To Trifid?" *Clip-Clomp. Clip-Clomp*. The centaur's hooves echoed against the cold, hard floor while he paced. "We know they aren't in Starling. There's nowhere left to hide in the ashes of your little forest. So, where should we burn next?" *Clip-Clomp. Clip-Clomp*. Despite the growing intensity of Sephdar's tone and demeanor, she locked her lips tightly and stared blankly at the large stone walls, refusing to answer.

"Wake up, Maia!" Spit flew from his raging mouth as he reared up, clashing his hooves against the wall in front of her and sending a cloud of dust flying through the air. "There is no safety with the Free Realms! Tell me, if the warriors are busy guarding Trifid, then who is guarding their homeland? They are an army divided between two fronts!" Sephdar softened his voice. "The only safe place is here. War is coming to Arcas, and your sisters will not escape it without my protection."

"Really?" Maia joined the conversation with a raised eyebrow and a sarcastic tone. "You're going to protect them here?" She motioned around the cell. "What lovely accommodations you offer!"

"Don't you understand that Cygnus brought you here for this purpose? Make no mistake, My Lady. I shared his food, his courtyard, and his vision long before you shared his bed!" Sephdar breathed deeply, regained control, and tried to appeal once more to her sympathy and reason. "Cygnus promised that the seven sisters would heal me. I will not rest until that promise is fulfilled. Please, get yourself out of this dungeon. Come with me to find your sisters peacefully. Fulfill your promised purpose, and I will release you all to live where ever you desire." He paused before asking again with a convoluted, concerned voice, "Where did they go?"

But Maia was not so easily manipulated. The screaming and insults and promises only strengthened her resolve. She had nearly become the lady of the White Palace, and if Cygnus had not been killed, she quite possibly could have been a queen of Arcas. She would not comply or grovel. Instead, she lifted her chin proudly, met the centaur's eyes, and replied with royal resolve.

"I will never help you find them. By the light of the three suns, you are nothing like Cygnus. If he knew what you really were, you would be the one caged. Go, four-legged beast." She motioned toward the door. "Gallop off and find them yourself. Or do you prefer to just stay here and aimlessly sniff the ground like your mongrel brothers you unleashed in my homeland?"

Her proud eyes were instantly thrown downward with a grunt as Sephdar reacted to the insult by clashing his backhand against her cheek. The old prisoner, Charles, had been sitting silently in a pile of straw, soaking in the conversation until now.

"Enough! Control yourself, Sephdar!" He stood as quickly as his feeble legs would allow and grabbed the adjoining cells bars. "You aren't going to win a lady by force. Leave her be."

"I don't have any more time to waste on winning a lady, old man." Sephdar clomped out of her cell and grabbed a whip from the weapons of torture lined against the wall. "Tie her up!" he commanded the two guards who accompanied him to the dungeon. "If her mind won't bend, then we will break her body."

"No! Sephdar, she's pregnant! Have a shred of decency!" Charles yelled and banged against the iron bars.

The men shuffled uneasily forward and stood on each side of Maia. She wiped and then licked the blood from her split lip. Refusing to be grabbed, Maia raised her arms, cueing the guards to stay back. She stood calmly, walked through the gate to the leather ties hanging from the far wall, and clutched the straps with her own freewill. Though silent, her face and body spoke volumes. *Go, ahead. Break me. Kill me if you have to. I'm already dead, anyway.*

The centaur snapped the whip against the wall several times then paced from side to side behind her, contemplating his best angle of punishment.

"Stop, Sephdar! This is madness!" Charles protested again. "The lady needs to stay healthy for their power to work. It doesn't matter if you find all of her sisters—if you injure the oldest Ilmatar, you will weaken the power of them all."

Sephdar seemed to contemplate Charles's words as he slowed his movements and wrapped the whip around his hand. He suddenly stopped to the side of Maia's face. Using the end of the whip, he pulled her face toward his to examine her state. Her teeth were clenched underneath the split and bleeding lip. Her unwavering, proud eyes still shot right through Sephdar.

"Perhaps you are right, Charles. She does not care if I beat her, but if there's enough life and compassion left in her—she may care if I beat someone else. Get the old man."

"What?" Maia yelled in a confused fluster. "No! Leave him alone!"

She twisted her body around, watching as the two guards fumbled with the lock and key to open Charles's door. With steadfast courage, the kind, elderly man walked out from the cell of his own will and stood next to Maia.

"It's alright." Charles smiled, touching her arm, hoping to encourage Maia to release her grip. "Don't waiver, My Lady. I'll be fine."

"Throw her back!" Sephdar commanded.

The guards grabbed her arms, pulling her toward the cell. Maia held the leather straps, kicking and yelling "*No! No!*" and refusing to return to her cell.

Charles had been kind to her since the moment she found herself trapped in the darkest place her body and her mind had ever entered. She couldn't bear to see his fragile skin sliced open at the end of a whip. And she couldn't bear to see him take her place in death, when more and more she longed just to escape this never-ending hell she found herself in.

Sephdar tightened the straps around Charles's wrists. The tips of his naked toes pressed against the cold rock floor while the rest of his body hung stretched out, suspended. As the tall centaur raised the whip, the lashing straps flew backward over the handle. No one heard the old man bellow when these thick strands sliced through his shirt and into the fragile flesh on his back.

The operatic scream hurling from Maia's mouth overpowered all other sounds, vibrating the dungeon and flinging the two guards off her arms onto the ground. The force of passionate power that flew from her body also threw her to the ground inside the cell. She immediately pushed up from the floor, held her growing stomach, and started running. But, unlike the Arcasian soldiers, the commanding centaur remained steadfast on his four black hooves. He kicked out a rear hoof, slamming the barred door in Maia's face before she could escape.

"ARH!" She banged her fist against the steal. "That's enough! Let him go!"

"I can do this all day, Maia," he taunted, hitting the whip against the wall several times, barely missing Charles's face. "Tell me. How long can a caged bird sing? You're looking a little weak there. Do you think you should be exerting yourself in your condition?" He pointed to her belly. "Better calm down, or you may be responsible for killing an old man and a baby all in one day." He raised the whip for a second time. Strips of red were already soaking through Charles' shirt.

"Stop! Please, I'll tell you where they are! Just stop!" she pleaded.

Sephdar smiled then lowered his arm. He could tell she was finally going to answer.

"Altair!" Maia lied. "The Hunter took my sisters to Queen Cassiopeia."

"Why?" Sephdar wasn't yet convinced. "Why go to the queen and not to the Free Realms?"

"Because they don't want to live in the Free Realms or in the kingdoms. My sisters want to live in Starling. They were going to the queen to buy rare furnishings and to seek out skilled laborers from the villages to help rebuild our home. Unfortunately, they will soon learn that you burnt up all of our resources to build with and will need to purchase that as well."

Sephdar bought the lie. He returned Charles to the cell then readied his army and his ships. He wanted to enter Altair quietly, and it was too risky to travel by land. People from Deneb or Altair or the Free Realms might easily discover them along the open roads and flat grasslands. And besides Cygnus's soldiers, few took to the Ligeian Sea. It was considered a cursed place of death ever since The Bridge War, when the waters of the sea ran thick with the blood of Earthians and Arcasians.

To reward her for compliance, Maia was "invited" along on the voyage. The centaur not only wanted to be cured as soon as he gathered the other sisters, but he also wanted to keep the Ilmatar close by. She was smart, beautiful, and powerful. If he entrusted her to his guards alone, she might easily find a way to escape in his absence. Though locked in a cabin and under Sephdar's constant watch, Maia hadn't completely given up on escape. In the dungeon, there were few variables, but here, the morale of the soldiers, the sturdiness of the boats, Queen Cassiopeia's response, and the uncertainties beneath the waters all could change her circumstances in an instant.

Charles warned the Ilmatar to be prepared. Sephdar would eventually discover her daring lie, and she would not go unpunished. *Unpunished.* The word imprinted across Maia's mind letter by letter as the boat ebbed up and down. Cygnus was dead. Her home lay in ash and rubble. And her lovely sisters headed the opposite direction. Maia debated whether there was any hope left worth fighting for, any future worth bringing a child into.

Aren't I already being punished? Don't I already feel a pain worse than death? How can I bring a child into this world of clashing kingdoms and wicked rulers? What kind of life can I offer?

Maia's power and life seemed to be slowly fading like the distant shoreline of the sea consumed by the growing shadowy chaos of the jungle. Was this trip her last grasp at survival or a willful step toward death? Yes, there would be consequences and soon. Maybe it would involve pain only for her, but most likely, that pain would also endanger her child. An innocent life hung in the balance of adult weights beyond his or her control. But that wasn't the only innocent life at risk. The unsuspecting people dwelling in the kingdom of Altair were also in danger.

Though she didn't think about innocent bloodshed when she first mentioned Altair, Maia knew that the idle Altairian army wouldn't stand a chance against Cygnus's trained soldiers. Of course, Sephdar would first request that the six Ilmatar leave Altair peacefully. But he journeyed with an army for a reason. The queen's men would inevitably respond with "They're not here," and the new lord would force his way through the entire kingdom like a roaring lion until he was convinced.

Still, not all hope was lost. In the palace dungeon, Charles told her to send word to Shedir—the most trusted advisor of the queen. If she could warn him, there was hope of victory against Sephdar, and hope of escape against her captors. Several days prior, Maia tied a message around a small bird and sent it flying to Altair on the waves of a song. She kept silent about her lie but warned Altair that Sephdar was coming prepared for war.

For Maia, a battle held the promise of death but also the promise of rebirth. Altair would likely suffer some loss because of her deception but so would Sephdar. More than anything at the moment, Maia longed for freedom from this new Lord of the White Palace. And the chaos of war enticed her with this freedom, whether it came in the form of a stray Altairian arrow or an Altairian rescue.

Now, Maia just had to wait for the shards of fate to explode and settle where they may in the remaining dust. Looking out at the Eridanus, she couldn't help but remember her own beloved little river that quietly flowed through Starling. She had already cried for Cygnus, for herself, and for her child, but now, she shed tears for her destroyed homeland. With a solemn, reflective tone, she quietly sang about her first love.

Lie near the waters blue
Listen to friends so true
Where volantis swim along
Starling, there I belong

"In the name of Queen Cassiopeia, the royal Flower of the Eridanus, you are trespassing in her majesty's realm. Stop rowing and lower your anchors!" shouted the soldier from a watchtower hidden in the jungle.

The warriors on each voyaging vessel paused their rowing. Every heart pounded in anticipation. Maia stopped singing and pressed against the ship, listening through the little window. A foreign army had not approached the jungle kingdom from the river in thousands of years, especially uninvited. Their arrival at the outer boundaries of Altair promised conflict. And this conflict could alter not only the destinies of Maia and Sephdar, but the destiny of the entire world.

Chapter 11

Andromeda and Perseus

"Son of Earth!" a young Cephid called out. Freezing in the middle of a ball game, the boy squinted his yellow eyes and studied the wanderers entering the gates of Deneb. Excitedly, he shifted his head to the side, shouting to his friends, "Hey-ya, guys! Jackson the Scorpion Slayer is back! I told you he would come back!" Every dirtied little face now turned from the game in the patchy grass and started running toward Jackson.

"You've been here before?" Nekkar questioned curiously.

"Yeah, but last time it was a bit different." Jackson felt both honored and embarrassed by the unexpected attention.

Like a mob of star-struck fans, the Cephid children surrounded Jackson and began to chant and bounce around him.

Red eyes! Red heart! Raised tail!
Shaula and terror came to our land.
Son of Earth! Sons of Arcas! Spears impale!
Beat the beast together, together stand!

Random children grabbed Jackson's legs, pulled his hands, and hugged him. Feeling slightly overwhelmed by the flattering attention, Jackson smiled and patted the little boys on the heads and backs, thanking them for the warm greeting.

"Wow, Son of Jack, sounds like you are some sort of hero in this realm." Nekkar elbow-jabbed Jackson in the arm.

With so many vivid memories of Deneb seared in his mind for the past six months, the kingdom almost felt like a new land to Jackson. The distressing makeshift hospital tents—once filled with the dead and maimed—were now replaced by tents of commerce and infectious laughter. The smells of blood and septicity had long vanished with better aromas of food and perfume.

Upon entering the city gates, Jackson and Nekkar's senses flooded with a sea of cuisine, crafts, and music. The carefree atmosphere delighted their famished and wearied bodies. At the first shop with customer-ready tables and chairs, they grabbed a loaf of bread, a vial of spiced dipping oil, and faced the merchant to pay.

"How much for the bread and oil?" Nekkar asked, reaching into his coin pouch.

Like every Cephid in the marketplace, this merchant had been studying the foreigners since they walked through the gate. Tall people were usually easy to spot, but with a herd of children following them, the two were impossible to miss.

"Ha! What use have I for gold, silver, or gems?" the savvy merchant shook his head as if slightly insulted. "Don't you know that you have entered Deneb where precious materials abound?"

"What can I pay with then?" Nekkar asked impatiently, waiting for the punchline answer the merchant was so obviously eager to give. He didn't have the energy to haggle with the locals. The merchant most definitely had his eyes on some worthy payment, but he didn't know how long they would have to dance around the topic before they would find out what it was. "You want the shirt on my back, the shoes from my feet?"

"No! None of that will do." With a straight face, the merchant waved his hand to dismiss the offerings. "I won't sell for anything *you've* brought." He then waited a moment to witness the reaction of disbelief on the strangers' faces before revealing with a smile. "I want to see what the Son of Earth brought in his bag from the dark world."

"I don't really have anything," Jackson shrugged.

"Show me." The merchant eagerly stepped around his storefront display and waited as Jackson removed the backpack, held it low near the ground, and opened it for the

Cephid to peer in. His yellow eyes seemed to glow slightly as he stuck his head near the open pack. As if sifting through fruit at a store, he touched and squeezed each item, mumbling to himself in disapproval and contemplation. The merchant had become an anxious customer.

"What is this?" He pulled out the sketchbook and was about to open it when Jackson snagged it quickly away.

"That's not for sale. Sorry." Jackson's cheeks turned slightly pink as he tried to shrug off the personal value of the book. "It's nothing special, just drawing paper, writing parchment, whatever you call it here." The little man returned to shuffling through the bag, and then pulled out the most unlikely trade.

"This! I will give you the bread and oil in exchange for this clear jug."

"An empty water bottle?" Jackson felt like there must be a misunderstanding. It didn't feel right to trade trash for fresh food. The Cephid held the bottle up to his head and peered through its clear plastic with the thin wrapper torn off the outside. He then knocked and tapped against the side, listening to the non-glass sounds. After unsuccessfully trying to pull the top off like a cork, Jackson showed him how to unscrew the blue, ribbed lid.

"Yes! That is my offer." The man handed the bottle back to Jackson. His face turned stone cold again as if this were a hard-core valuable deal.

"Um? Okay. Here, you can have the other one too."

The merchant held his prizes proudly as he returned to his booth with a crowd gathering around him to gawk at the alien purchase. Jackson and Nekkar sat down at a short wooden table and chairs to savor the bread and oil along with complimentary cups of fresh underground cavern water. While chewing on his second bite of dipped bread covered with tiny pieces of garlic and herbs, Jackson's enjoyment was interrupted by a swift *Wack!* against his head.

Jackson immediately turned, rubbing his scalp. "What was that?" His hair felt slimy and moist at the impact point and he noticed a bruised peach lying in the dirt behind him. The crowds of people in the marketplace seemed to be going about their business unaltered, so he shrugged it off as an accident.

Womp!

"Show yourself, little fiend!" Nekkar shouted in irritation while unconsciously moving his hand to his sword. He grasped at nothingness near his hip then remembered his sword belonged to Jackson now. His eyes shifted to the familiar weapon hanging on his friend, but the steel blade had vanished from its sheath. The Earthian was busy swiping sweet, slimy particles from the front of his shirt. *Ow!* Jackson's spine leapt slightly, and he threw his hands up in surrender, reacting to a sharp poke pressing his shirt into his back. Ordinarily, a sword to the back would have caused immediate panic, but Nekkar could now see the alleged fruit-throwing villain, and his expression quickly dropped from its ready-to-brawl façade to pure confusion, interest, and surprise. And upon hearing the villain's voice, Jackson knew his attacker's exact identity.

"What right does an Earthling have to come armed into my kingdom?"

A rush of mixed emotions ran over Jackson's body. He dreamed often about this moment. For the last six months, he replayed over and over again what he would say if he saw *her* again. Every touch, every breath, every word, every tingling sensation remained etched to perfection on the storyboard of Jackson's mind. Especially the kiss. The memory was definitely real but was the kiss? Could that brief moment in the caves be merely an illusion, an accident, or was there a real spark of interest hiding beneath that fleeting flare?

Yes, he'd rehearsed what to say to the purple-eyed, amber-haired princess, but one couldn't simply prepare the right words to say to such a creature. She was too unpredictable, too exotic, and too savvy.

"I don't know." He shrugged, casually cool. "How else am I supposed to protect myself against a princess who enjoys attacking unsuspecting guests?"

A gasp of laughter came from Andi as she lowered the sword. When Jackson turned to face her, he was greeted with a hug.

"I never thought I'd see you again!" She released her

arms from around him, stood back, and shook her head with spunky disapproval. "I can't believe that your band of interesting friends didn't mention that you came back here with them! And your leg!" She tapped the blunt side of the sword against his jeans. "It looks totally healed!"

"Yeah, my leg is fine," Jackson replied. "But what friends are you talking about? Who is here?"

"Rigel, Otava, and Merope, of course! Didn't you come with them?" Jackson shook his head. "We'll, they just arrived with news from the Free Realms."

"What news comes from the Free Realms?" Nekkar spoke up in official urgency, moving closer to join the conversation.

"Ha! If only I knew. A *princess* isn't allowed to concern herself with the politics of state." She rolled her eyes slightly as a teen does when her parents demand the formalities of court but never include her in the actual important matters of the kingdom. "We are much too busy attacking unsuspecting guests." Andi winked humorously at Jackson. "Who are you anyways? Your face looks familiar. Have we met before?"

"Oh, sorry. Let me introduce you to my friend from the Free Realms." Jackson stepped in to properly initiate the greeting. "Andi, this is Nek…"

"Princess Andromeda, at last we meet!" Nekkar interrupted, thrusting out his hand as if he were going to shake hers in greeting. Andi reached out as well, but instead of a handshake, Nekkar gently cupped her fingers in his grasp, bent over, and kissed the back of her hand. Then he stood, smiled, and looked directly into her eyes with a sly grin. "My name is Perseus."

Andi's face turned bright red as she removed her hand from his and looked to the ground. It was the first time Jackson witnessed a slight shyness and embarrassment by the attention given to her. Jackson stood with a blank look of utter confusion. He saw Nekkar kiss her hand and Andi's unmistakable reaction but didn't realize that Nekkar had just offered a very direct pick-up line to the princess. It wasn't a casual, broad comment to attract any lady. Nekkar's succinct introduction was aimed at Andi's very identity, at her very heart.

"Dude, what are you talking about?" Jackson softly punched him in the shoulder. "You didn't tell me your real name was Perseus," he spouted off like a confused young buck trying to decide if a rival had just entered into his territory.

"Oh, I'm sure his name isn't *really* Perseus." Andi crossed her arms over her chest to regain some control over her emotions. "That was my great grandfather's name." Turning to Nekkar she continued. "Ah, now I remember where I've seen your face. You were among those who entered my courtyard in Altair, hunting down the Son of Earth. I see that for growing up in the barbarian lands, you have at least been taught the royal histories." Andi jabbed a lighthearted insult at the handsome foreigner who had briefly unsteadied her wit by personifying the famous love story hero of the kingdoms.

Andi wasn't used to this sort of direct pursuit. In Altair and Deneb, she was still treated like everyone's little sister or like a porcelain doll that must be put on a shelf, out of reach. The destruction of ancestors during the Pillar Wars, and the marriage of the two kingdoms, left no legitimate royal suitors. And there was no hurry to rear heirs to the throne. Her parents created a lasting peace, and Arcas gave lasting youth to the last royal couple. Common boys from the kingdoms who were interested in her kept their distance because they were either scared of her parents or scared of her confident beauty.

"My father is Arcturus, commander of the Free Realm armies. Like you, I am well-bred and well educated. My parents still hold to the formalities of old, but I think—like you—I prefer freedom and adventure over needless tradition."

"Well, entering Deneb with Jackson certainly puts you at interesting odds with your people. Last I knew, the Free Realms were chasing Jackson to remove him from Arcas. If your father had succeeded in Altair, our people would still be under the terror of Shaula. I hope you come to Deneb peacefully because the Son of Earth is considered highly by my people." She admired Lodestar for a moment before returning the sword to Jackson, not quite sure yet if she could trust Nekkar.

"My Lady, I assure you that whenever I enter your presence, I come with only the most honorable intentions. Jackson is like a brother to me, and I will stand by his side against any foe from any realm. As you likely know, my people have control of Trifid and guard its Bridge to Earth, but a new evil has risen in Cygnus's place at the White Palace. I have come in the name of my father, Noble Arcturus, to seek an audience with your father King Alderamin on this account."

"I see. Errai!" Andi hollered and waved across the marketplace. A Cephid in official palace clothes scurried quickly to join them.

"Jackson!" He bowed as a show of honor. "The rumors in Deneb ring true today. It is good to see you again, Son of Earth."

"Thank you, Errai. It's nice to be back."

"Errai, Jackson's companion is a son of Arcturus from the Free Realms and has come to discuss important matters with the king. Will you please guide him to the palace?"

"Most certainly, My Lady." He nodded his head in agreement. He turned to Nekkar and added, "I cannot guarantee your words will be well received, but I can guarantee the king will at least listen to your request."

"That is all I can ask," Nekkar responded. "Son of Jack"—he turned to his friend and teased—"I hope you will keep hold of your sword while I'm gone. And princess..." He bowed then gazed into her purple eyes while raising one eyebrow dramatically. "May the hours until we meet again drift swiftly and beautifully like the breeze through your golden hair."

"Ohhh-kay." Andi tilted her blushing cheeks in disbelief at Nekkar's forwardness. "Good luck with my father, barbarian."

Though standing in a crowded marketplace with various people stopping to wave at Jackson, slap him on the back, or nod in recognition to the princess, Jackson felt like he was finally alone with Andi. He hoped she would stay around for a while, but he also didn't want to be a burden or an inconvenience.

"So, should I just hang out in the market until Nekkar comes back?" Jackson asked, not wanting to barge into Andi's day with his unplanned presence.

"Absolutely not!" Andi took charge of the situation with a grin. "I'm taking you to see the drawings!"

"The drawings?"

"In the caves, silly! You've made it into history, Earthling." She waved her arm in the air between them as if reading a headline. "Jackson, the Scorpion Slayer."

"Sure, that sounds like fun." Jackson tried to play it cool even though he was bursting with excitement to be back in the caves alone with Andi. "Oh, wait! Is there somewhere I can buy some rice on the way?"

"Are you hungry?"

"No." Jackson chuckled. "I brought something from Earth, but it was damaged in water."

"Ah, we do the same thing with our wet boots. Fill the toes with rice, and it draws the water out."

"Exactly."

While Andi bounced off to a nearby vegetable stand to procure a small bag of rice, Jackson memorized her every movement, every wave of her hair, and every curve of her body. He knew this visit would be short. He would be going to the Free Realms soon to face who-knows-what for his involvement in opening The Bridge with Cygnus.

"Here you go." Andi handed Jackson a small burlap bag filled with rice. He pulled his phone from his pocket and carefully shoved it into the middle of the bag then pulled the strings tightly around the opening.

"What is that?" Andi asked, peering over at the strange black device.

"I can't really describe it, but if the rice works, I'll show it to you."

"Deal. But I expect your alien toy to be worth the exorbitant price I paid for the rice," she teased sarcastically.

As they headed out of the marketplace together toward the vast, intricate caves, everything else vanished from Jackson's mind. The only world was Arcas. The only town was Deneb. And the only girl was Andi.

Amber, he thought. *Nekkar, her hair doesn't resemble plain gold that can be scratched or melted. It's amber like the clear, fair gem that allows light to dance through its varying yellowish-orange highlights with perfect clarity and exotic beauty.*

Jackson wasn't as brazen and bold as Nekkar to declare such praise out loud to the fiery princess. But perhaps the cool, dark solace of the caves could speak the words that the country-town Midwestern teen could not. At the cavern entrance, Jackson's heart beat a little wilder. His fingers could almost feel the vivacious energy of Andi's interlocking hand that he remembered so well. He shouted *Calm! Cool! Control!* to each nerve surging with expectation. But his heart whispered louder. *Just a brush of the shoulders, just a touch of the fingers, just an accidental kiss.* Though he knew—this time—it would be no accident.

Chapter 12

Divided Realms

"Yes?" King Alderamin called out in response to the knocking that interrupted his meeting. He was engaged in deep discussion with Rigel, Merope, and Otava about the current state of the kingdom realms.

"Forgive me for interrupting, My King," Errai apologized. "But a son of Arcturus from the Free Realms is requesting to speak with you on their behalf."

All present agreed to invite the Nekkar into the strategic exchange, and the king insisted that Errai stay as well. Nekkar hoped to urge the monarchies to finally join in the fight to protect all people from Sephdar and the open Bridge to Earth. He began his plea by describing the attack and destruction he witnessed in the Starling Forest several days prior.

"If I'd been there"—Otava raised his furry, clawed fist in anger—"by the Ursas, those fiery wolves would have been cooking in their own flames!"

"They may have destroyed your forest, but you helped rescue the Ilmatar," Rigel assured calmly. "Because of you, they did not destroy the souls of Starling."

"Yes. Thank you, Otava," Merope agreed earnestly. "I'm glad we got my sisters out of the White Palace and safely to the Free Realms. Alcyone was so eager to return home, but it sounds like there is no home to return to."

"So, who is this new *Lord* of the White Palace?" Alderamin inquired, emphasizing the title of lord since it was a stolen honor in this case.

"All I know is that the wolves called him Lord Sephdar," Nekkar answered with a solemn shrug.

"Sephdar. Sephdar." The king repeated the name as if he were retrieving memories.

"Wasn't that the name of the centaur, My King?" Errai questioned. "The archer from the Pillar Wars? I believe you banished him from the kingdom realms."

"The archer... the centaur... the THIEF!" King Alderamin remembered. "Yes, yes. How could I forget the one who fought for the kings then stole the crowns off our noble fathers' corpses before they arrived home for burial!"

"Didn't he return to his people in the Free Realms?" Errai asked.

"There's no way," Nekkar jumped in. "My father told me that neither men nor beasts were allowed into the Free Realms if they fought in the Pillar Wars."

"So, if he was banished from the kingdoms and the

Free Realms, where did he go for all these years?" Merope wondered.

"Trifid," Rigel answered assuredly. "There have long been rumors in my travels of a decrepit, infectious soul living alone in the old ruins among the black corvus. I'll bet that Cygnus took a true story, exaggerated it, and then used this ominous 'Gurges Ater' to manipulate everyone."

"Great!" Otava blurted out. "The bird-man lies and the horse-man steals, yet no one trusts the dependable bear because he looks too beastly! No offense to all of the naked toes present, but I say there is something scary in the stuff men are made of."

"I agree, Otava," Merope added solemnly, then expounded with a growing twinkle in her eye, "Men are quite beastly, are they not?" She teased, swatting the back of her fingers lightly against Rigel's arm. Everyone smiled and chuckled, enjoying a light-hearted moment in the midst of serious dialogue.

"Speaking of beastly men... Nekkar, your father brought quite the fury out of my queen when they first met. She graciously allowed a foreign military commander in her presence even though the Free Realms have remained invisibly distant for the entire reign of King Alderamin and Queen Cassiopeia." The king continued, curious how Nekkar would react to his accusations. "You are a youth, so perhaps you do not know the history. Your people left the kingdoms after The Bridge War and have been only loyal to themselves since the three great kings rose in wealth and power on Arcas. So, tell me. Why do Arcturus and Regulus suddenly feel the need to invade our lands? Why only now do they have the impudence to beg us to join them?"

"I know we have long been absent from the kingdoms." Nekkar spoke up with both confidence and restraint to defend his people from the charges of the king. "But we have neither been idle nor ignorant. Yes, at first the Free Realms traveled west beyond the dark river Antares and the Mystic Mountains to start a new realm apart from monarchies and Earthians. But as Regulus grew in wisdom and stature, he taught us that we are still brothers with those who remained in the kingdoms. After the Pillar Wars, we spent much time and great wealth to find and purchase the gems of old. We guarded the red gems far from the kingdoms to protect us all. Year after year, as the three suns rose upon us, the Free Realms kept our world safe from the darkness of Earth. But when the three gems vanished one day, we hastily followed the rumors of Gurges Ater and the stolen gems. The rumors led us back to the kingdoms and to White Wings, who often entered your gates. With all respect, Your Majesty, it was the Free Realms who lost blood against White Wings to secure Trifid. And because of our constant guard of the gems today, we are safe from Earthians trampling into Arcas and into your kingdoms."

The king stood and walked to the palace window. Everyone watched quietly, awaiting a response. The land below rolled in greens and grays. Deneb was quiet and plain on the surface but bursting with sound and color underneath. The king may have become complacent and visionless in regards to the future, but he was never careless about his people. Though he looked different, the same Cephid blood pumped through Alderamin's veins.

While trade blossomed at The Bridge in the early days, his father, Denebola, was chosen as the first king from among the young men. Denebola was the son of a noble and wealthy Cephid who married an esteemed—but much taller—woman from the kingdom of Vega. Thus, Denebola grew longer than his fellow Cephids and had dimmer eyes, but he was also as strong as an ox. Because of his mixed culture and great stature, he was chosen to lead the kingdom in trade and in war. After The Bridge War, Denebola built the castle in Deneb, the pillar, and enriched the caves with painted history and beauty. The land flowed with treasures from the trade he established with Earth.

But when Alderamin inherited the kingdom at a young age, without parents to guide him, his heart was weary. He maintained the kingdom and nursed his people's wounds from battle, but he never gained a renewed vision for the future. Though they hadn't lacked resources in the past, Deneb had grown rapidly in wealth and production since Jackson appeared months earlier. And Alderamin connected this increased prosperity with a restored union to Earth.

"It's interesting how concerned your people have suddenly become regarding kingdoms they abandoned and despised." King Alderamin returned to his chair among the group. "You see, Nekkar, we are not afraid of the Earthians as you are. The three great kings prospered in their trade with them. The Sons of Earth were our friends and allies. We do not know why that world was destroyed by water or why destruction followed the once prosperous union of our worlds. But when war did come, the Free Realms did not come to our aide. Your people did not fight to close the pillars. My fathers had to hire mercenaries like this very Sephdar to help. It was *our* blood that was shed"—he pounded his fist passionately against the small table holding their drinks—"to keep the dark waters of Earth from destroying Arcas. *Our* blood and *our* rule has kept Arcas in peace for more passings of the suns than any other age."

"True," Nekkar agreed. "Your blood shut the pillars, but now our blood guards The Bridge and has paid a high price for its security. King Alderamin, war and destruction are moving around the land at this very moment, seeking those it can devour. I survived against it but my men were consumed. And I agree with you that Earth is not to blame for our troubles. Jackson, the Son of Earth, helped me escape the fires in Starling and countless other dangers during our journey here."

"What!" Merope interrupted. "Jackson is here?" Rigel and Otava also perked with interested, astonished their young friend found a way to return.

"Yes, he just arrived in Deneb with me," Nekkar replied. "I count him as my friend and brother. After learning more about Earth's people and their ways, I'll admit that this present evil did not come from another world like we once believed. It came out of Arcas and must be defeated by Arcas. King Alderamin, if we remove the threat of Sephdar first, all the realms can then decide together how to deal with The Bridge to Earth."

"So, Rigel, you most recently came from Free Realms…" Alderamin turned his attentions to The Hunter who—though he'd sought refuge for the Seven Sisters in the Free Realms—did not swear allegiance to any land. "What does Regulus himself request of the kingdoms?"

"Regulus will be arriving to Trifid by ship. He is asking that you and the queen meet him there in three passings of the suns." Rigel handed him the official parchment, sealed with the running white horse of the Free Realms.

"Errai," the king instructed his most trusted advisor, "reply to Regulus."

The chamberlain immediately moved to the letter writing desk, setting a parchment, quill, and ink in front of him.

Regulus, Leader of the Free Realms,

Like you, I am eager to finally meet face to face. While I am willing to discuss the future of our world together, I regret to inform you that I will not be meeting you at Trifid.

As you are well aware, my Kingdom of Deneb is closest to the White Palace. If Sephdar proves to be on a path of conquest with his newly inherited army, I refuse to leave my people and my home unguarded.

I welcome the Righteous Regulus to instead enter my courts at Deneb. Upon your welcomed arrival, I will listen intently and consider joining forces. Until then, the king will guard his home and his people.

King Alderamin, Sovereign over Deneb

One and Only King of the Kingdom Realms in Arcas

Chapter 13

Chamber of Hearts

At first, the stroll through the caves was full of helmeted Cephids with their yellow, glowing eyes turning around every few feet to heartily welcome Jackson back and acknowledge the princess. Though their labor required intense attention and strength with each swing of the axe, they were a jolly people who appeared to work effortlessly and happily. Life was a treasure hunt with each day holding the opportunity to bring a new precious metal from the hard grasp of rocky darkness to the soft light.

At last, Andi and Jackson arrived in the halls of painted history. The princess rested her torch in a post on the wall near the newest illustration displaying the battle against Scorpius. The scene exquisitely revealed every detail of the final fight. Near the chosen entrance to the cave lands, Merope's hand was resting on the outside walls with musical notes and vibrations floating in the air around her.

Otava stood behind the caged scorpion raising his bear fist while King Alderamin aimed a spear at the red heart of the albino beast. Little Cephids crowded around the main scene while the elite fighters clutched to the dropped door holding down the scorpion's tail. Jackson looked like a true victorious warrior, raising a sword high while sitting atop the cage.

"Wow!" Jackson laughed. "Am I really that big and white?" He couldn't help but pick out the two differences that made him stand way out in the depiction.

Though feeling proud, overwhelmed, and flattered by the masculine portrayal of himself in the kingdom history, Jackson had to verbalize the obviously funny quirk. He looked like a white giant compared to the multitude of little, dark-skinned Cephids cheering from the sidelines.

"Well... you *are* a little pale," Andi teased. "But definitely a lot shorter in real life than in the stories." She nudged him with her elbow and laughed.

"Hey, I think I've grown since last time!" Jackson protested with a chuckle. He stood tall and moved closer to her, measuring down with his hand to prove that his stature now exceeded her own. "See?" He patted her head.

"Fine," she conceded. "I'll admit that you're taller, but it's only because you're wearing those alien shoes." She knocked her foot against his. "If you take them off, I'm sure it will be more like this." Andi stood on her tiptoes to meet Jackson's at an even height.

The playful bantering designed to challenge and tease was unconsciously luring their bodies closer. With only inches separating them now, their eyes locked together. They were no longer gazing just into each other's eyes, they were gazing into the deeper parts of the soul. It was a beautiful and terrifying and exciting sensation.

"Wonderful day in the caves, Princess!" a Cephid woman greeted with a small child in tow. Andi blushed and quickly turned away, putting some distance between her and Jackson.

"Yes, it's a lovely day indeed," Andi answered cheerfully. As the woman disappeared from sight, the two teens found themselves alone with an awkward quietness filling the shadows around them.

"So, what's the story with your great grandfather?" Jackson casually broke the silence.

"Which one?" Andi skipped lightly tracing her fingers along the wall as if she didn't know what he was referring to.

"Perseus. He must have quite the story if Nekkar wanted to steal his name."

Andi silently studied Jackson's face as if she didn't know how to begin telling him a story so personal, so important, and so powerful. Suddenly, her expression changed as she jumped up from leaning against the wall, lunged forward and grabbed Jackson's hand. "Come on!" She pulled.

"Where are we going?" Jackson grasped her hand back, reached for the torch, and ran to keep up with her.

"To show you the story!" She looked back with a sparkle in her eye.

"Show me?" Jackson forgot for a moment that all history in Deneb lived through more of a visual telling than an oral or written one.

"Someone has to educate you Earthlings!"

Jackson's breath increased, and his heart pounded more intensely as they twisted and turned through the maze of tunnels. Flames flickered behind them from the torch in his left hand as a fire of hope kindled in his soul. He didn't want to get too excited or imagine that she held a depth of feeling equal to his own, but things were definitely different than last time. Andi's hand no longer felt foreign, and his no longer tingled with sweaty insecurity. The reservations of being two teens belonging to different worlds—aliens to each other's home and way of life—had vanished. Now, they were indisputable friends. And maybe, just maybe, they could be more.

They raced deeper and deeper into the dark cave lands. Twisting and turning innumerable times, Jackson controlled the old urges of panic. He fought back the claustrophobic palpitations and calmed the cranial neurons screaming *Danger! Danger!* He was with Andi, and her courageous sparks of life spoke louder than fear. Unlike most others, her carefree courage wasn't foolish or rash. Andi wasn't afraid because she knew her way through the darkness of the jungle and the darkness of the caves. She always knew how to find the light again. She made Jackson feel brave, and at this moment, he felt braver than ever. Her hand grasping his protected his mind, so Jackson could fully enjoy the adventurous world around him.

"Here!" Andi stopped abruptly. "Now close your eyes."

"I already can barely see in here." Jackson laughed.

"Come on, just do it."

"Okay. Okay." Jackson gave in to the game, closing his eyes as Andi led him slowly. She pulled him gently forward, turning left. They entered a new sort of room in the caves. A large one where he could smell moisture, feel tiny wet droplets flying through fresh air, and hear the sound of crashing water.

"Open your eyes!" She released his hand and stood back to see Jackson's expression.

"Whoa." There were few words that could accurately describe the scene around them. "This place is amazing."

The large, open room held a pool in the center with a beautiful, curved bridge connecting the smooth rock floor on both sides. Flowing with tresses of soft blues and whites, a sparkling waterfall showered down into the pool behind the bridge. Light and water entered the cavern together from an opening in the rock ceiling high above. Blue and white crystals glistened around them while decorative, carved arches rose up on the walls like a cathedral.

"There they are," Andi pointed to the waterfall.

"Who?" Overwhelmed by the grandeur surrounding them, Jackson had forgotten why they'd come.

"My great grandmother and grandfather."

Jackson squinted hard, but the streams of whites and blues cascading down overwhelmed his vision. He expected to find drawings on the wall elaborately displaying the illustrated history of Andromeda and Perseus. Then, it dawned on him... Perhaps this was a different type of memorial, a final memorial.

"Is this their tomb?"

"No, silly. We call it the Chamber of Hearts. It's a shrine dedicated to them and the... *eternity of love.*" Andi swooped her arm through the air with an overly dramatic display like one would expect from a Shakespearean stage. "My dad built it as an engagement present for my mom because she esteemed her grandparents more than anyone else." She sighed a soft chuckle of irony. "Too bad *their* love didn't last."

"Your great grandparents'?"

"No. My parents'." She lightly huffed with frustration. "I'm told they were in love once, if anyone can believe it. They were joined on that bridge. They made vows to the *eternity of love.* But," she added matter-of-factly, "they rule separate kingdoms."

This was the first time Jackson had heard somber tones exit her lips. Even now, she tried to cover the melancholy with dramatic nuances and sarcastic smiles, but he could tell that her parents' separate lives affected her. Most days, Andi outshined the sad state of her family by living for the action and adventure and joy of the moment, but in this rare moment, the vulnerable truth came out.

"I know what you mean," Jackson empathized, opening his own fresh wounds so she wouldn't feel alone. "My parents just separated to different homes. Even when they lived together, they barely saw each other. And when they did see each other, they didn't seem to enjoy being together."

"I'm sorry." Andi smiled compassionately as a kindred spirit. "I know what it's like to live in two different homes."

"Yeah," Jackson chuckled in agreement. "Right now, I feel like I live in two different worlds."

"Well, that's what the Chamber of Hearts and the statue of my great grandparents are all about. They're supposed to be a reminder to choose each other over other people, other kingdoms, and other worlds."

Jackson nodded, then asked, "Statue? Where?"

"You still haven't found Andromeda and Perseus?" Jackson shook his head. "Come on. Over here!" She perked back up to her adventurous self. "Once you see them, you'll never have trouble finding them again."

Andi led the way around the pool of water, past the bridge to the back, near the waterfall. The misty air dampened their bare arms and faces. Behind the waterfall, a narrow path of rock protruded flat out from the wall, leading to the white marble figures. When one of the suns hit the open ceiling at the right angle, it would light up the statues, allowing them to shine through the billowing water in front of them. Andromeda and Perseus were holding each other, facing the water. Though standing, the young woman seemed to be tangled in some type of cord around her waist.

"So, are you finally going tell me this epic story about the *eternity of love* or are you planning to leave me in *eternal suspense*?" Jackson joked lightly.

"Oh, no!" she whispered anxiously, then jumped down into the water behind the figures.

"What's wrong?" he asked, confused and slightly worried by her odd behavior.

"Get down here!" Andi reached up and pulled on his arm. "Someone's coming!"

Concerned they were breaking some kingdom rule about entering the shrine, Jackson quickly dropped his backpack on the ledge and obeyed. He slid down into the water, ducking side-by-side with Andi behind the stone-fashioned lovers. The moving water lapped around the figures and soaked the squatting teens up to their ribcages. Both tried to ignore the fact their shoulders, arms, hips, and knees were touching in the snug hiding spot. Instead of focusing on the soothing sensation of warm bodies converging in cool waters, they focused on quieting their breath and heightening their auditory senses. The waterfall added white noise between them and the intruders, which required them to concentrate on listening. As true with anyone in their situation, they were curious about who had entered the shrine and why.

The thick boots of a man and light laughter of a woman echoed around the large cavern. Speaking with hushed, arduous voices, the two entered the Chamber of Hearts with conversation that only the other lover was meant to hear. For a moment, their focus moved to the beauty and grandeur of the waterfall as they moved toward the center bridge. Andi's eyes widened as she threw a glance at Jackson that shouted, *They are getting closer! I can't believe we are hiding here!* She smiled then quickly covered her mouth to quiet the nervous giggles that concealment often creates. Jackson returned a humored grin and shook his head as if to say *Lady, what trouble are you getting me into this time?* Even though Jackson didn't want to get caught eavesdropping or hiding behind a sacred monument, he also didn't want to leave her side.

"Come on, just tell me where the Son of Earth and the Daughter of Arcas are hiding," the woman demanded playfully. Andi and Jackson stopped breathing. "Ah, now I see them! Crouching behind the waterfall, enraptured in each other's arms," the woman remarked dramatically. The two teens froze and blushed, growing more nervous. Even if they were discovered, they hoped the seekers wouldn't have the audacity to come behind the waterfall to fetch them.

"I'd like to be enraptured in someone's arms…" the man commented with sly bluntness.

"Well, perhaps if your boat gets overthrown by the mighty Cetus, I'll come to save you too… Oh, wait, I think I already did that," she teased.

"I don't know if you can say you *saved* me when Mira the Wonderful clearly steered me to fall upon the dry shore."

"Mer-o-pe and Ri-gel!" Andi mouthed, pointing her thumb toward the bridge. She had quickly pieced the clues together.

Jackson nodded his head and smiled as if he understood, but he had no clue what she was trying to communicate. He was never very good at lip reading. He should have recognized the voices, but the Son of Earth was too busy thinking about the Daughter of Arcas hunkered down next to him. *Hold to your axe and hold to your lass; walk her through the caves that are cool and clean,* he recited the beloved song of Deneb in his head. He was starting to believe the Cephid people—that the best way to get close to a girl was to stroll through the caves. Touching side-by-side, their knees angled toward each other to keep their silhouettes from shadowing beyond the statues. The princess exhaled inches from his mouth, their silent breath mingling in the air.

"Details. Who needs useless details? You weren't moving—looked like death, quite frankly—and I woke you up." Merope pushed back playfully.

"Oh, no. Details are essential facts, My Lady. And the fact is that Perseus—the most legendary Son of Earth— saved Andromeda by facing the beast in the water at Andromeda's side, not from the comfort of the shore where you stood. See, it says right here." He read the plaque fixed to the middle of the bridge.

A shrewd man throws a blade.
A strong man throws a rope.
But Perseus threw himself,
And Andromeda held great hope.

"Yes, but a prudent *woman* throws a stick."

"And why is that?"

"Well, a thrown blade could hurt the entangled victim, and a thrown rope could drag down the rescuer. She's much too clever to enter the path of the beast, so she throws a stick and waits on the shore."

"It might be clever, but they'll never carve a monument to that type of valor."

"Oh, really? Pray tell, what type of gallantry becomes worthy of legend? If someone infamous like *The Hunter* found a lovely lady trapped in the waters of the great Eridanus, what would he have thrown? A rope? Himself?" Merope flared her eyes and lowered her brows, testing him to see if his wit could match his affections for her.

"I would have thrown the beast, of course." He

beamed with a champion's confidence. Merope started to laugh heartily at the ridiculously macho answer and soon Rigel joined.

Andi and Jackson relaxed a bit behind the frozen star-crossed lovers. They were no longer nervously hiding but enjoying the lighthearted conversations of a happy couple. The golden sun, flickering through the top of the waterfall, slowly moved until it glistened off something blue under the water. Jackson saw it first and pointed to it. Andi smiled excitedly and nodded her head before sinking under the water to reach it.

In moments, she surfaced again with her amber hair darkened and dripping. Andi opened her hand revealing a round, royal blue gem the size of a golf ball. Small, jagged white crystals decorated the outside of the stone. She lifted Jackson's hand from under the water with her free arm. Then, she put the unique gem in his palm for him to study.

With both of her hands free, Andi cupped them around his ear and whispered, "We call it a blue snowball. You can keep it if you want."

"The truth is, Meri," Rigel began with a more serious tone, "you did save me."

"Oh, you would have woken up eventually with or without me," she reasoned.

"No. I need you." Rigel grabbed her hand with tender strength. "I needed you when I followed your song through the forest, and I need you for the rest of eternity." He lowered to both knees then untied a small leather pouch from his belt.

"Rigel, what are you doing?" Merope giggled uneasily, not wanting to assume too much or too little from the gesture. Suddenly, she noticed the faded outline of where the three valuable ornaments once lay fastened to the thick brown leather around his waist. "What happened to the pendants on your belt?" she inquired. But he didn't answer either of her questions. His eyes and his thoughts remained fixed on her with urgent sincerity as he revealed his affections and his intentions.

"I wandered alone for a long time because I was afraid of getting too attached to a home and too attached to a heart. But I'm not afraid anymore. My home is wherever you are, even if that means we live in a tree house next to six women." He chuckled. Rigel pulled open the corded mouth of the pouch, revealing a pearl necklace. Shiny, white gems softly touched each other in a continuous string of pearls, but three, larger pearls accented the bottom. He stood up, gently placed it over her head, and then lifted her long dark hair, so the necklace rested on her neck. "No matter what beasts or darkness or waters or worlds avail us, I want to be in your arms, by your side."

"Alnilam?" Merope asked, looking down and noticing the expensive, rare azure blue pearls. Each of the three were the size of a large marble but each slightly unique in its shading. Rigel smiled with triumphant confidence, answering her question. "These are too much, Rigel. Please

tell me you did not sell your family pendants to buy this."
Merope looked honored and surprised and overwhelmed.

Rigel smiled warmly and lifted the pearls from her neck till they were resting in the strong palm of his hand. He then pointed to each blue pearl as he explained. "You see, the Creator made the golden sun, the crimson sun, and the coral sun. Like the shades of three suns, our seasons and colors may vary, but like the light of the suns, I vow that my love will always be warm, constant, and life-giving." He let the necklace fall softly to her chest and held both of her hands. "Merope, will you walk by my side for as long as the three suns rise upon us?"

Chapter 14

Shattered Mirrors

Sephdar descended with slow, calculated steps across the large plank of the ship to the Royal Pier of Altair. *Clonk. Clonk. Clonk. Thoonk!* As quick as reflex, the centaur fired an arrow into the thick of the jungle. The flying iron dagger ripped through the throat of a palace guard who had snapped a twig under his boots while trying to sneak upon the invading enemy. Within seconds, Sephdar pulled another arrow from the quiver on his back. The string stretched into the nock behind the corvus feathers the master archer gathered at Trifid while he wasted away in the forsaken ruins. The ebony fletching rose from the end of the wooden rod like perfectly styled Mohawks: tall, proud, and threatening.

Also tall, proud, and threatening, Lord Sephdar scoffed as he pushed the bloody courier—lying motionless on the pier—into the river below with his front right hoof.

The limp body floated downstream, staining the Eridanus with a surface line of red. Adhering to traditional formalities, this same courier had unrolled his message moments before and had spoken to the new Lord of the White Palace with a loud stateliness.

"The Royal Flower of the Eridanus has heard your request, and this is her gracious reply. 'The Ilmatar are not here. In the name of Queen Cassiopeia, you must return to…'" But Sephdar's spinning arrow stopped the messenger mid-sentence by tearing into his heart. Sephdar lacked patience for negotiations and formalities. His reply to the queen was the instant death of her messenger. If Altair would not hand over the other six Ilmatar, he would hunt them down and take them by force.

There was no time for Altair to respond to the startling attack. As the courier fell backward against the wooden pier, an army of black arrows pierced through the light of the suns from the White Winged ships and killed every visible kingdom guard. These guards watched over the riverbank from two towers built high in the jungle trees and from the Royal Pier, which also consisted of a large bridge, connecting Altair to the lands beyond the Eridanus River.

None questioned their violent leader. Sephdar's soldiers followed methodically, hitting the ground of Altair like drones programmed for death. Thanks to White Wings, the men were well equipped for battle. Cygnus had been patient and thorough preparing them for a day like this one.

To control the immense powers between the worlds, he trained them not just for war but also for conquest. Cygnus slowly gathered the crouching criminals, the wealth seekers, and the disenfranchised wandering the outsides of the kingdoms. In the southern shadows of the two remaining kingdoms, they'd been building, training, and waiting.

White Wings united them under a vision for the future. In this new world, they could all reign, controlling and sharing the wealth and power as trade ignited between two worlds once again. But Sephdar's rise to command came swiftly and violently. And whether these soldiers obeyed with fear, loyalty, or ambition, none had forgotten the future that was promised to them. White Wings' army was ready for a new dawn in Arcas, and they were ready to destroy the old to attain it.

The soldiers of Altair began their descent to the river. They marched in rows and looked official in their kingdom coat of arms, but their blades were dull and their senses were weak. After a few thousand years of inactivity, they were no match for the fresh skill and training of White Wings' army. The enemy attacked the Altairian soldiers quickly like giant waves crushing and consuming a marching army of ants. This fight was no battle. It was a slaughter. The Altairians fell rapidly on the outskirts of the fortified castle, washed away in a stream of blood, broken bones, and severed flesh.

Witnessing the slaughter before them, soldiers at the end of the line fled for safety. Arrows and swords may pierce flesh, but they could not penetrate solid rock. They believed the outer walls would protect them from the onslaught, but it would soon be clear that even the kingdom walls were not prepared for the day of battle.

"Raise the drawbridge!" Ruchbah shouted as he raced over the large wooden pass, lowered over the moat surrounding the walls. Father north, a section of the Eridanus River was dammed long ago to allow water to flow down and around the city moat before reconnecting with the river. Caph, a guard on the parapet, ran to the wheel holding the strong chains that controlled the bridge. He held tightly to the rusted metal crank and pulled with all of his strength.

"It's not moving! It's stuck!" Caph yelled frantically as he leaned back, using his body weight to help turn the wheel. Just inside the walls, Ruchbah twisted back to examine the drawbridge. *Creech.* As Caph pulled down, rotating the steel chains, the bridge raised a mere three inches. Thick vines, jungle moss, and weeds held firmly to the wood planks, forcing them to stay down. Over the years, no one had fought the jungle back or raised the bridge regularly to exercise its greatest strength. Like an unrestrained oppressor, the overgrown forest effortlessly held down the struggling, prostrated bridge from joining the very castle it was created to protect.

"Keep trying!" Ruchbah hollered fiercely as his eyes flashed with both dread and courage. He was not a man accustomed to action. He merely guarded the pillar, an uneventful job since nothing of value remained in the ancient gateway between the worlds. But when he heard the clashing of swords and cries of battle, Ruchbah remembered the wars of old. The adrenaline-charged instinct to protect the kingdom suddenly emerged from his long-forgotten youthful memories to the frontlines. Ruchbah rushed toward the top of the drawbridge. He raised his sword and *hack! hack!* hacked away at the thickest weeds.

Thunk! A black arrow drove into his thigh from the jungle as the shadowy army charged forward, rustling the wild trees of the Eridanus. With complete focus, Ruchbah dragged his pierced, bleeding leg toward the last group of vines and weeds. He cried in pain, standing as steadily as he could, and raising his weapon to slash at the remaining overgrowth.

"Ruchbah, leave it be!" Caph pleaded. "Retreat!"

"Just one more! Ahhh!" He screamed with power and pain while swinging the sword with all his might. *Snap! Snap!* "I've got it, Caph! Raise the bridge!" Ruchbah felt the drawbridge creek underneath him as he hobbled quickly toward the gates, using his sword as a crutch.

Thun-thun-thun-thun! Arrows whirled past his head, arms, and legs while the bridge slowly rose, snapping and breaking free of smaller weeds that still tried to hold it captive. Caph rotated the crank steadily as the heavy chains turned around the large wheel until a force suddenly halted the progress. Sweat dripped from his brow as he fought to keep control. The drawbridge froze about six feet in the air as enemy soldiers grabbed the wooden sides. Some merely hung down while others pushed their bodies up and crawled onto the tilted top.

Thoonk! A knife sunk into Ruchbah's back, causing him to jolt in the air then fall to the ground. The arrow in his leg splintered and broke as his deadweight flattened upon it. A soldier on top of the bridge, stood from his kneeled position, unsheathed his sword, and ran toward the body. Realizing the Altairian was dead, he stuck his boot on Ruchbah's back and pulled his large knife out, tearing the ruptured flesh farther.

Caph had now lost complete control. Gaining weight, the crank slid from his grasp and spiraled rapidly around and around until the heavy bridge thumped back to the ground. Caph joined the remaining Altairians fleeing into the castle as a last defense. Like a swarm of bees entering the hive, White Wings' army covered the lowered bridge in seconds, darkening the courtyard gate.

"Tear down every brick until you find the Ilmatar!" Sephdar commanded forty men carrying the parts to two catapults to the rear walls of the fortified city. Here, the palace towered high above the walls. Sephdar's men quickly assembled the massive weapons just beyond the moat. While others battered the inner door of Cassiopeia's palace, the catapults would batter the outer façade.

Thoop! Crack! Crash! A large puff of dust erupted from

the walls as the first boulder hurled against the palace. The casualties at Altair were quickly mounting to more than just individual bodies. The entire kingdom was falling into one massive casualty of war. Screaming, yelling, and wailing could be heard as the walls slowly crumbled on top of powerless victims, cowering for safety.

"My Queen!" Shedir raced into the throne room as quickly as his aged legs could carry him. "We are under attack just as the songbird warned us several days ago."

"Why do you bother to enter my presence so carelessly, Shedir?" Queen Cassiopeia appeared unconcerned while sitting on her diamond-crested glass throne. She held a small, decorative mirror in her hand and seemed to delight in looking at her colorful reflection bouncing off the mirrored walls into the hand mirror and then back again from multiple angles.

"A thousand apologies, most beautiful and royal Flower of the Eridanus." Shedir bowed and spoke rapidly, hoping to appease the queen's ridiculous formalities quickly enough that she would actually heed his warning. "We are under attack, My Gracious Queen. The gate has been breached and they are tearing down the castle walls as we speak."

"Why do you interrupt my time of beautiful solitude with your ugly, aged nonsense? Of course the gates have been breached! Every time I ask for a moment of peace, someone is clawing at the doors of Altair to gasp at my splendor."

"Queen Cassiopeia!" He paused to collect his frantic thoughts then spoke clearly and solemnly. "I have served this kingdom and your family since your father, King Algieba, opened the great Pillar of Altair. I'm telling you the truth. Our soldiers have fallen at the Royal Pier. The gate is breached, and the castle is crumbling around us!" When he finished pleading with the queen, the ground and walls rumbled like an earthquake, threatening to tear the palace apart.

"How dare you, feeble old man! My glorious castle is not crumbling!" The seated queen finally stood in frustration, believing Shedir's words shouted defamation. "My everlasting image sustains every wall, floor tile, and the very roof over our heads."

"I don't care about your image, Cassie! I care about you!"

In the desperate emotion of the moment, Shedir forgot all rituals and referred to her by the name he called her as a child.

Cassie had been such a sweet, young, carefree princess. Since Shedir and his wife KoChav never had children, when KoChav died, he focused his attentions solely on serving the Kingdom of Altair. His main task was to teach and guide the little princess. He'd always loved and cared for Cassiopeia as if she were his own daughter. But he'd never had the authority of a father or the command of a king, so she always knew she held all the power.

"Cassie? How dare you address me so informally! I am Queen Cassiopeia, the splendid, the perfect, the prosperous, the beautiful Flower of the Eridanus!" She gazed in her handheld mirror as she spoke, studying her eyes and lips while dramatizing each word.

A large stone burst into the mirrored throne room, her royal sanctuary. Glass fell from the ceiling as the foreign projectile shattered its way through the inner chambers.

"My Queen, please! I have a way of escape." He held out his hand, begging her to join him as the room continued to crack, splinter, and break.

"Can't you see that this kingdom will fall to the ground without my beauty shining around it? Even now, it shutters in pain and disbelief because you are asking me to leave."

"We must go—NOW!" He shouted at her for the first time in his life. He was too feeble to force her or drag her. Shedir's voice was the only power he had left to persuade the queen.

"Shedir, remove yourself from my presence at once!" she commanded, pointing her mirror like a scepter toward the door. "Can't you see my very anger with you is breaking these sacred mirrors? My beauty sustains this kingdom and you are trying to destroy it by refusing to give me the praise and adoration I deserve! YOU must go—NOW!"

A stream of tears fell down Shedir's face. He knew he could not save the queen. The old teacher hadn't really seen

Cassie in many, many years, but this could be the last time he would see a faint reflection of the girl he once knew. An obedient servant to the end, he shuffled out of her beloved throne room for the last time. As he closed the door, more large projectiles burst through the mirrored sanctuary. Shedir scurried around several hallways before stopping abruptly at one of the mirrors. He pushed his cane against the glass. *Click-click.* The mirror opened to a hidden passage, one of the only areas of the castle untouched by constant reflection.

Down.

Down.

Down.

Shedir felt the rocks pulsate around him as he scurried down stairs, deep into the foundation of the palace. At the end of the long secret passage, a small, dusty boat rested a few feet away from a pond that connected to the moat outside. Once he received Maia's note, he'd quietly prepared provisions and weapons, then placed them here in case an escape was needed. Shedir pushed the boat into the water and steadied himself as he entered the small vessel, which would quietly lead him through the jungle and then back south to connect with the Eridanus River. But his mind was not focused merely on escape. There was someone Shedir needed to go back for first.

He may have been feeble in body, but Shedir was not feeble in mind. He got in the boat and headed through the jungle, but turned right through a small canal leading directly back toward the enemy's armada. As the small boat wound around the larger vessels, the few enemy guards holding watch were too distracted by the siege of Altair to notice. It was easy to spot the prisoner's ship. It was the only boat with two armed guards. Two sentinels stood at the edge of the middle vessel enthralled with the battle beyond them. Shedir grabbed his crossbow and quickly eliminated them. The sound of the guards falling to the river below was drowned by the crashes, screams, and yells coming from the kingdom.

Shedir grabbed tightly to the railing as he descended into the belly of the ship. He followed a weak hum resonating through the wooden beams. At the back of the ship, there were only four officer's cabins. And only one cabin, the last on the left, was locked from the outside. Shedir's shaky hand pulled the chain off the large, iron nail. It rattled and clanged against the door as he opened it.

"So, did you find my sisters yet?" Maia asked, playing dumb while never turning from the window.

"No, but perhaps I can take you to them if we hurry."

Hearing the aged, unfamiliar voice, Maia bolted around.

"Who? Are you the friend of Charles?" she asked excitedly.

"Yes. I got your message. But the kingdom is falling fast. We need to go, My Lady."

The two hastily moved through the empty ship, descended the rope stairs falling down the side to the water below, and returned to Shedir's little vessel. The pregnant lady and the feeble old man were an odd pair rowing around war ships and then floating south down the mighty Eridanus. With just a small boat as their best transportation, there was only one place to go for swift safety: Trifid.

"Tell me where the Ilmatar of Starling are." Sephdar maneuvered over shards of glass and crumbled rock as he entered the throne room. "I know you are harboring them."

Cassiopeia stood in front of the last unscathed mirror on the wall. All others bore the cracks and brokenness of war, but it was as if Cassiopeia could only see the last remaining perfect one.

"How dare you speak this way to the Queen of Altair!" She did not move from the mirror but glanced at the centaur's reflected image then let out an astonished gasp. "Bow down on your beastly knees, you half-man thing. And without the proper attire! Who even let you in my presence? You, you, you filthy creature! Shedir? Shedir! Come hither at once!"

"There is no one left to answer your call," he mocked. "You may call yourself a queen, but look around. You are queen of nothing. You have no kingdom." He pulled back and aimed his loaded bow and arrow at her as a threat. "But if you want to keep your pathetic life, just tell me where the six sisters are."

Before she could answer, Albireo rushed into the room.

"Lord Sephdar! The castle is collapsing!"

"Did you find them?"

"We've searched everywhere and questioned everyone with breath, My Lord. There is still no sign of the Ilmatar in the kingdom."

"Then drag our guest of honor out and give her a tour of the kingdom. Maybe she can find them in the rubble!"

"You horrid, presumptuous beast!" Full of agitation, the queen burst into the conversation. The large mirror in front of her began to creak and crack. She turned from its dwindling perfection, and for once, Cassiopeia directly addressed the centaur. "You have no authority to give tours of my kingdom! And who is this guest of honor?" She raised her handheld mirror to her face again, blocking the dark lord from her vision. "Every creature with breath in his dusty lungs knows that only the Flower of the Eridanus who sits on this very throne holds honor in Altair!"

As the words exited her mouth, Sephdar looked at the queen with disgust and hate. He pulled back the arrow's string. As the long, feathered dart flew toward the queen, the roof above her started crumbling to the ground. The queen neither noticed the arrow nor the room collapsing around her. She simply stared at her image as a stream of blood rushed down her face while the rocks and rubble crushed her body against the floor. Sephdar never saw if his arrow hit the mark. Both he and Albireo fled from the collapsing castle and joined the rest of the army in the courtyard.

"I have fresh tea from your cabin, My Lord." Arkab swiftly but carefully met him in the courtyard. "But I also bring bad news." He held out the offering and braced himself for Sephdar's volatile response.

"What is it?" Sephdar reached for the tea with one hand while the other still grasped the warm leather on his bow.

"At the ship," Arkab began nervously, "both the guards and the Ilmatar were gone." Arkab and Albireo held their breath, waiting for an expected severe reaction.

"Good." Sephdar surprised his men with the reply. "I suspected she might warn her sisters somehow. No doubt, they rescued her during the battle. But no worries. Her little schemes are going to play nicely into our hands. There are only a few villages where they could be hiding, and they will be slow with the pregnant one. Let the men replenish, and then we will chase them down."

Albireo and Arkab saluted their commander, thankful no wrath had come upon them, and then left Sephdar to drink his tea in peace.

Though his men were celebrating their victory with pillaged food and ale, Sephdar stood alone, sipping on his tea with one hand and holding his stomach with the other. He won the battle, but the Lord of the White Palace was not satisfied. The lingering pain from Minaruja's bite fueled his anger further. He should have been cured by now. He should be controlling The Bridge to Earth by now, gaining wealth and renown in both worlds. But as the poison throbbed through his innermost being, it surged deeper into his soul. A slight smile escaped his menacing lips as he watched the men glory in power and victory over the Kingdom of Altair. These skilled soldiers were now his men. This swift slaughter was his conquest. And this victory was only the beginning of Sephdar's rule.

Chapter 15

The Announcement

King Alderamin stood in the hall outside the formal dining room, awaiting his grand entrance. It was a rare occasion to entertain guests who didn't belong to the kingdom realms, so he wore his best royal robe. Embroidered with spiraling reds, blues, purples, and bright golds from the collar to the ends of the tassels, the robe blazed with the glorious splendor of exploding fireworks. Alderamin's face, however, was also beginning to swirl with varying colors as the chamberlain approached him.

"Errai, where is my *prompt* and *proper* daughter?" Irritated, he accented the descriptors knowing well enough that Andi often avoided the formalities of old when it came to traditional princess behaviors. "Why is she not here yet?"

"I believe her garments got a little damp and required changing." He sugarcoated Andi's dirty, dripping-wet condition that she had scurried into the castle with. Errai also knew better than to disclose that a soaked Jackson had arrived with the princess through the back door. The Son of Earth had already made it to the dining room after a quick change of clothes, so there was no need to complicate the banquet by alerting her father of each trivial detail. "The princess should be joining us presently from her chamber," Errai assured the king.

"Enough. Enough, Sirrah. It's good." Andi shooed away the servant picking, pining, and perfecting her royal hair. "Nobody really cares what my hair looks like."

"I disagree. I believe I saw two young men in the castle who might care a great deal," she teased, layering an open satin-white robe over Andromeda's royal purple gown.

"Oh, stop," Andi scolded cynically, hoping to disguise the blush flaring to the surface of her cheeks. "I don't see why we should ever fuss about our garments and hair. If I dress elegantly for dinner, I'll splatter something in my lap, and if I dress like a princess for dancing, my hair will bounce until the tiara falls crooked."

"Well, regardless of any other man, you do it for your father." Sirrah straightened and fiddled with the details as Andi looked bored, watching in the mirror. "The king won't care if your appearance slowly unravels by the time the crimson sun sets, but he will care if you arrive at dinner dressed as any other than the only princess and heir of the kingdom realms."

"True." Andi opened her door and hastily walked out before turning to get the last word in. "But thankfully in Arcas that means that I will always be the heir and never the queen." She smiled then sped to the stairway.

Andi reached for her favorite sturdy, velvety drape hanging down from the ceiling to the floor. She gave it a little tug, sat sideways on the curved staircase then slid down the banister. Near the end, Andi gripped tighter and swung her legs out, flying, flying, flying around the corner. *Thump!* She surprised herself and her father with the sudden collision.

"An-dro-me-da..." he scolded, irritated by her tardiness yet slightly amused by her spunky athleticism.

"Sorry, Daddy." She widened her eyes as only a daughter can to soothe a father's frustration. She leaned up on her tiptoes and kissed his cheek. Alderamin's face melted into a slight smile.

"Well, you look like a princess, but you act like a jungle girl."

"Can't I be both?" Andi shrugged her shoulders innocently.

"Only if you swing to dinner on time," he insisted.

"I'll do my best," she agreed, slipping her hand through his elbow.

Errai entered the hall from the kitchen area, no doubt

checking on the progress of the feast. He seemed relieved that the princess had joined the king and that they both seemed to be of good spirits. Alderamin cued the chamberlain with a nod, so Errai opened the large door decorated exquisitely with homegrown gems. The dining minstrels began a new tune to welcome the royals to the table.

"All rise for King Alderamin and Princess Andromeda," he announced.

The two entered the dining hall with the stately, proud, and calculated strides of royalty, but the formalities wouldn't last long, for the guests standing around the table were not just diplomats or politicians seeking a favor, they were friends. The jewel-crested stone table was set with an open seat for Alderamin at the head, then Rigel, Merope, and Jackson filled the right side while Otava, Alfirk—a leader and warrior among the Cephids—and Nekkar sat on the left. The seat at the far end remained open for the princess.

The last thirty minutes before the royals arrived were spent reconnecting with friends and sharing adventures from the past few months. Alfirk quickly welcomed the Son of Earth and fellow Arcasians back to Deneb. He stood behind the table and used his whole little body to dramatize his spear perfectly piercing Shaula's eye. Jackson and Nekkar then described their collision in Starling and joked about the rocky start to their alien friendship.

Everyone became interested and curious about the red-and-yellow gem that Jackson found in his attic and used to return to Arcas. Alfirk wondered if the vanished gem somehow fell through the portal just as Jackson released it while Otava listed all the wretched creatures of the forest who might have stolen it. Rigel and Merope recalled trading Cygnus's transport gem with Regulus at the cabin in Starling after returning Jackson to Earth. The trade secured safe passage to the Free Realms and a ship in order to rescue the other six sisters. Otava then described with great enthusiasm his guest appearance as "chef" of the White Palace when they rescued the six sisters.

"So, as that White Palace cook—one could hardly call that poor man a chef—was shaking in his boots, I gave him a bowl of my well-crafted soup. He'd never seen an Ursa before so both his chair and his spoon were rattling with fear. Then, I lowered the fire's heat to a simmer, and I told him the Starling legend of the crab and the flying fish. Ha! Ha! Ha!" Otava rumbled a laugh of gleeful anticipation from the back of his throat. "Then... ha!... he starts touching his tingling fingers together, rubs his tongue on the roof of his mouth, and turns as pale as turkey meat. 'What is the name of this flying fish?' he asked with wide eyes—knowing full well the name of my secret ingredient. But before I could answer 'volantis,' he slumped over his chair like a giant slumbering slug."

Everyone chuckled at Otava's antics and dramatics.

Merope asked him to recite the poem that he sang while filling the rest of the bowls in the dining hall. Though he would never sing for a conscious crowd, he chanted the words in rhythm.

When acubens and volantis
Swallowed the mighty bee,
All three were bound to die.
But Ursa came round and feasted with glee;
It was the sweetest crab-fish fry!

"Then, I grabbed the dinner gong mallet and swung it three times against the round, copper bell hanging from the ceiling. Within minutes, the feasting hall was filled, and within seconds, the palace guards were sleeping sweetly."

The room was full of lively, loud conversation as Otava finished his story. Nevertheless, as Princess Andromeda and King Alderamin entered to join their guests, all eyes rested quietly on them. Jackson couldn't look away from Andi as she entered the dining room. In a normal, self-conscious state of mind, he would perhaps remember to glance to the floor or the wall and pretend he didn't notice her, but at the moment, she sparkled like the only star in a dark sky, and he couldn't look away. It was hard to believe this precisely decorated beauty was the same girl running around with him in the caves earlier. Jackson wasn't sure which version of her intimidated and excited him more: the beloved princess who adhered to age-old codes of dress and royal behavior or the athletic, fearless adventurer who could probably run faster and jump higher than he could.

But Jackson wasn't the only one who couldn't keep his eyes off Andromeda. While Jackson's interest momentarily froze him behind his seat, Nekkar's interest leapt him to action. As Andromeda approached the far end of the table by the two young men, Nekkar quickly bowed and pulled out her chair. She smiled cordially and placed her hand in his as he offered to help her sit. It felt pleasantly exciting to have this handsome, young foreign diplomat treat her like a lady and not a child. When the princess was seated, Nekkar kissed the back of her hand before releasing it. Andi immediately looked down at her plate and moved her hands to her lap as if everyone would notice a slight blush on the hand that was kissed.

"Don't worry, Jackson. It's just traditions and formalities," Merope whispered and nudged his arm. "She'll be dancing with you after dinner."

Jackson's face flushed as he wondered how she knew. *Am I that obvious?* Jackson felt like everyone was watching him, like his little secret was being shouted to the whole room of friends. They must know that he wished to spend every second with Andi. They must know he thought she was the most beautiful creature in the universe. They must know that he felt slightly threatened and growingly competitive as he watched his friend attend to her and kiss her hand. But really, no one was paying attention to

Jackson. Everyone was watching the king and waiting for him to be seated so they could also relax in their own chairs.

"I am privileged to host such an extraordinary reunion of friends." King Alderamin began the dinner. "Our people are grateful for the peace and prosperity that has lasted in the Kingdom of Deneb for many ages. Yet, since the arrival of our new friends who helped us destroy the Scorpius not long ago, our land has experienced increased wealth and growth. I am honored to share this meal with friends from many lands. May peace grow strong, may enemies flee, and blessings overflow on us all."

"Heed. Heed," the guests announced, raising their cups in agreement. Errai directed the castle servants to bring out the first dish.

"Merope, that's a beautiful necklace," Andi kindly noticed. "Are those Alnilam pearls?"

"Yes, thank you," Merope replied with a smile full of warmth and pride and slight embarrassment that someone brought attention to such an expensive piece of jewelry. The couple hadn't mentioned yet the pretty new pearl necklace dangling from her neck. But since she was nearby in Deneb, Merope hoped to send word to Maia soon. Even if Maia wouldn't attend their vows, Merope longed for some type of reconciliation with her oldest sister while she lingered in the kingdom realms.

"I think all the men will agree that the two pearls among us today far outshine any other priceless treasure," Nekkar complimented thickly, making sure to connect with

Andi's eyes so she knew the statement was directed entirely at her.

"Heed. Heed." The men raised their glasses again.

"A witless man chases beauty," Alfirk added his two-cents about relationships, "but a wise man protects it."

"Indeed," the king approved of the adage. "So, Merope, which man is The Hunter?" he baited. "Because I have many eligible men who—though they may lack in height—would swing a tall and mighty axe in your name."

Merope chuckled modestly while Rigel wasted no time to let everyone know his intentions.

"Well, then, we must ask the king at once if he will unite us before these short and eligible bachelors come offering her their own gifts of engagement!" The Hunter smiled proudly, knowing full well that Merope was pledged to him and him alone.

"What? Is this a serious proposal?" King Alderamin asked as the rest of the group stared back at the necklace then Merope's blushing face, piecing the clues together. With a masculine confidence, Rigel silently nodded his head once to answer the king's question.

"It's about time!" Otava suddenly blurted out.

Everyone laughed and congratulated the couple. The room suddenly filled with conversation about the proposal, wedding, and where the couple would live. And naturally, talk moved to the qualms and quirks and quotes of married life. In the new excitement, no one seemed to notice a shaky guard enter the room, kneel at the king's side, and hand him a letter. He quietly opened the correspondence and read its contents. Suddenly, the king stood, his olive skin flushed pale. The rest of the party stood with him in adherence to the proper custom.

"Have you verified the authenticity of this message?" he quietly asked the guard.

"Yes, My King. It just arrived by the ancient messaging system your father enacted between the kingdoms."

Alderamin clenched his fists and breathed deeply before raising his head to impart the correct message to his guests.

"Friends, the Kingdom of Altair is under attack. Errai!" he called the chamberlain.

Errai entered straightaway. "Yes, Your Highness."

"Our queen is in grave danger. Strike the gong immediately and summon the Cephid fighters. We are going to war."

Chapter 16

The Waves of War

"No, Andi." King Alderamin grabbed his daughter's hand tenderly, noticing she had changed into her riding clothes. "I won't allow you to come with us. You must stay here."

"But, Father, I know the jungle better than anyone. I can help."

"I'm already worried about finding and protecting your mother. The last thing I need to worry about is whether you are safe." He lifted her chin, tightened his brows, and solemnly gazed into her eyes. "No matter what happens I *need* to know you are safe. And our people need you. Your presence will speak life and comfort to Deneb. You must lead while I'm gone."

Andi nodded her head in agreement and fought to control the tears welling up, threatening to spill over onto her cheeks. She understood her father should focus on strategy and the battle ahead rather than worrying about his daughter's safety. But Andi also knew that Errai was really the one staying behind to care for the kingdom. The king wanted her to feel important and needed in Deneb, but the kingdom would run with or without the presence of the princess—as it always had.

For all Andi's life, her allegiance had been split between two kingdoms, never knowing which one she truly belonged to. The princess entered each castle as a daughter and a guest, a ruler and a foreigner. She knew the people of Deneb would not look to her for guidance in her father's stead. While the warriors hastened to Altair, they would look to one who was always present in the castle. They would look to Errai.

King Alderamin embraced his daughter and then kissed her on the forehead.

"I know I haven't always rushed to your mother's side, but today, we will emerge victorious together."

"I know, Daddy."

"Be strong, my dear, and do not worry. No one who threatens the queen will escape punishment." The king left the palace foyer and headed to the underground garrison. It was time to lead the Cephid army in the march toward Altair.

Outside the caves, Rigel stood leaning against a small tree, watching the warriors line up in front of the kingdom gates. Merope sat on the grass underneath the shade, tenderly petting the head of a small bird sitting on her finger. If any people of Deneb stopped to watch the couple and listen to the Ilmatar's quiet hum, they might think the two were relaxing in leisurely peace while the rest of the kingdom bustled in preparation for combat. Though calm on the outside, inside their mind and soul, a battle was already waging.

The Hunter and the Ilmatar owed no allegiance to the kingdoms. They had both purposely remained isolated from the realm affairs, but in their separation, a whitewashed darkness had slowly risen to power. Yes, Cygnus destroyed the freedom and serenity they had known for so long, but it also brought them back together. So much had changed since Jackson entered their world. They still didn't belong to any realm, but they finally belonged to each other. Could they simply run off now and smile and laugh for an eternity together while evil continued to destroy their world?

No. The peace of the future required the powers of the past. The ancient souls had been awakened, and they would not return to slumber until peace reigned in Arcas again.

"I suppose we'll have to postpone the wedding," Merope remarked with a sigh as she raised her arm, releasing the bird to flight. Rigel turned his gaze with sincere interest toward his dark-haired, olive-toned betrothed.

"I know. We're heading back to your sisters in the Free Realms, then?" Rigel offered the answer that seemed most logical, though it was also the answer he didn't want to hear. But his path was no longer his alone. No matter which direction they took today, they were going together.

"I don't think so." Merope forced a smile, stood, and wrapped her arms around her soon-to-be husband. "There's a palace of mirrors in the middle of the eastern jungle that I've been meaning to show you. A most fascinating sight. It'd be the perfect place for a bride to try on a gown."

"Really?" Rigel leaned back to look her in the eyes. "That's where you want to go?"

"If we're going to leave right now, then yes, that's where I want to go."

Pleased that she spoke the very words he'd hoped to hear, Rigel cupped his strong hands around Merope's soft cheeks and kissed her passionately. When their lips released, the two hugged tightly again. They knew this journey promised danger, but hand-in-hand, their individual fears melted into one unbreakable courage.

"So, how do you prefer to travel? By foot? By horse?" Rigel asked.

"By cloud." Merope beamed, pulling the powerful lyre from its leather case.

Jackson spotted Nekkar leading a horse out of the stables. He quickly jogged over to him, dodging horses and sturdy, short soldiers along the way. Since Nekkar was too tall to fit into the typical Cephid armor, the king told Errai to suit him with some of his own armor. He looked regal and strong and ready for battle.

"Hey, Son of Jack! It's too bad the journey is parting us, my brother."

"Yeah. Are you sure you don't want to come with me? I think your people are more likely to send help to Altair if you are asking for it instead of the alien from Earth and the Ursa from Starling."

"Friend, I wish I could. But I watched Sephdar's squadron attack and devour my men. I will not return to the safety of my people while they shed more innocent blood."

"I understand." Jackson pulled Lodestar out of the sheath on his hip, and held it out to his friend. "But if you are going to fight, you should at least fight with you own sword," Jackson offered.

"I'm a man, Jackson." Nekkar mounted his horse, puffed up his chest, and smiled mischievously. "I always have my own sword on me."

"Um, yeah…" Jackson squinted his eyes in sarcastic shock. "But you always have your mouth on you too, and it doesn't seem to be winning any battles."

"My mouth is going to win a battle when I save the kingdoms and Princess Andromeda thanks me with a kiss."

"Oh, shut up, Perseus."

"Yeah, that's what she said… before she kissed me!"

"Whatever." Jackson chuckled. "Go save the kingdoms."

"Seriously." Nekkar pulled on the reigns, trying to

steady his restless horse that could feel the anxious energy of war through the soldiers. "It would be dangerous for you to show up at Trifid without my sword and… without this." Nekkar reached into his cloak pocket, pulled out the red-and-yellow transport gem, and tossed it to Jackson.

"What? How?" he stuttered with confusion, relief, and irritation all swirling inside at the same time at the sight of his long-lost gem.

"It doesn't matter." Nekkar avoided answering the question, but his face told a story of both guilt and righteous justification. "The important thing is now you have it if you need it. Present Lodestar to my people, and they will listen to you as if I myself were speaking. It was an honor to know you, my friend."

Nekkar put his fist to his chest, and Jackson returned the gesture. Then, Nekkar cantered away toward the front line of riders, just behind the king. Jackson couldn't help but feel that if he and Nekkar ever met again, they would both be greatly altered by this moment, by the lingering questions, and by the journeys ahead. It was hard to be angry when his friend was headed to war. It was hard to be angry, but like any brother who acts like a punk, Jackson did harbor a strong desire to give Nekkar a swift punch.

Jackson rubbed his fingers over the transport gem as a thrilling relief melted over him. The traveling door between the worlds was finally back in his hands. Noticing him standing around, Otava called out for Jackson to join him toward the stables. Jackson tucked the gem safely in his pocket and ran to meet his traveling partner. Before the two entered the scuttle of horses and riders and equestrian tack, Rigel caught up with them. With serious intensity, he pulled them aside to speak with them.

"No matter what happens, you need to shut The Bridge down," he compelled in hushed tones.

"What about the gem at the top of the arch?" Jackson questioned, concerned about his ability to complete the task. "It's too high."

"Don't worry about that one." Rigel waved off his fear. "If you get the other two yellow Earth gems, and Otava gets the red gems of Arcas from behind the arch, The Bridge will close. That's all we need."

"Hey!" Otava protested. "Ursa Major, Rigel, I signed up to guide the little human to Trifid, not to touch those forsaken stones!" He was still uncomfortable and superstitious about any personal contact with the mysteriously powerful gems.

"You don't have to touch them with your bare paws," Rigel persuaded. "I'm sure you have enough tools and intellect to figure out how to get them without contaminating yourself." Otava's demeanor softened slightly, but he still wasn't convinced. "Everything is volatile and uncertain right now. The last thing the realms need is to worry about an open path to and from another world."

"We can get the gems," Jackson answered confidently for both of them. "But what do we do once we have them?"

"We wait until Sephdar and the White Winged army

is neutralized. The gems will be hidden until all the realms join together to choose a path forward. In ages past, The Bridge belonged to all the people, and so all the people must resolve its fate together."

In agreement, they parted ways with warm farewells and friendly embraces. As Jackson and Otava walked toward the cavern stables to ready their horses, a minstrel's song echoed through the cave lands, preparing the Cephids for battle.

The waves are raging in the east
No time for wine or feast
Those we love will soon be gone
By the lights of Arcas, march on

Fear inside let courage bestow
Great faith for justice to sow
Grab your sword, and hold your head
Souls fraying, the messenger said

The queen of beauty sheds a tear
Awaiting her king to come near
The darkness rises with our fate
May hope be strong, and death be late

The waves are raging in the east
No time for wine or feast
Those we love will soon be gone
By the lights of Arcas, march on

"I'm coming with you," Andi whispered in the stall next to Jackson. She threw a saddle on a sturdy Palomino as Jackson turned from the girth he was tightening on a dark brown Thoroughbred.

"I thought you were staying here to look after Deneb."

"Oh, they don't need me. Errai is more than capable of taking care of the kingdom. And I'm not going to just sit around here and wait it out while my parents are fighting some tyrant."

"Does your dad know you're coming with me?"

"My dad wants me to be some place safe. What can be safer than heading to a guarded fortress?" Andi smiled and spoke with an overly confident everything-is-fine voice, but she could tell Jackson wasn't buying it. So, she bent under the head of the horse and approached the shoulder-high dividing rail in between the stalls.

"Look, I can ride ahead of you, or behind you, or at your side, but I am going to Trifid." She grew serious, quiet, and more emotionally intense than Jackson had ever witnessed. "Our people are strong with an axe, but they are not prepared for the complexities of battle. They are marching head-on into lands they haven't dwelt in toward an enemy they've never been measured against. We couldn't even take down one scorpion without outside help." She released the halter from around the Palomino and lifted on the bridle. "My parents will not listen to me, but I believe Arcturus will listen if I come to him. If their warriors are as skilled as Nekkar, it won't take many of them to help us destroy this cowardly enemy. I know the secret paths through the Eridanus. I can direct them through the jungle."

"But…"

"Don't worry. I'm not planning on going to battle. I'll draw a map to show them how to attack the enemy on multiple sides of the forest. Then, I will either stay at Trifid until the fighting is finished or return to Deneb until I receive word from my father." She paused and studied Jackson's face to be sure he wasn't going to push the issue further.

"Now, I am going to walk this horse to the southern gate for Otava," she emphasized loudly as her alibi. Jackson smiled and shook his head as if to say *lady, you are going to be the death of me.*

The warriors were already marching out of the eastern gate, and he knew Andi's mind was made. Jackson was heading toward already rocky waters with the Free Realms, so he prayed this little journey with the princess wouldn't also destroy his good relationship with the kingdoms. But what else could he do?

"I have no idea how you are going to convince Otava to ride a horse." Jackson played along with a sigh. "But if anyone can turn a bear into an equestrian, you can."

Chapter 17

The Nebulous Lagoon

"I wish my charioteer, Auriga, was here with us," Andi lamented as the three continued their journey south. "He knows the landscape between the two great rivers better than anyone in the kingdoms."

"Hey, wait a sec!" Jackson remembered, twisting his backpack off and setting it between his legs and the horse's neck. "Let me see if my phone will turn on."

Pulling his phone out of the little bag of rice, Jackson wiped off tiny white particles clinging to the screen. Andi moved next to him, halting her horse to watch. He held his breath and pushed the little button, holding it firmly while he counted to three.

"Yes! It's alive!" Jackson celebrated with relief as a glowing icon appeared.

"Alive?" Otava asked uneasily as he slowly rode past them in a loaned chariot from Deneb, glancing suspiciously at the strange device. "I hope you brought a leash for your rice-eating alien pet."

"Don't worry. It's not a pet." Jackson laughed. "It's a tool."

"What does it do?" Andi asked curiously, observing the little buttons filling the screen.

"Well, it works as a map, keeps track of time, lets you... um..." Jackson tried to think of how to explain talking on the phone. "Send messages to someone really quickly...and come here, closer." Andi tilted her head in to watch the screen as Jackson held it out at a distance. "Do you see your face now?"

"Yes!" Andi was instantly amazed but then moaned. "It's a mirror, too? Please don't give a demonstration to my mom. She'll want to add it to her obsessive collection."

"Better than a mirror. Smile and I'll show you."

Jackson leaned in next to her, smiled, and *tap*!

"See? It takes a picture of anything you want, so you can look back and remember it."

While Andi marveled and tapped at the screen several more times, Otava grew impatient with the distracted teens who didn't fully trust his directions after a long, tiring journey.

"Well, I may not have traveled outside of the northern forest much, and I may not have any alien devices, but I can still pick up a good scent better than anyone in the kingdoms," Otava piped up, defending his role as the knowledgeable guide for the inexperienced youth he led toward Trifid. "And guess what I smell?"

"Water!" Jackson answered excitedly, looking the past the compass app pointing south.

"No!" the brown bear blurted out as if he'd been told the worst possible answer. He didn't notice that Jackson was looking to something in the distance. "With all that we've been through together, have I ultimately failed in expanding your understanding of the culinary arts?" Otava continued on in his passionate lecture, not allowing a moment of silence to pass for anyone to answer his rhetorical question. "You can't *smell* water, Son of Earth! I smell fish! And because my seasoned nose can smell fish, that means…"

"Jackson's right. It's water!" Andi nudged her horse into a joyful trot with her heel.

"No, no, Princess. You see, water itself doesn't have a scent. It merely carries along the smell of whatever food is brewing underneath it."

"I hope something tasty is brewing in the water underneath all that fog." Jackson patted his stomach, zipped his phone safely up again, and clucked to encourage his horse to gain speed.

"I'll race you!" Andi sped to a canter, holding the reigns back from a full gallop until she knew it was a real competition. She was always up for a playful rivalry and excited to jump into the cool waters of the Ligeian Sea.

Also feeling hot and dirty from traveling, Jackson

accepted the challenge with a firm thrust to the horse's side and joined the race. Still in his own world of culinary elucidations, Otava stood confused in the one-man chariot loaned from Deneb, staring blankly at the two young souls. With one last sniff of the increasingly salty air, he finally caught his own glimpse of the sea.

"Alright!" He growled happily, bounding out of the chariot. "I'll race you naked-toed cubs, but I don't need clompy feet to help me win!" The brown bear shot off the ground with his four massive paws. Feeling uneasy at the rear of the team, his driverless horse started cantering after them with the lightened chariot slightly bouncing behind.

The three gained renewed energy and spirit as they dashed forward. For a moment, Otava, Jackson, and Andi raced neck and neck. A thick, warm wind wrapped around them, caressing their faces and inviting them into the dense fog hovering around and above the water. Tinted with red and orange from the suns above and blues from the waters below, the vapors rose like hot steam merging into cool air. When they reached the water's edge, Otava threw his sack of weaponry over one shoulder, dove off the chariot and immediately began scanning the shoreline for fresh food. Andi and Jackson dismounted, dropped all their travel bags in the grass, and unsaddled the horses for rest and grazing.

"Whoa. I've never seen Arcas so shadowy dark outside of the caves," Andi remarked in curious wonder.

Growing up in the dense jungle and the pitch-black

caves, Andi wasn't afraid of darkness. Seasoned Arcasians would be hesitant to wander alone like she often did, hesitant to enter the few dark spots in a forever-lit world. But not this princess. Innocent courage guarded her heart and mind like shiny armor on a new soldier. The world she grew up in had been safe, protected, and peaceful, so Andi persistently felt young, strong, and invincible.

The travelers were so relieved to have reached the water they didn't notice the absence of waves as they approached the hazy blue. These waters rested quietly, only interrupted by tiny random ripples of insects above and small creatures wandering underneath. The two kids sat on the grass to remove their shoes so they could refresh their feet with a quick dip. The Ursa sniffed and skimmed his claws across the surface.

"This fog is so thick, it'll be like walking through cotton candy." Jackson chuckled lightly, imagining he was going to peruse through a new portion of the famous theatrical chocolate factory. "Too bad it tastes more like musty, salty fish."

"I'd rather eat musty, salty fish than chew sugared fabric!" Otava shook his head in humored disbelief while stepping into the shallow, still water. "Your people are quite strange."

"We don't eat cotton fabric." Jackson rolled his eyes. "It's just sugar that looks like cotton."

"Sure, we believe you," Andi added sarcastically,

smiling at Otava. "Don't worry, Earthling," she whispered loudly with a wink. "If you get a craving later, I'll cut the hem of my skirt for you to gnaw on. Maybe we can even find a bee's nest and sprinkle a little honey on top."

"What in the light of the three suns was that?" Otava interrupted his companions' teasing glances and laughter. The bear's hearty countenance turned severe as he gazed over the surface of the water. Whipping out his machete with a *thip,* the intense warrior instantly consumed the jolly chef.

Andi sank her toes quietly into the water to join Otava while Jackson pulled out his sword and walked next to her. His heart pounded in expectation and panic of some dangerous creature slithering under the surface, but Andi didn't notice the fear behind his eyes. She only saw his courage and his willingness to fight.

"What do you see?" she quietly implored, squinting through the fog.

"There!" Otava whispered. "It's an Ursa!"

"An Ursa? Here?" Jackson still couldn't see anything through the fog. "I thought you were the last of your kind."

"I was.... It's a little cub.... Oh, no. It's in trouble!" The burly bear rushed forward through the fog with his machete ready for action. "We need to save it!" he yelled, disappearing into the puffy, gray haze.

"I still don't see anything. Do you, Andi?"

"No, but we're going to lose that stubborn bear if we don't follow him."

191

"Yeah, we'd better stick together though." With the sword in his right hand, Jackson offered his left hand to Andi. It wasn't enough to see she was next to him as they headed toward an unknown danger; he needed to feel her next to him. Her warm palm touched his, but before their fingers clasped, she flung her hand away.

"Mom!" she yelled and sprinted away in the opposite direction of Otava.

"Andi!" Jackson called and then ran after her voice, but that sweet sound quickly became smothered by the clouds around them. The three companions now wandered separately up to their knees in water, each following something, each lost in the darkening haze.

"There you are, little bear." Otava sighed with relief, finally catching up with the cub. "What's wrong?" He searched the fog with machete raised ready. The little bear shook its head and shrugged his shoulders as if to say *Nothing's wrong*.

"What were you running from?"

The bark-brown creature excitedly waved Otava forward then took off running again. "Ursa Major!" Otava gasped—still breathing heavily from the last sprint. Afraid of losing the cub again, Otava put his machete away and swiftly followed.

Before long, hundreds of Ursas appeared out of the fog from all directions. They joined together forming a long, double line. Otava was overwhelmed with joy and bewilderment. All this time, he'd thought he was the last living of his kind. But all this time, Ursas had been hiding just out of his reach, growing in number and strength.

"Where is everyone going?" Otava inquired curiously as he joined the back of the line next to the cub.

There! He pointed at the large arch just becoming visible. It was The Bridge between worlds.

The older, wiser bear immediately felt dreadfully protective. He knew the Ursas were not safe. Their kind should be heading to the Starling Forest or the Free Realms—anywhere but Earth.

"No, No, No! We must tell them all to stop. Earth is not a good place for us! It's full of Bear-Eaters!"

Before Otava could protest further, a muzzle flew over his nose and tightened behind his ears. He pulled down on the tough leather with his claws, but it wouldn't budge. With a smack to the shoulder, he finally got the little bear's attention. Instead of helping Otava, the cub shrugged and pointed to his own face. Muzzled. The small Ursa was also muzzled but seemed completely unconcerned by the taming device and continued forward as the line moved.

Otava frantically ran to the front of The Bridge. Growling and rumbling from his throat, he tried to warn the others to stop and turn around. No one listened. Two by two, Ursas stuck their muzzled noses through the shimmering portal lights and disappeared. The more Otava protested, the faster they disappeared. Soon it was clear that the bears were no longer walking through the portal independently. They were being pulled through.

I have to save the little Ursa! Otava thought. If he couldn't rescue any others from the dangers of Earth, he felt compelled to at least save this dear little cub. He pulled out his satchel of weapons, grabbed a knife, and started cutting through the muzzle feverishly as he watched the long line of bears fade shorter and shorter on Arcas.

"Stop!" Otava roared as he burst through the cut leather. Now at the threshold between the worlds, the little bear didn't stop and didn't even look back. In a final attempt, the strong, brown beast grabbed a rope from his satchel and lassoed toward the Ursa as it vanished through the portal lights.

"Raah!" Otava yelped. The lasso wrapped around its mark, and tugged tightly against the large bear, burning his black pads as he skidded forward. He pushed back on his rear legs, but even his weight couldn't hold against the pull of The Bridge. Otava's back paws slid against the ground, rubbing raw as he tried to fight it. When his head passed through the lights, he opened his legs, gripping to the safety of Arcas against the sides of the stone arch.

Below, the little Ursa was swinging on the end of his rope over a deep ravine. The rope held only to the ankle of one rear foot. Of all the horrors that Otava could imagine on Earth, nothing prepared him for the sight underneath him. Every single Ursa that went through The Bridge landed to their death on the rocks below. Their furry bodies covered the ground like rugs—still soft and warm, but lifeless.

"Hold on!" Otava yelled. Even though they had only just met, this cub felt precious to him. It was the only other breathing Ursa around, and he was determined to save it.

Finally, trying to fight back, the cub pulled and tore at the muzzle until it loosened and fell off.

"Good!" Otava encouraged. "Now reach up and grab the rope."

The little bear curved his body and extended his front claws up, but before he could grasp the rope, the rope slipped off his foot. The line now held tightly only to the curve of one claw.

"Why didn't you listen to me?" Otava scolded in frustration and sorrow. "I told you. I told you this cursed world is full of danger. Every creature who enters it is forever plagued with death and darkness!"

The little bear bent his head to look up at Otava. He pointed at the older bear, and for the first time, spoke.

"This darkness... didn't start... with us," it wheezed faintly. "It started... with... you."

Otava screamed as the claw started to crack and splinter. *Snap!* The claw broke off and the little bear fell down, down, down. As he flailed in the air, the face morphed until it no longer looked like a young Ursa. It looked like a young man. Otava roared and roared in ultimate distress as he watched Jackson's face and body smash against the ground in disjointed brokenness. Only a lone claw dangled in the wind on the end of the rope.

"Mom?" Andi cried out to the dazzling, colorful figure walking away, just out of reach. "What are you doing here? Don't you know your kingdom is under attack?" Her words started as questions in her mind but left her lips as accusations.

Just like a beautiful flower, the queen had adorned the castle. But underneath the precious jewels and perfect appearance, she had become a weak, flimsy, and powerless leader. While Cassiopeia reflected brightly from her throne within the castle, The Altair Kingdom faded outside the castle. And for the first time, the princess's anger boiled over into confrontation.

"What is your problem, Mother!" Andi's eyes filled with the waters of emotion. She swallowed hard to contain them from overflowing down her cheeks. "Don't you care that your people are fighting for you? Do you care about anything other than yourself?" But just as a tear escaped the prison of her mind, staining her youthful cheek, the queen turned around to face her daughter.

Andi studied her mother for clarity, for answers. It had been many years since she'd seen the "seated queen" standing, let alone outside of the castle walls. Her eyes appeared sincere and clear. Without a word, Cassiopeia removed the diamond crown from her head. Her rainbow-colored hair dissolved into natural amber as it fell to her shoulders. One by one, all the jewels and sparkles disappeared from the queen's clothing and skin into the fog. Cassiopeia now looked like the strong, innocent bride depicted in the historical halls of Deneb. The woman standing before Andi was a woman she'd heard about but never seen. With a warm smile, this new mother and new queen extended the crown through the fog toward her daughter.

"What are you doing, Mom?" she asked with a softened voice. Andi had never seen her mother without the crown upon her head. In fact, her mother had never extended a real compliment to Andi, yet the queen now extended the crown—the most precious symbol of her unique beauty and power—to her confused daughter.

"I don't want it." Andi shook her head.

"I'm sick, Andi."

"Keep your crown, Mom." Andi scoffed at her mother's ridiculous comment. Stoically over dramatic—this was the queen she was used to. "We live in Arcas. A little sickness never killed anybody under the three suns."

"It's not my body, Andi. My heart and soul are sick."

"What do you mean?"

"We've had it all wrong for so long. Many of our ancestors thought the physical darkness of Earth would destroy Arcas. They believed that the nighttime, aging, and diseases of that world would ultimately annihilate the light of life within us. Yet, while we worried about darkness coming from the outside, we already had the darkness growing within us."

"But, you can fix that," Andi encouraged. "You can change your heart and soul. Go back to Altair! Be a gracious and strong queen who leads your people to a better future with better purpose."

"No, my dear Andromeda. Death in the body lasts for but a moment, but death in the heart and soul lasts forever."

"So, you're just going to give up? You're going to pass your crown and your mess off for me to fix?" Andi's voice grew with passion and anger once again. "No! For once in your life, you are going to stick around and fix your own mess!"

"I'm sorry, Andromeda. I can't fix the kingdom, and I can't fix myself. You must take the crown. Lead the people to a new king, the coming king. Only he can heal the darkness in the heart and soul, only he can destroy the darkness consuming Arcas." The queen placed the crown on Andromeda's head and walked away.

Overwhelmed by the weight of the crown and the weight of the words, tears streamed down Andi's face. She instantly removed it and ran after her mom. She reached through the fog, but when she grabbed her mother's arm, it burst into a million shards of glass. Queen Cassiopeia exploded, leaving tiny mirrors of shrapnel floating upon the waters around the princess.

"Mom? Mom!" she cried, searching through the fog as her knees bumped into the floating mirrors.

Andi was surrounded. Looking down into the reflections, she saw the crown upon her head. The princess reached up to pull it off again, but her arms wouldn't move past her waist. *Chink! Chink!* Her hands were suddenly bound by golden shackles. She yanked and yanked, but the chains slowly pulled her back, back, back toward something. When she whipped her head around to see the monster pulling her, it was her mother's throne.

The two arms on the diamond-crested glass throne consumed the gold chains until Andi was forced to sit. Then the royal chair liquefied around her legs, torso, arms, and head like thick lava seeping around her. The princess was no longer a body with freewill. Every muscle hardened to glass—becoming one with the chair—until her mouth was the only part of her body she had the power to move.

"Help! Help!" Andi screamed over and over again.

"Princess!" Otava's gruff but compassionate voice burst through the cold, hard throne holding her captive. "I've got you, little lady. You're going to be fine." His strong, furry body and face were dripping wet. He dove his paws into the waters and lifted out the sitting princess who was writhing in the shallow water.

"Have you seen Jackson?" Otava asked with quiet concern while carrying her out. Still hyperventilating, Andi could neither speak nor open her eyes, but she did answer. Her hand tremored as it slowly rose from her chest and pointed back toward the thick center of the fog.

Chapter 18

The Water Bearer

"Annn-diii! Ooo-tavaa! Where are you guys?" Jackson yelled, still searching aimlessly for his friends within the ominous vapors.

"Hi, Jackson!" A familiar figure happily kart wheeled through the floating clouds.

"Andi?" Jackson ran toward amber hair that almost glowed in the haze. "What's going on? Where did you go?"

"I'll show you. Here," Andi commanded, offering out her hand to him. Feeling strangely confused but excited by the offer to grasp her hand again, Jackson walked forward and reached his hand toward hers.

"No!" She instantly withdrew her hand as if his fingertips were repulsive or dangerous. Jackson blushed in embarrassment at the misunderstanding. "I don't want your hand. I want the transport gem."

"Why? Is something wrong? Is Otava okay?"

"No, Son of Dirt. Thanks to you, none of us are

okay." Andi smiled brightly, speaking with her usual bubbly voice, but the words stabbed him with accusations. "You stole the ancient gems. You opened The Bridge. You brought darkness into our peaceful world. You brought darkness to my home."

"I'm sorry." Jackson's eyebrows clenched with stress as he looked to the ground shamefully. He couldn't bear to hear the disappointment in her words echoed within those beautiful, lavender eyes. But he glanced up again when another recognizable voice entered the fog.

"Don't worry, Princess." Nekkar smiled confidently as he interlocked his fingers in hers. "We don't need the Son of Jack or his gem or MY sword that he's trying to wield. I, *Perseus*, will save Arcas just as Perseus saved Andromeda."

With the red-and-yellow gem in one hand and Andi's hand in the other, Nekkar pressed on the four corners and drew a doorway between Jackson and the new couple. Jackson wanted to run or cry or throw up to remove the horrible tightening in his gut. His body refused to move though his mind raced in circles. *Did I give the transport gem back to him? I don't even remember pulling it out of my pocket. Why do I even have Nekkar's sword? I don't know how to fight. The Free Realms don't want me at Trifid. Why am I even here?*

The Son of Earth stared into the dancing archway of blues and oranges. Like a magnet, the lights slowly drew him in. The mystical doorway beckoned him onward with the promise of escape. If he could remove himself from this present embarrassment and criticism being hurled at him on Arcas, perhaps he could find happiness again on Earth. Jackson stepped into the portal directly through the front door of his home.

What luck! he thought, knowing from experience that random passages between the worlds rarely take you exactly where you want to go.

"Mom! You're home?" Jackson asked, amazed she was whistling happily and cooking over the stove.

"Of course, honey! This is my favorite place on Earth!" She turned around and wrapped her arms warmly around her oldest son. "I'm so glad you're back. Go say hi to your father in the living room."

Jackson felt tears of relief flow down his cheeks. She was his mom again. She was Dad's wife again. She was home again. Jackson wiped his eyes as he walked through the hallway to the living room. Relief—it spread from his head to his feet like a warm shower on a cold day. Life could go back to normal now. No more Arcas. No more princesses. No more adventures.

His dad was sitting on the couch reading the newspaper. Beautifully normal.

"Mom told me to tell you I was home," Jackson spoke clearly, announcing both that he was back and that he knew the separation was over. It was time to apologize for the past and secure a better future. "I'm sorry for… everything."

"I'm glad to hear you say that, Son… of Earth," he replied.

The smooth, clear intonation stung Jackson's nerves with a thousand shocks. Without a second thought, he yanked his sword from the sheath. The man set the newspaper down.

"Now, now, Jackson. Is that any way to greet your new father?"

"Get out of my house, Cygnus!" Jackson stood his ground, clenching Lodestar with both hands. He didn't think of how big and strong the opponent was. He felt no desire to run or hide. All Jackson could think about was getting the lying, white-winged villain out of his house and away from his family.

"You couldn't kill me before, Son, and you won't kill me now." Cygnus smiled calmly using his charm and controlled disposition to manipulate Jackson's emotions as he stood up from the couch.

"Here ya go, honey," Lori entered the room toward her son with a fresh-grilled sandwich on a plate. "Jackson! What is wrong with you? Put that sword down!"

"Mom, get out of here and call the police!"

"Don't talk to your mother that way," Cygnus scolded as if he had the right to, as if he were protecting Lori from Jackson, the intruder. "She made your favorite, a turkey sandwich. Now, be a good boy, put the sword down, and eat."

"No!"

"Jackson! Obey your father, or I'm going to call the police!" Lori demanded with an anxiously quivering voice.

"Good! Please do call the police, Mom. I would love to see them haul off this alien monster and lock him behind bars!"

"That is a great idea, Son of Earth. Don't worry, my darling," Cygnus tenderly addressed Lori. "Just let the police haul off the monster."

Ding-dong-ding-Ding-dong-ding. All heads instantly turned to the front door. Lori walked briskly over to open it.

"Oh, thank you." She sighed when she saw the faces on the front porch. "We invited this man into our home, and now he is threatening us."

Two officers entered the room, then immediately pulled out their pistols and aimed them at Jackson.

"Sir, put your weapon down," one warned.

"Me?"

"Yes. Do you see anyone else in this house with a weapon? Drop the sword, get on your knees, and put your hands on your head," the officer ordered.

Reluctantly, Jackson raised his free arm in surrender and slowly lowered his knees to the carpeted ground, setting the sword next to him. As soon as both hands rested on his head, a cold, hard handcuff pressed against and around one wrist. The officer manually bent his cuffed arm down behind his back, grabbed the other wrist and joined the two in the bonds of chained steel.

"Let's go." The two officers lifted him to his feet.

"Wait! You need to arrest him too!" Jackson pleaded and motioned with his head and body toward Cygnus. "He's dangerous. The last time I saw him he tried to kill me!"

"You were the only one with a weapon today, boy. No one else is getting arrested."

"This is crazy! Don't you see the strange, winged man in my house? My mom is not safe here with him!"

One man in uniform continued to lead Jackson to the door as the other stood in front of Cygnus.

"So sorry about this intrusion, Lord Cygnus." He bowed slightly. "I hope you and the misses have a good day."

Jackson noticed the encounter. *How can they know Cygnus?* Something was wrong with these policemen. *Badge. Badge. Where's his badge?* Jackson searched the man escorting him outside. *There!* On the man's chest shined a silver badge. But it did not bear the emblem of a state or a county or a city. Brushed over with a pale white, the badge bore wings. Curving above the wings, it read "Prince" and underneath "of the Air." These men did not belong to the local police force. They belonged to Cygnus.

Without a second thought, Jackson jerked away and raced toward the woods.

"He's getting away!" the uniformed minion yelled to the house before chasing after him. Cygnus appeared on the front porch, still calm, collected, and in charge.

206

"You can't escape, Jackson," Cygnus hollered coolly. "All the people of all the worlds serve me and me alone. Corvus, get 'em!"

A huge, black raven rattled the patrol car as it exited the back seat. Like a trained dog, it fixed its eyes on Jackson, raised its wings, and chased after him with unequaled speed and focus. The running officer stopped to breathe as the bird passed him in the air. The black monster jolted up, over, and around, dodging branches that filled the space in the forest. He was gaining on Jackson. *Drip. Drip. Plop.* Jackson both felt and heard large drops of rain cool his arms and head as he escaped with the urgency of a fugitive. He turned back to see the bird inches away, extending his claw to grip the boy's back.

Swoosh! In an instant, the sky opened and poured buckets of rain on Jackson's head. He was blinded momentarily, but the handcuffs slipped off. Sticking his arms out, he felt for the trees he would collide into any second now. When Jackson squinted through his moist eyelids, the world appeared distorted like he was trying to focus through a bubbly, wet windshield. As he blinked and rubbed his eyes, the woods, raven, and his house dissolved around him, falling into the water that swayed gently below his knees. He couldn't see Cygnus or the officers or his mom.

Jackson rested his hands on his knees. He breathed and breathed and breathed, staring at the rippling water below him. His heart still pounded and his head spun with a consuming chaos of adrenaline. *Where am I? Did I use the gem and jump back to Arcas? Where's Cygnus? Where's my mom? And what did they do to my dad?* Nothing made sense. All that was left was fog.

Fog… and a hairy man?

Shaggy, wet, aqua-blue hair framed the man's face. Behind the long beard and wild tresses, his matching aqua-blue eyes glowed with compassion and concern. His clothes were tattered like one who'd survived a shipwreck. He was watching Jackson and holding an intricately decorated, large clay jug by the handle on each side. The jug was empty and aimed sideways as if he just poured it out.

"I'm sorry I didn't reach you sooner. It was a bad one, wasn't it?" he asked gently.

"I don't understand what just happened," Jackson replied honestly. But then the adrenaline kicked in again, and he reached for his sword. This man could be dangerous. He certainly looked like a vagrant. But the sword was gone.

"You dropped your sword in the water, back there." He pointed. "I've been waiting a long time for you, Son of Earth. And now you are here, which means the end is near." His eyes sparkled, and he nearly laughed in glee as if the end was a good thing. *He's either some type of prophet or he's crazy*, Jackson concluded.

Suddenly, his wild blue head turned to the side, and the man shrieked. "Oh, no! You get away from me!" Jackson looked in the direction of the threat, but he saw nothing. Only fog. The man quickly dunked his jug in the water and poured it over his own head. He breathed deeply, then opened his eyes.

"Ah, that's better." He sighed and smiled. "You see, the water washes away the dark visions. When you are washed, you think clearly. But once your head starts to dry, the dirty dreams come back through the fog."

Jackson touched his own hair, still dripping.

"So, you threw water on me?"

"Yes. My name is Melik." He put his fist to his chest, the typical Arcasian sign of peace. "But many call me the Water Bearer."

"Do you live here or something?"

"Yes. The Lagoon is my home… for now"

"Why? This must be one of the most horrible places to live in all of Arcas."

"I choose to live in here because I know the secret to escaping the darkness. If I leave, many poor souls will remain tormented, lost forever in the fog."

Jackson felt both amazed by Melik's sacrifice and incredibly sad that the man had to constantly fight back his own nightmares in a world of endless light.

"Do not worry about me," Melik consoled, sensing Jackson's heaviness of heart. "Some day soon, a king will come and break the fog forever. Then, I will leave."

"Oh, we need to find my friends!" Jackson

remembered his mission with the mention of a king. "Have you seen them? An Ursa and a girl?"

"I helped the Ursa, and I believe he found the girl. Her screams stopped right before I found you. Don't worry, they made it out of the fog."

"Thank you. How do I get out so I can join them?

"Those in the clouds of The Lagoon walk in constant darkness, but those who bury themselves in the water will spring out into new light."

"Okay... What does that mean?" Jackson didn't want to wait in the haze until the nightmares came back. He needed to find Otava and Andi without wasting time unveiling riddles. "Can you please just point to the way?"

"Tell me the truth, Son of Earth." Melik walked up to Jackson and put his hand on his shoulder. He was still kind, but he became serious. "Do you think I'm crazy or a liar or do you believe that I know the way?"

"I believe you. I just need a guide."

Thwoosh. Thwoosh. Thwoosh. Thwoosh. The sound of hooves galloping through The Lagoon interrupted their conversation. Strong and swift, the violent centaur charged toward them. He had fire in his eyes and venom dripped off the end of his arrow.

"Watch out!" Jackson warned in terror. "Sephdar is right behind you! He is pulling back his bow!"

"To escape the dark vapors, you must cleanse yourself in the water. Those who bury themselves in the water will

210

spring out into new light," Melik instructed as clearly as he could, unruffled by the threat, just as the warring centaur jumped over the water bearer to attack. Hooves soaring high in the air, he twisted his human torso, and shot the arrow directly at the heart of the Son of Earth. Jackson dove under the water. He opened his eyes just in time to watch the black arrow disintegrate into nothing at the surface.

Underneath the waters, the fog disappeared and everything became clear. The light of the three suns pierced down, sparkling off the pale sand. Melik's bare feet sunk slightly in the smooth, soaking grains ten feet away. Jackson saw the man smiling in satisfaction through his aqua-blue beard. He dipped his jug into the water and walked away.

Ah! Jackson shielded his eyes from a blinding shot of light. Something large and shiny was reflecting off the suns from beneath the surface. It was reflecting too brightly to decipher the shape. But the shoreline rested just fifty meters beyond the object, so Jackson swam toward it. *My sword!* Jackson reached out, grabbed the handle, and then surfaced for air.

It was an amazing contrast. Above, visibility remained shallow, clouded by the shadowy, thick grays. Immediately, Jackson lost his direction and his path to the shore. He sheathed the sword and dove back into the waters. The shore rested just a few strokes away.

Otava! Jackson swam faster after recognizing his large, furry friend. The Ursa was down on all fours, sniffing the fog over the lagoon. Nearby, Andi rested in the white sand on the dry shore. Whether from lack of air or nervousness, Jackson's chest tightened. He knew the visions were fake. Cygnus had never entered his home. Andi had never told Jackson he screwed up Arcas. Nekkar barely knew Andi, and the two were definitely not a couple, but he could still see them standing together against him, holding hands. The image was disturbing, and the fresh nightmares haunted him.

He wasn't necessarily afraid of Andi being interested in Nekkar. She was her own person and had the right to choose another. Honestly, he wanted her to be happy. But Jackson now felt the need to protect himself from both Andi and Nekkar. He'd trusted in his parents' loyalty to him and their loyalty to each other. That didn't work out so well. If he didn't love, if he didn't care, then he couldn't be hurt when loyalties failed.

"Jackson! You made it out!" Andi jumped up and ran over to him, throwing her arms around his back. He felt the warmth of her tone and the warmth of her arms, but he didn't have the energy to break down the walls the fog had built around his heart. He stood like a statue—numb—not cringing away but not hugging her back.

"Are you okay, Jackson?" Andi backed away from him, holding his shoulders sincerely and examining his face. Her eyes were sad and tired. *Screams.* Jackson remembered what Melik heard in The Lagoon. Screams from the girl full of life and courage and beauty. He never wanted to hear that sound. *What did she see?* he wondered. Jackson wished he could wrap his arms around her. He wanted to hold her tight. He wanted to wash the horrors out of her mind and comfort her. Maybe he couldn't open his own heart right now, but he would do everything in his power to protect her heart.

"Yeah, I'm fine." He pried out a cumbersome smile.

"I've never been so happy to see a Bear-Eater," Otava teased with somber overtones, slapping him on the back.

"Oh, guess what?" Andi's tone lightened with good news. "We found the Ligeian Sea, finally!" She pointed to the waters crashing against the sand in the distance. "We hopped right into that nasty lagoon, not realizing the real sea was just past the fog."

"Great. Where are the horses?" Jackson asked, eager to get himself and his friends far away from The Lagoon.

"They ran away. After the Water-Bearer drenched my head, he told me something spooked them and they took off toward home. But... someone else arrived while you were lost," Otava explained, motioning at the crashing waves. Just then, a dark head and body emerged from the sea. Blue flames burst under his feet as the horse galloped across the white sands toward them.

"Alnitak?" Jackson asked excitedly, remembering the famed war horse well. "Is Rigel here?" His spirits rose at the mere prospect of The Hunter's presence.

Alnitak had rescued Rigel before and carried him safely past the wings of Cygnus's army. Jackson could still smell the scent of the horse's fiery breath when his four-legged body lunged from the cliffs of Trifid. And he could still feel the cords of his mane in his hands and the strength of the magnificent beast carrying him safely through the air and into the Ligeian Sea.

"No. He's not here for Rigel." Andi squeezed Jackson's arm. "He's here for you."

Chapter 19

The Royal Couple

King Alderamin tightened his grip around his axe as they approached the southern, natural bridge hidden within the wilds of the jungle. The tall axe was carved and jeweled throughout the iron head more beautifully than any sword, a weapon worthy of the cave land king in both power and design. Alderamin lifted the axe from his belt, signaling his men to ready their own weapons. Damp with sweat around the girth and breast strap from the long journey, the horse beneath him lifted its front hooves to plant them on the rock path hovering high above the river. With each quiet stride toward the castle, the king's heart pounded more loudly of both courage and fear. Make no mistake; the king was ready to wield his weapon in defense of his queen, his bride. But Alderamin was not ready to look Cassiopeia in the eyes.

Nearly ten years had passed since Alderamin last saw the queen face-to-face. Though the kingdoms traded freely, it was obvious they were separate. Two different kingdoms, two different crowns, two different beds for Princess Andromeda to lay her head. Of course, the royal couple hadn't planned it this way. Their marriage was meant to unite Arcas. Their union would join the kingdoms under one rule, one purpose, and one future. But the two young lovers never truly figured out how to merge into one.

In the early years—when they still looked at each other with wonder and excitement—the two often split their time: a few months separate, a few months in Deneb, a few months in Altair. Alderamin and Cassiopeia loved their time together but also loved their own kingdoms the best. It was difficult to not always feel a bit out of place in the other's home. Both entered the extra castle like an honored guest but never like an equal partner and ruler. The ruling life was complicated and intense for a couple thrown into power so young. It became increasingly difficult to maintain any type of normalcy in marriage because the two were not just committed to each other; they were committed to their people, to an entire kingdom that demanded their attention. As time passed, the queen became increasingly critical of her foreign husband and the king became increasingly aloof toward his foreign wife.

Life just seemed easier apart. Separate, they could raise the little princess by their own standards and rule each kingdom by their own decrees. Still, King Alderamin often imagined a royal reunion, full of parties and painted portraits and magnificent pomp. Since living in Arcas gave them endless time, it was easy to put off treading through the awkwardness that years of separation had shoveled between them. It was always understood that the reigning family would all gather together again someday. But the king never wrote a letter of invitation. He never mounted his steed and galloped off to lift his lady from her throne and into the setting golden sun once more.

Now, it was too late for such glitz and gallantry. Today, Alderamin entered the kingdom not like a husband, or a king, or an honored guest. Today, the king silently crept into the back of Altair like a bandit. He'd sent Alfirk and Nekkar—along with half the Cephid army—straightforward to approach the kingdom from the main crossing over the Eridanus River to the Royal Pier. Alderamin, however, led the rest of the army in from the back, hoping to catch the enemy fighters unawares. Step by step, the king rode toward his bride. This threat of death had summoned the royal couple together again, but would it rekindle a fire of passion or disgust in the queen?

"Halt!" Alderamin shouted a whisper through the silence in the troops, holding his axe high to command them to stop. The king froze for a moment then yelled loudly in panic as he galloped toward the castle, "Make haste to the castle! Find the queen!"

This wasn't the sort of behavior of a king who wanted to storm the enemy unnoticed. But as the Cephid riders kicked the sides of their horses to swiftly release them onward, they soon understood the cause of alarm. At the highest point on the bridge, the fighters of Deneb witnessed what the king saw over the tree line.

Smoke.

Smoke.

Smoke.

Billowing puffs of black and gray trailed down the path of the river. The battle was over. And the enemy had left a burning path of evidence from the castle down to the last Altairian village depending on the river and the kingdom for its livelihood.

King Alderamin's horse jolted to a stop. The once-solid brick wall around the castle was filled with holes, cracks, and breaks. The largest opening crumbled through half of the outer wall, filled the moat with a jagged footpath of rock, and continued its destruction into the rear of the castle. The royal charger would never make it over these uneven pieces of broken brick. Diving off his horse with axe in hand, King Alderamin climbed over the rocky rubble paving his way to the queen. The Cephids quickly followed suit, their small, steady bodies lunging to the ground one by one behind the crown. Everyone knew the enemy was long gone, but all entered the city with weapons ready.

Once inside, each man's adrenaline of war instantly drowned under the sorrow of complete devastation. Bodies lay everywhere. Battered, motionless limbs stuck out of piles of rock from the crumbled palace. Altairian soldiers, who once adorned the queen's world with jewels and praise, now ornamented the courtyard with their lives. Sword and spear piercings oozed like scarlet ribbons flowing from their garments to the ground underneath them. Arrows of darkness covered many others. The black feather fletching stood above each chest and limb, pinning the bodies down while waving ever so slightly in the breeze as if to taunt the dead by their ability to move. The stench of death, which had saturated the courtyard air over many hours of constant sunshine, filled every healthy nostril with the sweet yet grossly metallic fumes.

Though the castle had several large holes and breached entrances, the king ran around to the front door as if he expected Cassiopeia to be waiting on the threshold for him. There was no need to knock or turn the knob. The upper half of the door hung sideways on one hinge, splintered off from the bottom that was rammed firmly against the foyer wall. Alderamin paused for a moment, nervous about entering his wife's domain with the dust and sweat of travel covering him. She hadn't always been so particular about how people entered her presence, but the queen had changed through the years. The more Cassiopeia dwelt on her own image, the more critical she became of others. All others threatened to spoil the beauty and perfection she had built around herself, the perfection she required of herself.

Crack-Crunch. Crack-Crunch. Crack-Crunch. Each step

Alderamin took landed upon fractured mirrors. He looked down the hall, expecting to see life, hope. But instead, the king saw a thousand broken reflections of himself. His dark, burdened eyes and concerned brows surrounded him endlessly, reminding him that he'd failed. The king had failed to protect the Kingdom of Altair. He'd failed to protect the queen. He'd failed to protect his family.

"Shedir? Shedir!" Alderamin cleared the sorrow from his throat and blurted out as if the old man would suddenly appear, answer all his questions, and guide him to his beautiful wife, who was hiding in safety.

"My King!" a labored, raspy voice called from a pile of toppled wall. "I knew you'd rescue us!"

He ran through the hall, searching reflected image after reflected image until he found a figure with lighter skin than his own. The servant had nearly disappeared into the large pieces of rock covering his stomach and legs. He wore the dull gray garments of the palace with a mirrored fabric sewn into the front to reflect the queen's beauty when he had the privilege of entering her chamber. His rock-colored apparel camouflaged him within the bricks and probably prolonged his life.

"Help me!" Alderamin shouted to his men as he shoved his axe under a chunk of the castle holding the man down. In seconds, the short miners surrounded him and heaved the boulder off the injured servant. All held their breath as they examined what was left of his poor body. The servant's ribs were crushed. Shards of bone breached through the skin and each time his lungs lifted, the covered, fractured bone visibly separated under the skin. The king kneeled down in compassion and grabbed his hand.

"Yes, I'm here, brave son." He had seen the wounds of war before. The king watched the dead and the injured return from the Pillar Wars as a youth. Even recently, he'd held in his arms those who had been attacked by Shaula, the scorpion that invaded in his caves. But he'd never walked on a battlefield fresh with casualties. At this moment, Alderamin forgot about pride and crowns. All he could think of was comforting the soul in front of him who was fading away from an Arcasian life that he thought would never be taken from him.

"The ships…" he breathed, "they bore the flag of White Wings."

"Cygnus is dead, my boy. Did you see who led the army?"

"They took orders"—*gasp*—"from a centaur. Skilled with a bow… made for the throne room." He averted his eyes briefly in shame. "I'm sorry," he apologized, laboring to communicate with each heavy, raspy breath. "I could not… Wall… fell. Castle… breached."

"You did well, soldier. The kingdoms are honored by your bravery today." The injured man seemed to smile in relief to the king's praise. "Did you see if this centaur left with the queen?"

The man took one last breath, turned his head slightly back and forth as if to say "no," then passed out of their world forever.

"My King!" Alfirk entered the hallway. "Survivors are arriving from the nearest villages, but there are few—mainly women and children."

"Get this man's body out of here, and join him with his Altairian brothers in the courtyard. Have the women tend to the wounded. Order every man to seek out signs of the queen. She may still be here! Mark every searched room and lift every brick until we find her!"

Continuing boldly through the hallway, the king searched for his wife. Crumbled wall, broken mirrors, and dusty, crushed bodies decorated the once pristine residence of the queen. *This is my fault. I let these walls crumble.* Though Altair fell in a day, he knew that years and years of lethargy were to blame for its collapse. *It wasn't the Altairian soldiers' job to protect the queen. It was my job. I am the king. There is no other king in Arcas. I wasn't here when the kingdom needed me. I wasn't here when she needed me.* Though his men's boots stomped and crackled loudly on the broken glass, all Alderamin could hear were the condemning thoughts circling his mind.

At the instructions of Alfirk, the Cephids' dark bodies quickly infiltrated the castle. Usually the halls were well lit by the light of the three suns bouncing off of the mirrors, but light was dim and distorted in the wounded palace.

Born with the ability to see in the darkest places, the little miners' eyes glowed yellow each time they turned into a shadowy hall.

"Mark the door!" *Scruuutch.* "The queen's not in this room!" *Scruuutch.* An axe scraped across a heavy wooden door each time a room was cleared. "Someone's alive! Come quickly!" another shouted for help.

King Alderamin squeezed the handle of his axe until his knuckles blanched. He could no longer control the passion inside him. Water flowed to his eyes while anger fought like a dam to hold back the flood of sorrow. With no destination in mind, he began running, running, running through the glass and the blood and the toppled bricks. He had arrived too late to outrun the enemy, but perhaps he could outrun the guilt.

Suddenly, the scenery changed. Everything felt untouched as he reached the back hallway. Every mirror was still perfectly intact, every wall still standing. And there was his light brown face in image after image with blood-shot, yellow-brown eyes looking back at him.

"RAAAAAHHHH!" He viciously swung his axe right and left, shattering each image that now looked detestable and pathetic to him. *Crash! Crash! Crash!* Shards of glass blasted from the sharpened edge of his axe as it collided with the mirrors covering every wall. But the last unblemished mirror that he swung the heavy weapon into didn't respond as the others. His axe didn't just sink into the glass; it sunk into the wall itself. The king jerked and yanked, but the iron head stuck firmly. In anger and frustration, he kicked the mirrored wall.

Click-click. Alderamin froze as the wall sprang open. Grabbing the edge of the solid door that was hiding behind a reflective façade, memories fell upon him like rain saturating a thirsty ground. *I know this place,* he realized, peering into the dusky staircase. Entering the dim passage, he slowly exhaled and inhaled to tame the wild breath of emotions that exited his lungs moments ago. For a moment, the world behind faded. His fingers traced along the stones on the passageway, but what he felt was a hand interlocked in his, pulling him forward. Pulling him Down.

Down.

Down.

"Shhh! Someone will hear you!" Cassie giggled with a feisty excitement.

"But many suns have passed since we both presented ourselves to the people of Altair." He stopped on the stairway and wrapped his arms around her, pressing his lips against the side of her head. Her hair smelled like the roses that grew around the kingdom. *"And aren't we supposed to be entertaining guests tonight?"* he asked, touching his nose to hers, and lightly wrapping his finger around an amber strand of curled hair.

"That is exactly my plan." She danced her fingers up his arm to his broad shoulder. Then the queen removed the crown from her head, and released her hair to cascade past her neck and

shoulders. "*Tonight, I am entertaining my most important guest, uninterrupted. Only he gets to tour the secret parts of my palace.*"

It was rare for the young king and queen to get time together, and even more rare for them to be alone. They kissed and kissed on the dark staircase before continuing hand-in-hand to the secretively scenic under-the-castle waters of the moat. In front of the dimly lit waters, a lush rug lay complete with candlelight, sweet treats, and drinks. Alderamin smiled. Right at this moment, he felt more like a king than any other time. And his wife, his queen, was the most lovely of all women in the kingdoms, of all Arcas.

"*And if the Old Miser comes looking for us?*" *he asked, twirling her around then pulling her close for a dance.*

"*He won't,*" *she answered confidently with a sly grin. "Who do you think set this up for me?*"

Suddenly, a muffled clamor of voices below interrupted Alderamin's dream, snapping him back to the painful present realities.

"I don't want to listen to your silly song! I've heard that same out-of-tune lyre play more times that I can count! White Wings and his Sullyfat music man always played it for me," the voice huffed like she was bored. "Their nauseating tunes never equaled the serenading sound of my illustrious tone." The sickly noises of someone coughing and spitting echoed through the passageway. "Don't you see this ugly place is making me ill, Ilmatar! I order you peasants to give me my mirror at once so I can look at something worthy of the eye!"

"I'm sorry, My Queen. Your mirror fell into the water," another voice spoke softly and sadly.

"Dive into the water and get it then! The Flower of the Eridanus is wilting before your dull eyes, and you can't even give me the one thing that will bring me comfort!"

"Cassie? Cassie! I'm here! Don't worry, I'm coming for you!" Alderamin burst out, speeding down the long, curved stairway. He heard a splash, and then the soft strums of a lyre, along with the deep humming of a woman's voice. Queen Cassiopeia continued to rant and rave about all the injustice and ugliness around her until the music overwhelmed the sound of her voice. When the king arrived at the landing in front of the waters, he saw Merope strumming the lyre while Rigel watched a cloudy song lift the queen's body off the ground.

"What are you doing!" Alderamin shouted frantically, rushing forward.

"It's okay." Rigel stepped in front of him, holding him back with firm but compassionate hands. "Merope is trying to help her. The queen is injured."

The king understood and waited anxiously, watching the cloudy, colorful music spin around his wife. Caph emerged from the water, climbed out, and held the mirror up victoriously. But his face fell when he saw the king. As one of the few soldiers who survived, he didn't want to see this hurt and devastation in the king's eyes. He didn't want to look at him and explain how they failed to keep the castle, how they failed to protect the queen. The king never looked his way though. His eyes were focused on what was left of his bride, floating in front of him.

Dark arrows pierce the flesh
Rocks crush and break the bone
Mend all together again
Return her as she's known.

Rigel, Alderamin, and Caph stood still, listening to the Ilmatar's deep song, and the lyre's powerful strum. As the melody quieted to a hum, the cloud returned the queen softly to the ground and slowly evaporated around her body, now lying still and quiet. Everyone waited for a response from the queen.

"Caph, did you find my mirror?" she asked calmly.

"Yes, yes, My Queen!" He scurried over to her and placed the small hand mirror on her limp fingers. Alderamin waited, not wanting to upset or interrupt her.

Cassiopeia slowly lifted it and looked in the glass.

"What happened to me? What have I become?" A tear rolled down the queen's cheek, streaking the powdery glitter painting her face. "I do not recognize this woman." Alderamin couldn't stay back any longer. He lunged forward, fell to his knees beside her and grabbed her free arm.

"I recognize you. You are Queen Cassiopeia, the most beautiful ruler over all in the kingdom realms."

As he approached her, he could see a mix of dried and fresh blood surrounding the hole in her stomach. The wound was not healed. Hearing his voice and feeling his hand, the queen set down her mirror, and for the first time in many years, she looked directly at her husband. It was as if a fog had lifted from her eyes, dissolving into the lyre's cloud. Her vision was clear. She not only saw her husband for what he was, but she understood what she had become.

"You came." She smiled and breathed out. "Thank you for coming."

"I'm sorry. I'm so sorry, Cassie. You're hurt." He leaned down, whispered in her ear, and pet back the hair on her forehead. Alderamin's voice choked and the tears finally released. "I should have been here."

"No, no. I'm sorry. I've been lost, so lost." She winced and held the wound throbbing within her. "But I see clearly now. I see you, Al-der-my-man." She smiled again, weakly, but warmly. "And you are a good man, a good king, and a good father." Trails of tears rolled down her cheeks again. "Tell Andi that I love her, and that she's beautiful. Our daughter is everything I wish I could have been. She will make a good queen."

"I know. She's just like her mother. But you can tell her that yourself because I'm taking you back to Deneb with me. She's waiting there for you."

"I'm not going to make it… to Deneb." She shook her head with a sad smile as if to say *I love you, but we both know what is going to happen here.* Her breathing grew more shallow. The air seemed to crack and shatter as it exited her lungs.

"No!" He shook his head back and forth, holding her tightly against his chest.

"My dear, I will not make it out of Altair today."

"No. I'm taking you home with me right now and you are going to live." The king lifted her limp body from the ground.

The others stood quietly behind with wet eyes and tight throats. Merope looked at Rigel painfully and shrugged. He knew her mind. Merope didn't understand why she couldn't heal the queen. Why she didn't have enough power to stay death. Rigel looked back at her solemnly, pointed at his head, and mouthed, "You did heal her. You healed her mind." The two wrapped an arm around the other's side and squeezed tightly. They couldn't help feeling they were intruding on a scene in which they didn't belong, but they could not move for fear of interrupting it.

"Do you see the door in front of us?" Cassiopeia asked as Alderamin walked her toward the stairs. Her face instantly changed as if she was looking at something amazing. Determined, the king continued forward, carrying his bride just as he did across the threshold the first night they were wed. "It shimmers like the three suns glistening off a still water. It's the way between the worlds, Alderamin."

"Stay with me, Cassie," he whispered. "Don't go through any doors,"

"But I'm so unworthy, so dirty and ugly. I do not deserve to enter such beauty."

"You are the most worthy and beautiful person I know. You just stay here with me."

"It's opening... They're letting me in..." she whispered as her soul parted from body.

"No. No. No. Stay with me! Cassie, NOOOO!" He felt the stillness. Her breath was gone. "Don't go! Come back to me!" Alderamin cried, falling to his knees with his wife cradled in his arms. For what seemed like hours, the king kissed and hugged and pleaded with Cassiopeia to return. But she was gone. Her body became heavier and colder. When his lungs could no longer wail and all the tears had dried to extinction, he lifted her once again, and carried her body up the stairs to meet what was left of her people.

Chapter 20

Argo Navis Sails Again

Axes chopped and hacked vigorously through the greenish-brown vines one by one, releasing *Argo Navis* from his jungle prison. By order of the king, Cephids and surviving Altairians were now working together at the northern end of Altair to unleash the kingdom's ultimate beast of war. Normally, the people would shudder at the face of Eltanin, the dragon who betrayed the kingdoms and led many to a fiery death. But as the iron face of the beast emerged from the grip of the jungle, the people felt new hope and new power.

Sephdar would not escape unchallenged. Whether taken by vengeance or by justice, blood was required from White Wings' army and their new leader. King Alderamin would not rest until the villains paid their debt to the kingdoms with their own lives. And now, he was awakening the vessel of reckoning that had long been slumbering in the forest.

Argo Navis was the watery dragon of Altair, the ultimate naval weapon. Its bowsprit rose into the air with the carved likeness of Eltanin. Similar to the powerful dragon, this crafted beast soared over the waters with the power to hurl flames from its mouth at any enemy. Wooden scales and faded, chipping paint decorated the outside while the interior, metal mouth of the creature displayed black soot and charring from past fires of attack. The renowned war ship became famous for its speed and power during The Bridge War, but it retired near the boating village of Rana after Eltanin's deadly betrayal of the kingdoms in The Pillar Wars. The Sons of Earth were banished back to their world, Eltanin was banished to a desolated Vega, and *Argo* was banished to a dry dock.

The village of Rana rested at the north most tip of the kingdom. Since Sephdar never went farther than the castle, this little village and its people remained untouched from the attack. Rana was a quiet town filled with those who used to serve in the royal Altairian Navy. Though a few still braved the waters from time to time, most led a safer life of fishing from the shore. Years of inactivity had stolen the adventurous spirit from the sailors and replaced it with fear. The more people refused to ride their boats down Eridanus, the more Mira ravaged the river, randomly exploding through the waters riding the mighty Cetus. The river belonged to the beasts now, and men of the eastern kingdom knew to stay clear of it.

Nekkar, however, was born in the far west. He had traveled by horse through prairies, by foot over mountains, and by ship in the Ligeian Sea. The son of Arcturus did not fear these strange waters, so he led the charge to unleash the war ship. Though the Cephids much preferred the underground life to one at sea, their righteous rage over the death of the queen fueled them with fresh courage. Sailing the infamous *Argo Navis* down the Eridanus to catch the White Winged fleet was little to ask of them. At this moment of rage submerged in billowing passion, every Cephid man would saddle Eltanin himself if it meant bringing the tyrant army to justice.

Grabbing a sturdy vine, Nekkar climbed up the side of the ship. *Thud!* He jumped off the flat railing and onto the main deck. Letting his fingers glide along the rails, he walked from the main deck to the forecastle, near the dragon's head. As the young man's boots echoed through the hollow body of the ship below, he realized something felt strange about this old ship. He petted the smooth, glossy back of the dragon's brown, spiked head, imagining the real beast from the stories of old. Each scale was chiseled to perfection and highlighted with greens. Nekkar rubbed his fingers together after touching the dragon. No dust.

Nekkar bent over the side of the boat, examining Eltanin's face again. On the outside, the beast looked weathered and old. The ship's exterior was covered in cobwebs and bird droppings and jungle debris, but the inside of the boat was clean and unchanged by the tropical forest around it. The deck rested unprotected in the wilds of the Eridanus but seemed untouched by creature, weather, and wear. Someone was protecting *Argo Navis* all these years. Someone cared for the old ship and may not be happy that it's going away, going to war.

Suddenly, Nekkar felt like he was being watched. He reached for his sword, but muscle-memory failed him. Nekkar pulled the sword as if it were Lodestar, long and straight. But he was wearing a sword of Deneb now, thicker and curved at the end. The weapon was only half unsheathed when a rope flew down from above, tightened around his body then jerked him onto his back. Before he could stand, a body flew down from the sails and shoved a knee into his chest. In seconds, ropes bound both his hands and feet. A small blade slid against his neck from the flying cowboy as another shadow moved from the stern to the forecastle where Nekkar lay bound and confused.

"What think you, Markeb, of this tall one from Deneb?" the moving, rhyming shadow asked the one who held the knife at Nekkar's throat. When he reached the tied-up foreigner, he peered suspiciously down at him, studying both Nekkar's looks and demeanor to judge his purposes. Like many in Arcas, this man's face did not age with time, but looked slightly darkened and leathery from long, endless hours in the suns' light. He wore a dusty, old hat embroidered with the dragon-faced ship, the retired image of the Altairian navy. Though the Eridanus ran with fresh water, the captain looked like he'd been soaking his long, matted hair and beard in chlorine then rubbing it with algae. The base browns of his tresses were drowned out by streaks of bleached blond and a greenish tinge. "He carries no axe. His eyes are not yellow, yet he dares steal my ship like a vagabond fellow."

"This ship does not belong to you," Nekkar spouted back, unafraid. "It belongs to the Kingdom of Altair in service of the queen."

"*Argo* does not belong to Captain Tycho, ya' say? Go ahead and stick yer hand in my cabin, for I bite like a moray." Perhaps, he'd gone a little crazy over the years, spending too much time pacing a docked ship, but the leader of the vessel evidently could not speak without ending in rhyme.

"He's up to no good, Cap'in," Markeb warned as Tycho stood over Nekkar, studying him. "We ain't laid our eyes on the Flower of the Eridanus since *Argo Navis* floated through the canal to her eternal rest away from the waters."

Two more *Argo Navis* sailors and territorial enthusiasts of the old war ship joined the group on deck. One climbed up from the hull and the other crept up from the stern. These two kindred—but very different—spirits, Asmid and Aspid, joined the small ragtag team who guarded the vessel.

"We're surrounded, Cap'in! Hundreds of these little people throwing axes around *Argo*! They're going to scar her," Aspid complained in a frantic whisper, petting the foremast as if he were comforting the soon-to-be-wounded ship.

"Let me light 'em up!" Asmid shook his fist, ever ready for a fight. "I'll ignite thee flames in thee belly of thee beast and char 'em out of thee Eridanus!"

"Really? Will you add to the trail of flames already flowing down the river?" Nekkar spouted in disbelief, feeling the pressure of both the knife at his throat and the increasing distance between them and White Wings' army. "We are not the enemy. This ship is the only vessel that can bring justice upon the army that just destroyed Altair."

"Climb the mast, limber Aspid. Do his words reek of truth or of rotten squid?" Captain Tycho ordered, waiting cautiously to discover the truth of Nekkar's claims. Unconvinced that they could trust this warrior who wore the brand of neither kingdom, the small band of sailors watched Aspid scurry to the top of the mast and peer south over the trees.

"By the great river!" Aspid softly shouted, alarmed by the sight but still trying to remain unnoticed by the Cephids working below. The thin, keel-of-a-man slid back down the mast as smoothly as if it was a fireman's pole. "The kingdomless one speaks truth," Aspid affirmed to the captain once his feet landed upon the deck. "There's smoke in every village from the castle to Theemin."

Captain Tycho nodded his head at Markeb, who responded by removing the knife from Nekkar's throat.

Sorrow and solemnity replaced the distrust and irritation in his eyes.

"No one provoked those attacks," Nekkar explained, standing to his feet. "Sephdar, a centaur, has taken over White Wings' army and is stealing, killing, and destroying all that is good in the kingdoms."

"Sephdar?" Markeb asked, jumping through the memories in his mind. "Isn't he the one they call the Black Hole?"

"Aye," Asmid jumped in, always eager for a tale of blood and brute. "Thee seamen from Achernar were out on thee waters fishing that day. They say Minaruja attacked whilst he rested on the lower banks where thee water mixes between thee fresh Eridanus and thee salty Ligeian." Asmid replayed the event using one arm as the sea serpent and one as Sephdar. "Thee venomous beast burst from thee water and grabbed thee centaur right in his torso. Minaruja's serpent head shook him back and forth and back and forth like a rabid dog shaking a helpless rabbit. Her mouth frothed and foamed until thee archer regained his bearings. He pulled an arrow from thee quiver and shot it straight into her snout. They say thee angry beast flung him halfway to Trifid. To thee ruins he stumbled with a black hole in his middle and a black poison ever pumping through his veins."

"Then let the smoke billowing through the forest confirm to you that it is not just his body that is poisoned, but also his soul. It would have been good for Minaruja to win the battle that day, for Sephdar has become ten times the deadly viper, attacking the innocent all over Arcas from land and from the water," Nekkar laid out his case.

"The innocent? Ha!" Captain scoffed. "My boy, have ya' seen war? Have ya' walked through its bloody door?"

"Yes." Though still quite youthful, the son of Arcturus defended his experience. "I have wiped the blood of war from my sword, and I have seen my men die before my eyes."

"Then ya' know that none are innocent. All carry crimes for which they must repent."

"But that doesn't mean that we stop fighting for the good that remains within us," Nekkar challenged. "That doesn't mean that we allow evil to reign freely, destroying all the good that remains."

"Aye. But look to the current today in the river. Such a sight makes even the bravest sailor quiver." Captain Tycho pointed to the Eridanus with a cautiously wild expression. Nekkar stepped near the railing on the hull of the ship, then looked past the dry dock and the man-made canal to the river. The rapids seemed slightly swift with little ripples of white rapids highlighting the surface, but nothing seemed abnormal or dangerous to the Free Realm warrior.

"I'm sorry, but I don't understand your rhymes and riddles. You once led the Royal Navy of Altair, and now you're afraid of a few rapids?"

"By the great river, I'll throw yer scrawny bones into

thee rapids, and ya' can see why thee cap'in stays off the Eridanus!" Asmid threatened, moving toward Nekkar with no weapon but his brawny arms.

"Captain Tycho is welcome to stay off the river," a deep, official voice entered the conversation, "but *Argo Navis* will sail."

"King Alderamin," the captain bowed once he turned and saw the king. The other sailors immediately followed his gesture of respect and fear. "Where be the gracious queen? Did she also come to my humble marine?"

"The most beautiful Queen Cassiopeia has passed from this world, but her death will not go unavenged. What say you, Captain? Will you set the dragon ship free once again and sail with me?"

"My soul mourns for the loss of the queen, but dangers lie under the river with Mira, Mira unseen," Tycho warned with an ominous tone. "The river has become wild, My King. Prepare yer troops to make the fight a land thing."

"Captain"—Alderamin stood in front of him with fire in his eyes and passion in his voice—"will you sail with me, joined in war as with my father, King Denebola, or will you forgo justice and glory by watching idly from the shores of Rana?"

Tycho quietly pet the railing of his ship. He looked from his sails to his men to the face of the king before finally answering.

"Markeb, ready the sails!" Tycho commanded resolutely, yanking a key from a chain around his neck. "Asmid and Aspid, release the beast from his jail!"

The three scurried around with an anxious excitement. They'd seen rapids like these before and it worried them that travel by ship was risky, but to sail the flaming dragon across the waters was worth the risk, especially with their captain at the helm. Asmid and Aspid grabbed vines and swung to the ground next to the dry canal where the vessel was docked. Two gates met together in the canal, locking out the river's waters. Using the captain's key, Asmid wiggled the iron into the keyhole while Aspid directed Cephids to shove large wooden beams into the gate braces.

"One, two, heave!" Asmid bellowed. They pushed and pushed against the beams, fighting the water to open the gates. "Heave! Keep pushing, men!" The side with Asmid's powerful strength pushed forward first, sending a small stream of water into the dock. Then, *whoosh!* a flood rushed through the dock and lifted the vessel above the braces that stabilized it from below.

"HoooRaaah! HoooRaaah!" cried the men, raising their fists in joy as they watched the dragon's head rise above the water once more. As some climbed into *Argo Navis*, others sped away to join the rest of the naval fleet waiting at the Royal Pier. Though a few were stolen and a few burned, most of the ships docked at the kingdom were left untouched.

Sephdar believed that no one was left in Altair to come after him, and no one was fast enough to catch his rampaging fleet. He and his men relaxed leisurely at the pillaged village of Theemin, enjoying an abundance of stolen food and ale while dividing the spoils. But *Argo Navis* rounded the canal, entered the Eridanus, and sailed onward to avenge the queen.

Captain Tycho grabbed the helm at the back quarterdeck, feeling life and energy surge through the ship to his innermost being. He breathed deeply and shouted for all aboard to hear.

"Swift is the booty and speedy is the prey.

If *Argo* hunts, fires of justice will spray."

Chapter 21

The Battle of Acamar

Sephdar quietly sipped on his tea as his men reveled in the fresh spoils of war. By the time White Wings' fleet reached Theemin, the people of the village had long spotted the trails of smoke down the river and fled in fear. Houses, pots of stew, and valuables were left abandoned. The army walked through the spoilage feeling like gods, taking all they wanted without confrontation or consequence. They sang and danced and occasionally exchanged blows over a prized jewel all while drowning the memories of blood and death with strong ale.

Though Sephdar had reached a high point of glory and power, the ache in his gut gripped him with an ever-present bitterness. He wasn't content with the victory over Altair. Most would celebrate in the newly attained wealth, but the things he desired most still eluded him. Maia had escaped during the first battle and not one village down the river unveiled the presence of an Ilmatar. All seven sisters who were supposed to heal him had now vanished, and Trifid remained controlled by the Free Realms.

The Free Realms, Sephdar thought with disdain. *The land I once called my own cast me out. They sullied my name among my hoofed relations. They stole the Ilmatar from me at the palace. They stole The Bridge to Earth from the ruins I rebuilt.* He squeezed an empty, stolen teacup in his gloved hand until it crushed. *Arcturus will feel the heat of my wrath just as Altair did. They will see my power and quiver before me. Then, there will be none left to stop my reign. Whether I find it on Arcas or Earth, I will take my healing just as I will take the crown. I will be king of not just one world, but of the way between worlds.*

"Lord Sephdar," Albireo interrupted his leader's silent schemes, "the corvuses have reached Starling. Lupus has agreed to join us at Trifid, and they are all eager to take back the fortress with us."

"Good. Gather the captains of each ship. It's time to plan our final attack before we return to the water and continue downstream to Trifid."

But before Albireo could follow the command, shouts of chaos erupted from the banks of the river.

"Dragon!" Arkab ran up breathless. "A dragon's flying down the river!"

"Impossible!" Sephdar barked. "There are no more flying dragons in Arcas. Get everyone to the ships!"

"Fire! Fire!" men from the shore shouted.

Sephdar galloped to the bank and into his lead ship. He gazed into a thick steam floating upon the waters until he saw it. The large mouth, head, and nostrils of a dragon emerged through the vapors. *Thoom. Kist. Thoom. Kist. Thoom. Kist.* The centaur shot arrow after arrow straight at the dragon's head but every shot dissolved into a puff of dark smoke as the creature spewed flames from his mouth. He stared in disbelief as his archers shot hundreds of arrows from their anchored vessels lined against the shore. But the beast continued on, neither blinking an eye nor twinging his skin under the attack. Sephdar stared at the rapidly moving creature until something billowing and dark green became visible in the air.

"What kind of sorcery is this?" Albireo commented in confusion to his leader. "His wings stay upright in the air, and yet he still flies over the water."

"Not wings." He squinted through the scope to bring the soaring objects into focus. "Sails! It's no dragon, just the old dragon-faced ship of Altair!" he explained. "Sound the trumpets, Albireo. All those on land must gather to the ships. Set the sails, and make haste down the river to the hills of Acamar! Once there, we will gather to the high ground and send fiery arrows upon them while they chase our empty ships."

After the trumpets had sounded and all men were gathered to their vessels, Sephdar shouted a battle cry for all within earshot to hear. "We left their dead on the castle grounds. Now we will bury their living under the water!"

Argo Navis steadily crept closer to the back of Sephdar's fleet. Like a shark pursuing a school of fish, it was only a matter of time before the beast opened his mouth and consumed the slowest and most concentrated section of ships. Powered by flame and steam and hundreds of rowing Cephids, he was still the fastest vessel in all of Arcas. The strong, short-armed men of Deneb chopped swiftly through the water in perfect rhythm and harmony as if they were swinging pickaxes to chop through rock. Cephids also powered the rest of the Altairian Navy, working swiftly to keep up with *Argo*.

Though the royal navy had remained stagnant since the Pillar Wars, the Altairian ships were still the fastest and most efficient war vessels in Arcas. All men from the kingdom learned at a young age the art of sailing and watery warfare. Those who survived Sephdar's attack now manned the sails and decks while preparing their weapons for assault.

Sephdar neared the hills of Acamar feeling confident. The ache in his gut surged into further anger and vengeance. In his mind, the leaders of the kingdoms and the Free Realms had all wronged him. *So what if I swiped a little gold in the past?* he reasoned. *Didn't I fight and risk my life for them all? I killed Sons of Earth to insure the safe havens of Regulus and Arcturus. I brought down the dragon to sustain the reign of the king and queen who gave me no thanks but threw me out into the wastelands.*

Sephdar did not feel that his punishments fit his

crimes. He had been rejected and banished. Not only left to wander alone, but he was also left to die alone after Minaruja's debilitating strike. Now, it was his turn to be on top. He had destroyed Altair. He would sink Deneb. And then, he would take back Trifid.

The lead ships rounded the last bend of the great river. The southern end of the Eridanus widened to roughly ten miles and continued to grow larger as it joined into the Ligeian Sea. Sephdar surveyed the area, looking for the perfect spot to drop anchor, hide in the hills, and destroy his enemies. But a surprise was waiting for him around the last turn. Just past the bend, a strange cloud billowed upon the waters. A deep hum floated in the air. Focused on the ambush, neither Sephdar nor his men noticed the oddities. The lord quietly shot his arm downward, signaling for the anchor to be released. In ship after ship, the heavy iron sank down, down, down until it *thunked* against the bottom of the river. The front half of White Wings' fleet was now fixed in place.

"FIRE!" A shout rang out from the cloud followed by *phoonk, phoonk, phoonk, phoonk*! Harpoons fired into the air, breaching the hulls of the front three ships. Sephdar's men fell against the mast, down to the deck, and against the side rails from the instant jolt. The centaur, however, remained steady on his four-hoofed legs. He could see the fear in everyone's eyes as if some force of unmatched power controlled fog. But something felt familiar about this cloud.

Sulafat! Assuming that a small band of local pirates swiped the mighty lyre, he charged his men to attack head-on.

Little did Sephdar know he was facing a much greater threat than a random pirate attack. Behind the lyre's cloud sailed deep-sea fishing boats and crews from Achernar. This village rested on the eastern corner of the Eridanus River and the Ligeian Sea, and it was the last place down the river that swore allegiance to Queen Cassiopeia. Rigel and Merope had used the lyre to fly hastily to Achernar. They described the destruction, the death of the queen, and King Alderamin's plan of attack. These burly fishermen baited the biggest and most dangerous creatures of the sea. To them, Sephdar was just another vicious, devouring beast that needed to be removed from the waters. They did not join the fighting for mere treasure but for justice. While Merope provided the team of boats with cover, Rigel commanded the assault with his knowledge of war and leadership presence.

"Aim your arrows toward the cloud! It's just an illusion. Mere flesh and blood hide behind it!" Sephdar commanded.

The men regained their ground, grabbed their bows off their shoulders, and aimed into the foggy haze. But before Sephdar could return fire, another jolt knocked his men to the deck again. Boats from his own fleet were ramming into each other! He glimpsed behind to see his ships colliding. Then he witnessed the cause of commotion and chaos.

Argo Navis had reached the back of the fleet. Captain Tycho rammed and set fire to any ship in his way. He was making a path for the Altairian Navy. One by one, the dragon hurled flames into his vessels. The back line of ships was blazing, and *Argo* pushed forward on the right side. The kingdoms were corralling and surrounding all sails bearing the emblem of White Wings.

Fiery men jumped overboard to cool their melting flesh. Others swung inward from ropes, gathering to the safer ships in the center. Thousands of arrows whizzed in the air toward both armies. Infuriated by anyone challenging his perfect plans, Sephdar lined his bow with three arrows and led the attack from the frontlines.

"Pull!" a voice yelled from the cloud, still clothed in mystery. Suddenly, the harpoons inside the speared lower holds of White Wings' ships were yanked tightly and pulled forward. Water poured heavily into the ships from the breaches and the increased pressure dragging them forward. The wooden frame splintered and cracked from the thick, sharp iron.

"Fire, men, fire!" Sephdar screamed, releasing his own flying daggers at the faceless enemy. But of the hundreds of arrows that flew from the front lines, very few made it into the cloud. For like a harpooned whale being bound by its captors, a huge fishing net came flying over the sails of the head boat. It caught both topmasts, halting arrows mid-air and trapping men from escaping the front ship. Like the harpoons, once the netting grabbed hold, it tightened and pulled forward. The front hull sunk deeper, tilting the entire ship.

"Abandon ship!" Sephdar hollered as he galloped uphill on the deck, grabbed a rope, and leaped high over the water into the vessel behind him.

Snap! Rip! Crack! The topsail and foremast broke under the net's pressure as men scurried around to vacate the ship. Sephdar's ship sank headfirst, broke in half, and gradually fell below the water. Shouts of glee erupted from the cloud. The frontline of ships was now completely abandoned to the harpoons, nets, and deck-flooding waters.

Captain Tycho sailed aggressively toward the enemy, but all the while, he cautiously studied the water. The Eridanus River crashed wildly between ships and erupted underneath from vessels sinking down, bubbling over, and sizzling up. He had no doubt they would win this battle. Tycho was the battle-tried and loyal captain of *Argo Navis*, after all. But life on the river was not as it once was, ruled by men. Different creatures now ruled the realm underneath Eridanus's surface, and disruptions in their mysterious, veiled kingdom hardly went unnoticed. Yet for the sake of the queen and the sake of his beloved ship, the strangely lyrical and obsessively devoted captain continued on to destroy the murdering trespassers. These tyrants deserved to fall into the lands and hands of the beasts hiding beneath the dark waters.

The captain's battle strategy was simple, yet proving most effective. While the generals of Deneb initially suggested they ram the enemy and instantly board them, the captain and naval officers of Altair gave great wisdom for fighting on their native waters. Ramming required great shipman skills from all present and could risk having ships taken by the enemy. Instead, each Altairian ship would act more like a dog herding cattle: get close enough to nip their heels, but not so close to get kicked in the teeth. *Argo* would burn Sephdar's outer boats as the rest of the fleet circled around, pushing the enemy vessels to the center. Next, a rain of arrows would fall upon those fleeing to the inner parts while fire caught sail to sail amongst the tightly packed ships.

While Captain Tycho steered, Markeb described each enemy ship's location from a high perch near the main mast sails. Aspid shouted, "Fire!" through a tube on the deck down to Asmid in the hold below where the flames were fed. Asmid growled and laughed under the hatch as he pumped a large bellows up and down using the ox-like strength of his arms and hefty weight of his body. The bellows forced a huge gust of air through a pipe into the oven, hurling another burst of flames out the dragon's mouth.

"Swift is the booty and speedy is the prey. If *Argo* hunts, fires of justice will spray." Tycho chanted the rhyme over and over with eyes wildly focused and rudder shifting rapidly for each assault.

250

"Remember, men, only fire upon my signal!" Caph reminded the men of Altair. "Arrows shot from a close range cause the most damage. We want to be sure our attack descends upon the real enemy and not our own men." All those who survived Sephdar's slaughter and could hold a bow raised them in the air and waited for the command.

"FIRE!"

Over two thousand arrows whizzed into the sky, darkening the light of the high coral sun. To lessen the risk of their own boats catching fire, they did not light the arrows first. Instead, they fired through the flaming sails of the enemy's ships. Some of the flying darts then lit in the air before hitting both man and vessel. The archers now stepped back as Cephid men held their axes in one hand and rope in another.

"In the name of King Alderamin and for the honor of the queen, swing hard, men of Deneb! ATTACK!" cried Alfirk. He was the first to fly from the boat with axe raised. Alfirk rammed his feet into the hull of a flaming ship, swung his mighty axe down with a roar, and chopped a hole where the waters rose above the keel. Streams rushed into the abandoned boat, weighing it down deeper into the water. Cephids hacked their mighty axes at hull and mast, collapsing the sturdy vessels of war. The men swung back to the Altairian Navy and stood aside, waiting for the enemy watercrafts to be covered—forever lost from sight and memory under the Eridanus. Each ship sinking below the surface cleared a path for attacking the next line. The archers fired the next assault by air as the last Cephid returned.

The men of Achernar rowed steadily forward behind the lyre's billowing cloud. The fishing boats formed a line following the haze that blocked the whole way down the river. Dread filled Sephdar's men as they gathered on the second row of southern ships and reloaded their bows. They knew danger waited behind the cloud for another round of strikes, but they still couldn't see what the danger was. They aimed their arrows blindly. But before they could shoot, a new threat suddenly distracted them. *Argo Navis* rushed upon the rapids next to them with unmatched speed. Great fire spewed from his mouth, spreading across the river in a mystical pattern, chasing wave and foe.

"Head to the center boats on the east of the river!" Sephdar commanded, irritated and angry. In moments, his next line of ships would either be flaming from *Argo* or sinking from the mysterious fighters behind the cloud. He needed to regroup and recharge his men. Since the dragon ship approached from the western side of the river, they could fight their way through the Altairian ships surrounding them on the east. Once they took down a few vessels, they could reach the banks of the river and attack from solid ground. But Sephdar never got a chance to plan this counterattack.

Falling from the blue sky, large planks lowered

instantly down from pulleys on the Altairian masts to White Wings' ships on the east. A spike at the bottom end of each plank crashed and splintered into these unscorched decks, creating a secure bridge. Nekkar and hundreds of mounted Deneb fighters burst atop the planks and soared on to the nearby enemy ships. Though the Cephids were short, their axes rose tall. With one swing atop their horses, they tossed men overboard, smashed skulls, and sliced through torsos. Nekkar led with righteous fury, remembering every face and name of his men who were ambushed and murdered unexpectedly in the Starling Forest.

All men who bore the emblem of White Wings were either collapsing in their blood or scrambling by rope and water to reach other ships. Loud cheers erupted from the mounted kingdom warriors as they took over four enemy vessels. All the momentum, spirit, and courage rested on their side. Victory sat securely within reach. All they had to do was extend a little and claim it.

"You see, my love?" King Alderamin squeezed Cassiopeia's hand gently. "We will make it home to Deneb today, together. And nothing will ever be able to part us again." King Alderamin knew the kingdom realms were winning the battle. He heard the cheers and watched the winged flags burning in the sky, but the feeling of victory trickled down from his throat to his gut like sugary ale. Amid the sweet flavor, he could still taste a bitter sting.

The queen lay on a decorated bed of silk and jewels.

253

The king refused to leave her behind in the heartbreaking wreckage of her kingdom. She sailed with them on *Argo Navis*, and the king had stood by her side during the voyage and the battle. He gave her one last kiss on her cold, stiff, and perfumed hand. Then he grabbed his kingly axe and prepared to board the enemy vessels that were now filling with the fearful spirit of self-preservation. Boat by boat, Sephdar's army was lowering their weapons and surrendering in hopes of mercy.

"King Alderamin!" Tycho bellowed from the quarterdeck, startling the king from his thoughts of final judgment and justice. The captain's eyes were wild with alarm, and he held firmly to the wheel that guided his rudder. "The water be cold, so ya' better take hold!" he warned.

All of the sudden, he was steering *Argo* away from the other ships to the right edge of the river. No one understood the captain's strange words and actions until they saw a huge tsunami of a wave spiraling down the water.

"It's Mira! Mira! A monster! The serpent! Minaruja!" voices cried out as they grabbed rails or masts and held tightly to *Argo Navis*.

Cetus, the mystical monster of the Eridanus, fought through the fleet with Minaruja coiling around his watery body, striking his venomous fangs at the double Mira nymphs riding on top. The king dropped his axe, ran to hold Cassiopeia, and grabbed the railing closest to her. Like a string of erupted ocean mines, a sudden domino of destruction flowed down the river. Ship after ship exploded, collided, and capsized. The monsters of the sea held no respect for flags or sides. In mere seconds, they had tossed men and boats of all allegiances—with an equal violence—into air and water. Man's destruction and bloodshed now appeared trivial and small next to these uncontrollable beasts of nature.

The iridescent, translucent Miras spewed water and strange, high-pitched sounds into the air as they twisted, dove, and dodged the serpent's attacks by yanking the bridle controlling Cetus. *Argo Navis* swayed sideways to the right as Cetus exploded ferociously through the middle of the Eridanus. Men and heavy objects tumbled off the dragon ship into the marshy riverbank. *Argo* then swayed hard to the left, throwing other items from the left side of the deck into the middle. Still, many held tightly to the boat, including the king. The dueling creatures finally disappeared past the waves of the Ligeian Sea. Debris, halves of ships, ripped sails, and bodies were scattered everywhere in the river from the hills of Acamar to the delta of Achernar. The massive waves settled into swift rapids, but only those still clinging to *Argo Navis* remained upright, afloat.

King Alderamin stood, watching as men coughed and swam and fought their way to shore. The great walls of Trifid Fortress stood in the distance. And soldiers were marching out of Trifid toward the delta! *The Son of Earth made it*, he thought, regaining his breath and remembering that victory was moments from his grasp. *They are joining us! The battle is still ours!* The king looked for his axe, but it was missing. He scanned the grasses of the marshy bank in search of a glimmer from the steel blade. What he saw along the marsh, though, was not a blade but a centaur. Sephdar shook the water from his four-legged body as he climbed out of the river.

"SEPHDAR!" Alderamin shouted. Everyone on land and the waters seemed to halt and listen to the king's voice. "The day the queen fell is the day you also will fall!" With fury in his eyes and strength in his legs, Alderamin jumped off the ship and into the marsh. At this moment, any weapon would do. He grabbed a wooden plank with nails sticking out the end and ran toward the centaur, violently knocking down every white-winged, dripping-wet uniform in his way.

"They've lost their weapons!" Sephdar hollered to his men. "Get to shore and fight. Destroy the rest of the kingdoms then take back Trifid!"

Every man quickly followed their leader and returned to the battle both on land and in the water. Though a few still carried a sword sheathed to their side or a bow around their arm, most axes, swords, and spears were lost to the bottom of the deep, dark waters. Broken pieces of ship, floating arrows, and fists now became the primary weapons. Bodies wrestled between the waves and debris, struggling to beat their enemy to dry land. Strategy no longer existed in this battle, only brute force.

Chapter 22

Boots at Trifid

Andi held tightly to Jackson as they rode Alnitak bareback across the shores of the Ligeian Sea. The coral sun was setting in the west, the golden sun blazed high in the sky, and the crimson sun peeked over the eastern horizon. Though Otava ran solo, far behind the blue flames flaring from Alnitak's hooves, his large satchel of weaponry rode with the stallion. Jackson could feel the warmth of Andi's body with her arms wrapped around him as they rode. After their nightmarish experiences in the lagoon, it felt comforting for both to be so close to each other.

Alnitak galloped with unmatched speed through the sandy beaches. The pace was swift, but the ride remained smooth. The Son of Earth still didn't understand why the warhorse came for him, chose him. But he was grateful as if some force in the universe was silently affirming his presence in Arcas. As they rode, Andi slowly relaxed her check against his back and drifted to sleep. Jackson felt needed, trusted, and strong. If only her warmth and closeness could last longer—just a few more hours or days. Actually, he wouldn't mind if he could feel this closeness with the princess every single day for the rest of his life.

His journey with the princess upon the great Alnitak was quickly nearing an end, however. Shimmers of blues and oranges danced in an arch extending over the water on top of the Ligeian Sea. The Bridge still blazed with otherworldly light, an open passage between the worlds that probably no one on Earth even knew existed for all these months.

"Andi?" Jackson nudged his shoulder gently to wake her.

"Hmm?" She stirred, slowly opening her heavy eyes.

"There it is. The Bridge to Earth."

Andi woke up and sat up straight to witness this ancient wonder with her own eyes. With a slight yawn and stretch, the princess put a little distance between their bodies, pretending that she fell asleep purely out of accident and exhaustion. It was one thing to fall asleep against Jackson, but to hold tightly while awake would infer a feeling entirely different, a feeling entirely more intense than friendship. Though the princess may have wanted to continue holding tight, she wasn't ready for Jackson to know that.

"It's so big. It's beautiful," she remarked in awe of the awakened relic.

"Yeah, it's larger than I remember. But when I saw it last time, I was in a lot of pain and a bit delusional."

"I still can't believe Cygnus tricked us all into believing in some made-up enemy. Gurges Ater," she huffed with a slight boogey-man voice. "And my parents just foolishly believed everything he said for all those years. They never left their kingdoms to verify the threat. They never even questioned Cygnus."

"Yeah, but it was easy to believe him. Every lie was glazed with horror and honey and a little bit of truth. I just hope Arcturus understands that I am here to help."

"You carry Nekkar's sword. The Free Realms will listen to you," Andi encouraged.

"As long as they don't think I stole it. I'm not exactly the most, you know, welcomed and trusted person in Arcas right now."

"Well, then it's a good thing you brought a secret weapon with you!"

"I don't know," Jackson lamented with frustration. "My phone was my only secret weapon, and it's stuck in my backpack at that creepy lagoon." Jackson patted the bag resting down both sides of the horse in front of his legs. "At least Otava's arsenal made it out, but I doubt any of these weapons will win us good graces at Trifid."

"No, silly Earthling." She lightly smacked his side with a twinkle in her voice. "I'm the secret weapon! If they won't listen to you, they will most definitely listen to the only heir of the Kingdom Realms."

Alnitak raced to the gates of Trifid Fortress. The fortress seemed quiet, empty. Alnitak flared his nostrils loudly and pawed at the ground as if he were anxious for the two to dismount. Jackson held Andi's hand to help her balance as she bent her leg around the back of the horse and let her feet drop to the dry sand. Jackson held to the thick, black mane and twisted his own leg around to join her on the ground. After pulling Otava's bag of weaponry off the stallion, Alnitak nickered a quick farewell, turned back toward the west, and galloped away. Otava ran up to join them, panting wildly.

"Where... are... the guards?" Otava asked, pressing his paw against the door to rest and catch his breath. The portcullis was raised, leaving only the huge steel and wooden double doors blocking their entrance.

"There's only one way to find out." Jackson pulled Lodestar from the sheath at his side and knocked the blunt end of the sword loudly against the right door. *Boonk. Boonk. Boonk.*

Sounds of *Bang! Clash! Crash!* directly followed as if someone was startled by the knocking.

"Who's there?" a tired voice called out.

"We've come in peace bearing Lodestar, the sword of Nekkar, the son of Arcturus," Jackson announced his well-rehearsed line.

"Arcturus is gone," the man shouted from behind the raised wall covering the parapet walk. "You'll have to come back later or wait until he returns."

The three looked at each other with bewilderment. Alnitak was gone, Otava was exhausted, and Andi and Jackson were starving. After the long journey, Princess Andromeda was not about to sit quietly outside the fortress and wait.

"In the name of King Alderamin and Queen Cassiopeia, open these gates!" Andi demanded using the most royal voice she could muster. "We will wait inside for Arcturus to arrive, thank you very much."

"And who do you think you are, milady, the sparkly princess herself?" The man huffed out.

"Yes, indeed. I am Princess Andromeda. Now, I would like some warm food and a place to rest, please, while I wait to speak to your leader."

A roar of laughter rumbled out, but upon hearing her female voice speak so commandingly and confidently, his curiosity grew until the man reached his hands up, grabbed the wall, and stood. He looked curiously at the bear, the boy, and the girl then smiled in disbelief.

"By the Flower of the Eridanus, you *are* the bloomin' princess! Welcome, Princess Andromeda to Trifid Fortress protected by the great Free Realms."

"Thank you," she beamed, satisfied her title still carried some weight and purpose outside of the kingdoms. "Now, could you please display some of your wildly raved-about hospitality and let us in?"

"A thousand apologies, but we don't answer to the

king and queen around here. I was told not to let anyone else in until I see Arcturus himself at the door."

"Fine. If this barbarian doesn't want to open the doors for a princess who is weary from travel, I guess we will just have to find another way inside. Otava, get your grappling hook!"

"With pleasure, Princess." With great dramatics, Otava opened his pack, meticulously went through each weapon, and then grabbed the grappling hook.

"You can't just barge in here! I'll shoot!" the guard protested while seemingly stumbling around to retrieve his weapon.

"It looks like you have three choices," Jackson negotiated. "You can let us in as peaceful diplomats. You can shoot arrows at us and face the wrath of Nekkar, Arcturus, and the Kingdom Realms. Or you can stand there while a boy, a bear, and a princess take Trifid from you and hold you prisoner until Arcturus returns."

Otava started to swing the hook around and around like a medieval cowboy. The Ursa could have merely hooked it to his crossbow for a straight shot, but swinging it felt much more dramatic at the moment. And they were working very hard at causing enough of a spectacle to sway the guard to open the gates. They could tell he didn't want to be there alone. He was left there, and it definitely wasn't because he was the most gifted and dangerous guard.

"Alright, Otava! Let's take the wall!" Andi commanded.

"Stop! Stop!" the guard shouted. "Fine. I'll open the door. Just wait here and don't start climbing up the walls!"

"Thank you, good sir," Andi replied cheerfully with a curtsey.

It seemed to take hours for the guard to make his way down the parapet, walk to the gate, and lift the bar locking them out. When he pushed the heavy door open, they knew why he was the lone soldier at Trifid. He stood just inside, slightly irritated that they smelled his weakness and now could see it. The guard walked with a good leg on one side and a crutch on the other. A stump that ended just above his knee hung down, hovering in the air. His crutch was made of a long branch cut short where the one stick split into two. One of the white winged flags from the fortress was ripped and wrapped around the top to soften the split where his armpit rested.

"Make yourself at home, Princess," he invited them in with a shallow, slightly perturbed bow. "My name is Boots. And yes, I know that's ironic, but I did wear two of them before the Battle of Fornax." He tapped his crutch against the ground underneath his stump.

"I'm sorry for being so forceful," Andi apologized sincerely as the travelers accepted the invitation and entered the fortress. "We really are very tired and will feel much better waiting in here. If I may ask, where is the rest of your army?"

"They went to fight Sephdar, the new lord of the

White Palace. He apparently thinks that Trifid should belong to him now that White Wings is gone. If you run up to the parapet, you might be able to see something."

Jackson, Andi, and Otava scurried up the staircase to look out. Boots slowly hopped and hobbled up the stairs behind them. They couldn't see much from the top of the fortress, only puffs of smoke floating above the thicker trees and brush surrounding the mouth of the river.

"Look to the sea," Otava pointed. "I think this battle started on the river."

Though they couldn't identify military banners or distinguish details, it was evident that debris from over a hundred ships floated around The Ligeian. Some vessels were still mostly sticking above water while others were floating out to sea, slowly sinking. The sea looked as if a tsunami had pummeled the army of boats against the shore only to drag and dump the remains back into the waters. Andi could feel her stomach float to her throat. *Is my mother home safe?* she wondered. *Where is my father?* She prayed her family and her people were still standing.

"How did you know that White Wings' army was coming?" Jackson asked. Since he was tasked to warn Arcturus, he wondered how word reached Trifid before they did.

"Oh, yeah... they are actually still here, probably sleeping," Boots explained. "Rode a boat all the way down the Eridanus to warn us about Sephdar. They were quite an odd pair traveling together from Altair." He chuckled with a

264

slightly perplexed look. "A bent-over old man and a tall pregnant lady."

"From Altair? An old man?" Andi asked anxiously. "What is his name?"

"I don't remember… Shed-something? He was kind of funny, told us we could just call him Old Miser."

"Shedir!" Andi's heart leapt with joy. "Please, take me to him at once!"

They made their way back down the parapet stairs past the second raised portcullis and walked toward the inner courtyard. Though their feet were slowly following Boots, their hearts raced with excitement and anticipation. Finally, they would hear some news from Altair. It made them glad that the Free Realms were already warned, already fighting offensively against Sephdar.

In their haste to meet Shedir and Maia, however, they missed a large ship sailing in from the distant west and dark clouds gathering in the distant north. Looking like armed forces of bees and ants, one black cloud swarmed in the sky and one black cloud darted on the ground. They raced toward the delta connecting the river to the sea in near parallel unison. But these creatures were much larger and more dangerous than mere bees and ants, for their claws could tear flesh and their bite could snap bone.

Chapter 23

Three Arrows

King Alderamin charged Sephdar, swinging the wooden plank right and left to defend himself from Sephdar's arrows. The wet and frustrated centaur loaded arrow after arrow, shooting them at the advancing king. Five arrowheads stuck into the broken shipboard, lining it with long, feathered rods. Other arrows ricocheted off the makeshift weapon or swooped inches past the king's body then plunged into the bodies of surrounding fighters. Alderamin surged forward with passion and power exploding from his soul to his fingertips. For the first time since he became lord of the White Palace, Sephdar's haughty eyes flashed with fear. The king was coming for him, and he was coming with unmatched vengeance.

"Rha!" The king bounded forward much quicker than his adversary anticipated, swinging the plank's nails directly into Sephdar's extended arm. The centaur shrieked, dropped his bow, and reared his front hooves in the air to release the board that was momentarily embedded in his flesh. Alderamin held tightly, so the nails ripped through Sephdar's muscle and skin as he rose in the air. His hooves returned to the ground as his hand covered the painful strips of bloody, throbbing tears.

"My King!" Alfirk cried out while fighting to reach him, crashing an axe into the skull, ribs, and legs of enemy soldiers. But he wasn't just carrying any axe. Though most of the Cephids lost their weapons to the water, Alfirk saw the jeweled flicker of the king's axe as he swam to shore. He dove to retrieve it from a small sand dune near the bank and had been battling through the mess of wet soldiers to return it to Alderamin. The king turned his eyes toward Alfirk, his most skilled soldier. Seeing his axe, the king nodded his head, agreeing to the next move. In an instant, the axe and plank both soared through the air for a weapon exchange.

The king's strong hands gripped the axe, melting into the handle as if the weapon were an extension of his body. Sephdar pulled his second weapons of choice—a long blade from each side of his girth.

"Your axe may be tall, but you are king of a little people," Sephdar warned, holding his swords out at an angle, prepared to defend or attack. "Surrender, and I will let you and your little ones safely return to Deneb."

"Ha!" King Alderamin mocked, wielding his axe diagonally across his chest. "There are times when it is necessary for a king to surrender for the good of his people.

But a true king never surrenders his people to a thief and a murderer. No, he fights. And look!" He pointed toward the Free Realms rushing into the battle. "Even Arcturus has come to fight with me. Today, you will pay for your crimes with your life, and all the people of Arcas will rejoice over your broken body."

The royal axe flew through the air with great power and speed. *Ching! Zank!* The thick double-pointed head collided with the long blades from Sephdar's right hand and then his left. *Clash!* Both swords rammed into the sharp ends of Alderamin's axe. The two struggled to hold their stance with weapons extended, their bodies a few feet from each other. As the king glared with righteous indignation, he saw hollowness in the eyes his enemy. There was no light in his eyes, only emptiness. There was only one cause that the centaur fought for, self. Self-gain, self-comfort, self-preservation—they were all things that proved useful in small amounts, but a large dose of self poisoned the soul. At this moment, muscle against muscle and blade against blade, the king knew that Sephdar couldn't win.

Twisting his axe and jumping in the air, the king landed his wide double-blade on top of the two swords. Sephdar tried to yank his swords back, but Alderamin quickly ran underneath. The swords were kept steady in the grooves under the axe blades with the weight of the king holding them down. When he reached the centaur's tall body, the king jumped sideways in the air, never releasing his grip from the handle. Heavy boots rammed into Sephdar's poisoned gut. He screamed and dropped his right sword to clasp his stomach.

As Alderamin's axe fell to the side from the fallen blade, he quickly swung under and around in a hook then twist motion. The second sword was yanked from Sephdar's weakened stance and spun out of reach. The king stood tall as the large, pained centaur lifted his bloodshot, hate-filled eyes. He raised the weapon and swung it right up to Sephdar's throat. Then, he stopped. The centaur went into self-preservation mode. He bent his red-rust colored knees and lowered himself to the ground in surrender.

"You've won, thanks to Minaruja. I should have known that sea serpent's bite would lead to my death one way or another."

"No!" Alderamin was now eye-to-eye with the reclining centaur. "Forget Minaruja. You brought about your own death. I should have cut off your thieving hands after the Pillar Wars. I should have known that the same beast with the audacity to steal the royal jewels would also steal royal lives."

"But you are a merciful king, and you care for the lives of your people." Sephdar pleaded for his life, but really, he was buying time to catch the king off-guard. For out of the corner of his eye, he spotted his bow. It lay just within arm's reach, but he had to get the blade off his neck to grab it. "Spare my life and you will spare the lives of your own. I will call my men off. We will retire to the White Palace and never again enter the Kingdom Realms."

But there were no chances left for Sephdar, and the king did not move his axe from the centaur's throat. Not even the punishment of death could equal his crimes. Like the venom of Shaula, the venom of Sephdar had to be destroyed.

"A king does not lead to war without a purpose, and a king does not wield his axe in vain."

With the double edges angled sideways, King Alderamin swung his axe back, using every muscle from his heels to his jaw. But just as the blade reached Sephdar's neck, claws bolted down from the air. One talon grabbed the axe in between the king's two hands, and another wrapped around his left extended arm. The huge corvus lifted Alderamin ten feet above the ground, and Sephdar seized the opportunity.

In seconds, he reached for his bow, pulled an arrow out of the sheath on his back, and aimed at the king's heart, floating above the ground. Alderamin fought and kicked in the air. He let go of his axe with his right hand—though he refused to release his weapon completely to the dark creature. The king pulled a knife from his war vest to counterattack. The ends of the talons around his left arm were digging into his skin and cutting off the circulation. As the knife penetrated its lower chest through bumpy, leathery avian skin, both he and the raven shrieked in pain. The corvus instantly released the king and fluttered wildly in the air. But the last king of Arcas fell to the ground with Sephdar's arrow sticking out of his heart.

Sephdar stood, shivered the dust off his back, and smirked. The king was gone.

"My King!" Alfirk screamed, stabbing the nailed board into the side of an enemy combatant. He grabbed the enemy's sword off the ground and ran full speed to Alderamin. But Sephdar saw him out of the corner of his eye and kicked backward. The iron shoes clad to the centaur's feet shot into Alfirk's chest before the short warrior could make contact. He flew backward and lay motionless on the ground.

Sephdar watched with pleasure as the wolves and ravens joined in the battle with speed and ferocity. The corvus swooped quickly over the fight to the frontlines, picking up short Cephids, then throwing or dropping them from deadly heights. The little men fell to the ground with broken limbs, snapped necks, and disoriented minds. At the other end of the battle, Lupus and his pack of wolves tore into the men of the Free Realms. The wolves' bite broke flesh and bone, and their saliva combusted into flames on the men's clothes.

Before long, the combined realms were losing men and losing ground. Arcturus's numbers were already thinned from the Battle at Fornax, and Regulus had not yet sailed to Trifid with reinforcements. The Cephids and Altairians fought hard, but with their powerful axes vanished below the water, they were no match for giant birds, wolves, and White Wings' men. As Arcturus continued to fight, he saw the beasts herding those still standing from the realms into a circle. They were surrounded and souls who continued to fight were being released from their battered bodies in rapidly increasing numbers.

Suddenly, the fighting stopped. Between the Free Realms and the Kingdom Realms, only a few hundred men still stood on the dry land. Their breath huffed heavily in and out, wearied and overwhelmed from continuous fighting. Weapons and broken ship pieces aimed outward in defense while the wolves growled, snapped, and bared their smoldering teeth. Corvuses circled above, waiting for a command to strike again.

"Arcturus! Arcturus!" Sephdar hollered over the crowd. "King Alderamin is dead, and I have your sons. Surrender so you and your sons and the rest of Arcas will live."

The crowd remained silent until a thin line parted between the living bodies. Arcturus walked through the center toward his adversary's voice, his sword still raised. When he reached the end, he saw Muphrid suspended in the air by two corvuses, and only ten paces away, Seginus lay on the ground with a wolf standing over him, snarling inches from his face.

"Is all this blood shed worth it for a silly bridge that leads to a dark, dying world? Your other sons have fallen. I

272

heard that one was lost to the fires in Starling, and another passed on this battlefield earlier. Are you willing to lose them all today?"

Arcturus tightened his jaw and fought back the tears. He knew Trifid would return under White Wings' banner today. They no longer had the numbers or the advantage in the fight. He still trusted Regulus and his plan, but he was losing hope in seeing that plan endure. Their leader was supposed to bring reinforcements, supposed to come and instruct the Free Realms on what to do with The Bridge to Earth. But Regulus wasn't here. Once again, he hadn't made it in time for the fight, and Arcturus had to make the decision.

"What do you want?" Arcturus asked with eyes focused and voice low and clear.

"I want your men to drop their weapons and surrender. Then you, Arcturus, will escort me safely to The Bridge. Once I see that you have left it unharmed, we will let you all return to your own lands. We do not want your lives. We just want back what is ours, and Trifid was rebuilt by my hands, not yours. Or"—he shrugged—"we kill your sons and wipe you all off the face of Arcas right now."

"Tell your beasts to release my sons. Then I will agree to your terms, and we will surrender Trifid. No more blood needs to be shed today."

Sephdar nodded at the wolf who slowly stepped off Seginus and crept backward. In unison, the corvuses opened their talons and Muphrid fell to the ground. When Arcturus saw that his sons were released safely, he dropped his sword. With no other leader to follow, every man of the realms also dropped their weapons.

Seginus and Muphrid were bound with rope from the battered ships and led behind their father as an assurance that he would follow through by handing over Trifid. Nearly fifty others who appeared to be leaders and the strongest warriors were also bound, including Nekkar, who was assumed to be from Altair since he had clothed himself with the garments of the kingdom to avoid friendly fire before they sailed down the river.

The walk to Trifid felt long and weary. Bodies lie everywhere, some writhing in pain with life-threatening injuries while others begged to be carried away from the battlefield. Sephdar's army assured them along the way that as soon as Trifid was theirs again, the realms would be free to return and care for the wounded. As they neared the walls, the prisoners felt the sting of defeat but also enjoyed the sweetness of breath still entering their lungs. The king and queen were lost, the gate between the worlds was lost, but their lives were not yet lost.

Arcturus commanded Boots to open Trifid. The one-legged man refrained from arguing or asking questions to verify the command. The scene of bound leaders, surrounded by enemy soldiers and beasts on both ground and air, answered every possible question he could have.

Arcturus entered the gates of the fortress he had worked so hard to take. The noble man showed no sadness or weakness, just inner strength and resolve that he had made the best choice, the only choice he could at that moment of decision.

Andi and Jackson sprinted with all their might to The Bridge as Sephdar entered with Arcturus. Moments before, Boots discovered the returning soldiers from the watchtower. It was too dangerous for any of the others to be seen until they knew who was arriving as the victor and who as the captive. As far as anyone outside the Free Realms knew, Boots was the only soul in Trifid. When Boots saw Arcturus and his two sons bound, he turned back without a word then flicked his wrist out as if to say *Go! Now!*

With Boots' direction, Otava used his expert skills and tools to get Shedir and Maia safely outside the walls without being noticed. In the meantime, Jackson and Andi made haste to The Bridge to remove the gems. She could remove the red gems of Arcas, and he could swipe at least two of the gems of Earth without assistance. The gem stuck at the top of the arch would be too difficult to obtain, but with five gems removed, it should shut the portal down effectively enough.

Focused on the glimmering blue and orange lights within the portal, they ran right past a .44 magnum on ground in front of the arch. No Arcasian had yet dared to move or touch the strange alien weapon still lying outside

The Bridge. They hurried on, but the two didn't have time to remove the gems. As Jackson rubbed his hand over the left, front side of the arch, where a yellow gem glowed and rotated, the centaur and Arcturus came into view.

"Jackson, they're coming!" Andi warned. "Forget the gem! Get back here!" She pulled at his arm until he scurried behind the arch with her.

They ran back to the pillar standing waist high behind the arch. The two bent down and hid. Though one couldn't see past the lights at the front of the portal, the back worked like a lit-up and shimmery one-way mirror. One could still see beyond the open arch. Sephdar and Arcturus moved to where the peninsula angled straight out to sea roughly fifty paces away. They paused, looking at The Bridge and talking. The open portal amplified the sounds in its path, so Andi and Jackson could hear the conversation between the two leaders.

"There's your bridge." Arcturus presented it with his outstretched hand. "I hope you enjoy your union with that dark, forsaken world."

"I am pleased to find it unaltered. I spent many long years rebuilding all of this with my own two hands. I left to just run a few errands for Cygnus, and before I knew it, you stole all my hard work. Be sure to warn your people that if anyone else ever tries to take Trifid or touch my gems, I will tear all of Arcas apart and kill without mercy. On that day, not one prisoner will be released, not one will be left alive."

Albireo hurried up to them with a tea and handed it the centaur. Sephdar gladly accepted it and then Albireo showed him one more thing, hoping for additional favor with the man-horse who had become the most powerful ruler of Arcas.

"One of the men saw a pile of flags that once were raised above the fortress," Albireo explained. "We painted arrows over the White Wings on it. Since Cygnus is gone and you led us to victory this day, we would like to raise this flag high in the sky as a sign that Trifid now belongs to you: the skilled archer who became a lord one day and a king the next."

Sephdar was pleased by the three black arrows covering the white wings on the flag. He tried not to seem too excited by the triumph or the honor, so he merely nodded his head in approval. Albireo ran off with the flag to the main pole at the front of the fortress where the captives waited for Arcturus to return and release them.

"Tell me, if the Free Realms took Trifid, why did you attack the kingdoms?" Arcturus asked, sizing up the character of the new conquering ruler.

"Because they were in the way of something I needed."

"And what of the Queen of Altair?"

"There is no queen. Not in Altair, not in all of the three-sunned world."

Andi's eyes went wide in disbelief at the realization that her mother was gone. The princess covered her mouth with both hands and dropped her face to her knees as tears streamed out uncontrollably. Arcturus could hear the arrogance in Sephdar's voice and feel the dishonor in his cavalier justification for bloodshed. The centaur had no regard for life or limits or sacredness.

"Oh, yes..." Sephdar seemed to remember, though this requirement had never left his mind. "There is one more thing you must do before I let you all go. Since the king and queen are dead and I have risen as victor, you will proclaim me to the people as the one and only ruler left in Arcas. Then, all the captives—including you and your two sons—will be freed to their homelands."

"I will speak to the people," Arcturus seemed to agree. But the noble leader and father had no intentions of proclaiming the violent, prideful centaur as king. There were some things that the deep parts of his soul would never surrender to no matter the cost. As the three-arrowed flag rose high in the sky over Trifid, he had other plans. Plans that would prove deadly for more than just one.

Chapter 24

Darkness Reigns

"We can't do it, Jackson." Andi wiped the tears from her eyes and tried to whisper through heavy, jerky breaths. For a several minutes, they'd stayed slumped behind the pillar—stunned by the fate of her parents. The king and queen never asked for war. They tried everything to stay out of it, and in their hesitancy, they were slaughtered. "If we take the gems, he'll kill them. He'll kill them all."

"I know." Jackson sat quietly next to her with his hand resting on her back and his head solemnly bowed to the ground.

If they removed any of the gems now, there would be a massacre. Sephdar would hunt them down, and kill anyone in his way. It was time to give up closing The Bridge. Jackson drew a portal. Their souls were so heavy that they no longer cared about where they would end up on Earth. Hand-in-hand, Andi and Jackson entered the lights.

What they didn't notice as they entered their small door between the worlds is that, at the same time, several bodies walked through The Bridge into Arcas. The first man strolled in confidently like a blaze of white light. Three others followed behind. While the men in back looked around with a lot of excitement and a little bit of fear, the leader immediately noticed the activity at the front of Trifid. Bending down without a word, he picked up the .44 magnum lying on the ground and continued forward toward the gates.

Andi and Jackson landed in a busy subway, surrounded by moving bodies. Oddly enough, no one noticed their arrival. Everyone was too busy talking, texting, reading, and speed walking. Just a few paces forward, and they would return to Arcas—safely outside the fortress walls, they hoped.

"I don't know if I should continue with Nekkar to the Free Realms or go home," Jackson confessed while they still held hands, not wanting to lose each other. He didn't want to mention *if Nekkar's still alive*, but they both knew it was implied.

"Yeah, that's a tough choice," she agreed solemnly. "I need to return to Deneb to comfort what is left of my people." Andi knew these events legally elevated her to queen—the last monarchy in the kingdom realms—but she didn't dare speak this truth. The new role that would inevitably be thrown upon her was too terrifying, too enormous, and too ill-timed.

"I'm sorry" was all Jackson could reply as he squeezed her hand sincerely. He knew those two words weren't enough. He wanted to spend the whole day in a soliloquy, apologizing for coming to Arcas the first time, for believing Cygnus, for opening The Bridge, and for pushing Cygnus to his death through the portal so the horrible Sephdar could take his place. He was sorry he came back. His simple longing for a peaceful retreat to Arcas was met with death.

"For everything," he added, hoping it would imply how awful he felt that her parents, her world was destroyed.

"Don't be sorry. It's not your fault. This all was bound to happen with or without an Earthling walking amongst us. And if my world was going to fall apart, I prefer it falling apart with you around." Andi smiled through her slightly red and swollen eyes. "Plus, your world is strange. I think I would have left it too," she joked.

Jackson quickly drew a door right into a subway wall decorated with graffiti where no one was standing. When they walked through the portal, they landed in the middle of the prisoners, just outside the walls of Trifid. Andi swiftly used her right hand to cover her head with her cloak while the left remained tightly clasped to Jackson's. The crowd of prisoners around them slowly shuffled aside, making room for them. The people were too beaten down, too sorrowful to notice who had entered their midst.

As the weapon-wielding victors guarded the prisoners, everyone watched the walls of Trifid, anticipating the announcement of their fate. If all went well between the two leaders, they would be free to return home soon. Maybe not with the pomp and praise of victory but at least with their breath and lives. Muphrid and Seginus were standing near the front gates, positioned strategically so most of the crowd could see them. Nekkar—still believed to be a member of the kingdom armies—stood near the back, anxiously waiting as the lives of his father and brothers teetered unsteadily at the end of their enemies' swords.

It was time! Sephdar and Arcturus appeared overhead on a raised parapet platform above the people.

"Slaves of the Free Realms and the Kingdom Realms," Sephdar began, setting his teacup on the wall that reached just above his girth, "for thousands of years, Arcas has remained separate from Earth. Though many are wary of keeping an open door to that dark world, the three suns have shone favor to our cause by granting victory to my army three times now. So, a new flag flies over Trifid to remind us that those who clothed themselves with White Wings' coat of arms..." Sephdar paused dramatically, sweeping his hand over the crowd to all those who fought with him.

"The forgotten people!" Sephdar's men grunted and agreed.

"Those like me." He placed his hand on his stomach. "Who were cast out of the realms simply because of an injured past!"

"Heed! Heed!" His men nodded their heads and shouted.

"Now it is our time to rule, and we have proven it! Together, we have conquered Altair!"

"Yeah!"

"Together, we conquered the beasts of the river!"

"Yeah!"

"And together, we conquered Trifid!"

"Yeah!"

"So now we stand victorious at Trifid. A forgotten city of ruins we rebuilt with our own blood, and we took back with our own blood!" he shouted, raising his fist and his bow in the air victoriously.

"Sephdar! Sephdar! Sephdar!"

"We've heard that our visionary, White Wings, may have been killed with one arrow, but my leadership has shot back against our foes threefold. I tell you today that The Bridge between worlds belongs to us who have fought for it. And this door will remain open under our control. As Lord of the White Palace, I have shown my strength, and I assure you that no one coming from that portal will overtake me or harm the everlasting life of Arcas. This bridge will bring new prosperity and new opportunities to us all. Perhaps my healing, all of our healing, will now come to us from The Bridge between worlds."

As Sephdar finished, the man who held the .44 magnum continued quietly forward watching Arcturus walk slowly to the edge of the high wall.

The centaur could not contain his victorious smile. He knew Arcturus, a leader admired by many, was about to declare Sephdar's throne in front of both his allies and enemies.

"Today, a king and a queen passed from this world, both killed by this violent archer. I am told that it is my duty to proclaim to you now the new ruler, the new king over all Arcas." Arcturus could see the eyes of his enemies perk up with pride and the eyes of his friends drop with sorrow. The good people of the realms had fought hard to preserve their kingdoms, their rulers, and their sovereignty that had survived for thousands of peaceful years. But they had awakened to the danger too late, and the enemy had grown too strong.

"So, I proclaim to you today," Arcturus continued with a clear and booming voice. "There is a new king coming: one who rules with both justice and mercy. There is a new king coming: one who you can trust and love. There is a new king coming: one who holds the hidden secrets about the way between the worlds."

Sephdar puffed his chest, ready for the grand reveal.

"But this beast"—he pointed accusingly while maintaining a straight, calm face—"this centaur who murders a defenseless queen and ravages little villages." Arcturus sped up his words to be sure that every last one of them was heard before they silenced him. "This bastard archer—Sephdar—who was rightfully kicked out of the Free Realms and rightfully banished from the Kingdom Realms is NOT. OUR. KING!" Arcturus ended with a defiant shout then waited for the reaction.

The crowd murmured restlessly. Sephdar's men seemed nervous by Arcturus's words and accusations. Instead of proclaiming their new leader as king, Arcturus had emphasized that Sephdar was neither worthy of kingship nor worthy of a title above archer. Though their hands were bound, the prisoners' confidence and insolence was freed. They remembered the fallen king and the queen. They remembered the slaughter and the pillaging and the burning. Sephdar's promises no longer felt like a freedom from battle and death, but more like an eternal imprisonment to a wicked ruler.

The prisoners began chanting softly:

"Not Our King! Not Our King! Not Our King!"

All eyes were fixed on Sephdar as his face exploded with rage. He would not be mocked, and he would not allow defiance in the midst of his clear victory. Without a second's thought, he whipped an arrow out of his sheath and *Thoong!* The flying dart flew into Arcturus' chest, and he fell forward against the wall. After a moment of shocked hush, the crowd erupted into angry shouts as blood spilled from Arcturus's body over the wall to the ground below.

"No!" Muphrid and Seginus screamed out, lunging forward. The guards standing by the sons grabbed their tied arms, sending blows into their stomachs and faces until they were lying on the ground, powerless to get to their father. Nekkar, who had finally cut through his binds using a sharp edge on his belt cried out, rushing through the crowd in his family's defense. But as he pushed forward person-by-person, ready to fight, a hand reached out and clasped his tightly. He turned with blood-shot passion in his eyes to see who was obstructing his way.

Andi didn't say a word to him as Nekkar whipped back to look at the cloaked face of the one pulling him back. The princess looked not just into his eyes but also deep into his soul. Fresh tears compassionately streamed down her face. Nekkar immediately turned his eyes away from her gaze. He breathed heavily from grief and pain and anger, but he didn't let go of her hand. Her eyes and her tears had said it all. *I'm so sorry. I lost my dad today too. No good will come of fighting right now. Please stay here with me.*

Nekkar knew Andi was right. He returned a squeeze to her hand as if to say, *Okay, I'll stay* and stood next to her, feeling the warmth and comfort flow between their sorrowful hearts. Jackson stood on the other side, holding Andi's other hand. He'd never seen someone good die, not like this, not right in front of his eyes. He rubbed the gem. If he had to, in a moment, he could whisk them all away. He would draw a door and take Andi and Nekkar and as many prisoners with him to the safety of Earth before closing the portal again.

They all watched in horror as the furious centaur lifted a wheezing, bleeding Arcturus up from the wall. Suspended in the air, all eyes fixed on the fading father. With his last burst of breath, Arcturus gasped and pumped one fist in the air.

"Not! Our! King!"

In his final effort to show power over Arcturus, Sephdar ripped the arrow out of his chest. The noble captain roared in pain as the crowd roared in anger. Like a boiling cauldron, blood bubbled up and out of his body, overflowing on Sephdar's hand to the ground below. In seconds Arcturus fell limp. Sephdar hurled his lifeless body into the crowd of prisoners below.

"Not! Our! King!

Not! Our! King!

Not! Our! King!" the prisoners bellowed with full force, pulling their arms apart violently to free them from the ropes.

Standing at the edge of the wall with blood on his hands and hatred erupting out of his soul, Sephdar spewed his ultimate command over the roar of the crowd.

"Kill them! Kill them all!"

But before another prisoner fell at the edge of a sword, deafening shots rang out over all the voices. *BANG! BANG!* Sephdar's four-legged body stumbled to the side, knocking off the tea cup, which spilled and then broke against the ground. Wounded and bleeding, now his body was the one leaning against the wall with blood pooling on the stones beneath. He turned his face in shock toward the one holding the gun while gripping the wall with his bloody hands.

"You?" he gasped with wide eyes and stunned fear. "How?"

The air shook again as the man answered with another shot from the pistol; this time the bullet went straight through Sephdar's head. The centaur's body toppled over the wall. His bloody cloak flew up, landing over his face as he slammed against the ground. Sephdar's exposed torso revealed the true nature of this man-beast: a swirling, poisonous black hole. The entire crowd outside the fortress went silent as they gazed at their infamous "Gurges Ater" now bleeding, lifeless, and dead.

All eyes then turned up again to the fortress walls as a figure came forward to address them. The three men following stayed to the side and out of the way as he set the gun down on the wall where the teacup left a faint liquid circle on the brick. Andi, Jackson, and Nekkar continued to hold hands and threw glances of confusion and concern to each other. No matter what came next, they were in it together.

Clothed in glistening garments, the handsome man looked over the crowd with authority and frustration and concern. No one doubted his identity now, though they all doubted whether he was actually real, alive, and standing before them. The people gasped as he stretched out his enormous white wings. The wingspan seemed so much bigger and the feathers prettier than anyone remembered. And when they looked at the wing that was horribly wounded, they saw that it was whole and completely healed.

No command was issued from above. No word spoken from the crowd below. But every person of every allegiance bowed in awe and approval.

Except three who now stood alone.

APPENDIX

STAR CHARTS

No matter the race, language, culture, or location of a people, the stars play witness to their triumphs, their failures, and their history. These millions of witnesses pierce through the black sky, bringing light when eyes see dimly, bringing hope and beauty when hours feel darkest. Some look to them for enjoyment, some look to them for heroes, and some look to them for revelation. However you look at them tonight, know that it was under the same sky, the same ancient lights, that Jackson found himself the night that his life and his destiny changed forever…

Contained in the next few pages are simplified Star Maps of the constellations that were a source of inspiration for this novel. There are 88 modern-day constellations, many of them have been used as characters, places, and creatures in the World of Arcas series. Familiar star names from the story are also labeled for your enjoyment and exploration of Arcasian mythology. Just as the people and creatures in the World of Arcas have ancient ties to Earth, these familiar constellations also hold an ancient place in our hearts and history. On any clear, dark sky, one should be able to find some of these constellations blazing through the atmosphere and waiting to be discovered, pointed out, and dreamed about. So grab a pair of binoculars or a telescope and explore the evening sky with us.

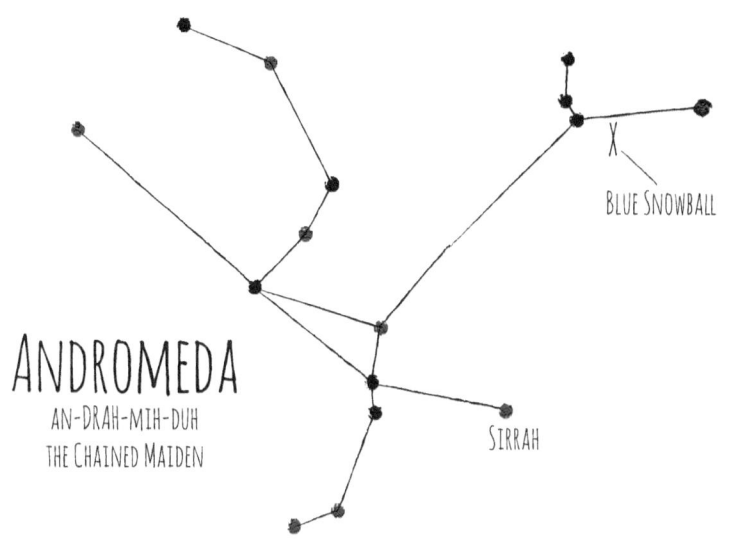

Andromeda
an-drah-mih-duh
the Chained Maiden

X
Blue Snowball

Sirrah

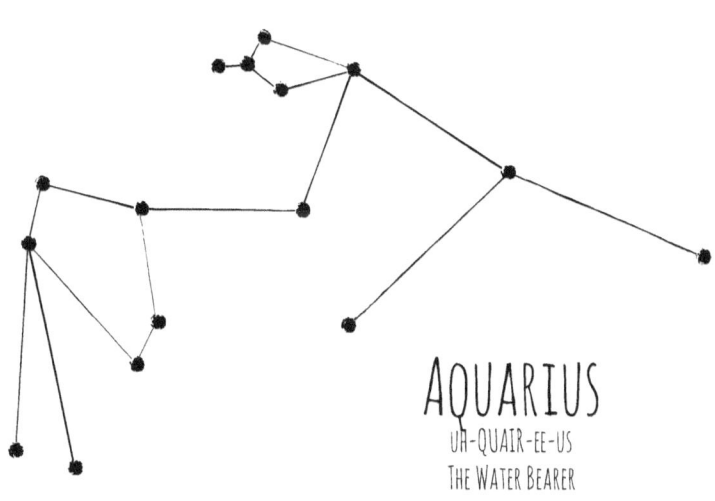

Aquarius
uh-quair-ee-us
The Water Bearer

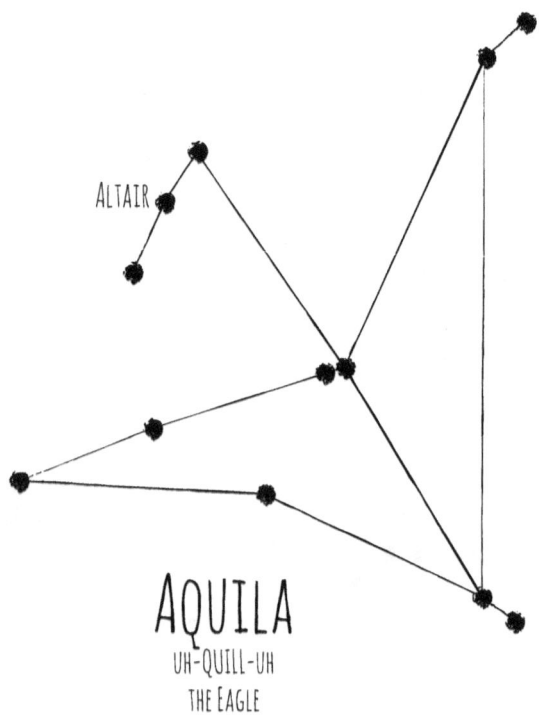

Altair

Aquila

uh-quill-uh

the Eagle

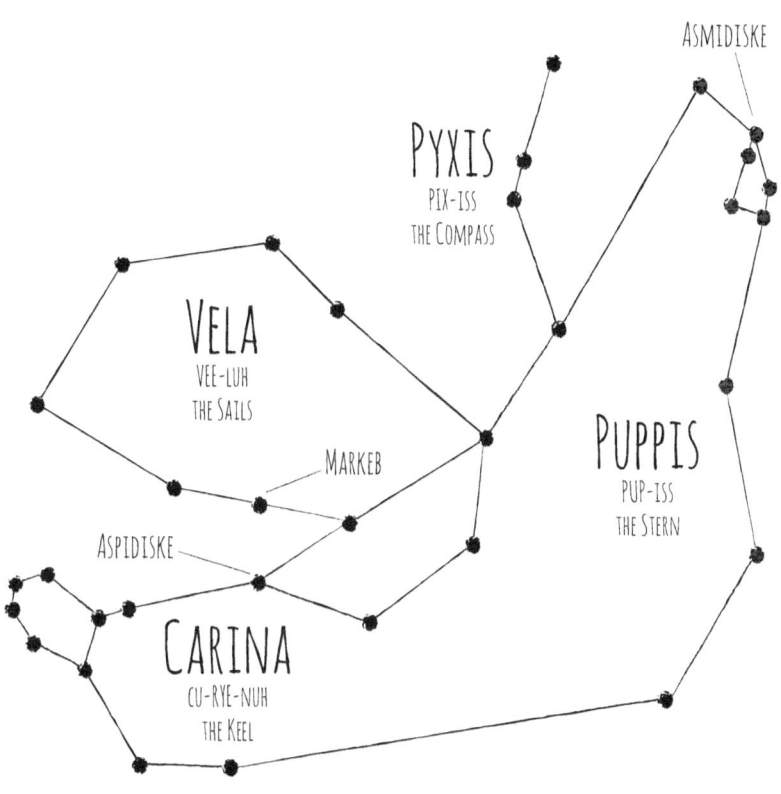

Argo Navis

Argo Navis was one of the original 48 constellations listed by Ptolemy. In 1752, it was split in to the four constellations above because of its massive size. The chapter "Argo Navis sails again" is a reference to this original constellation.

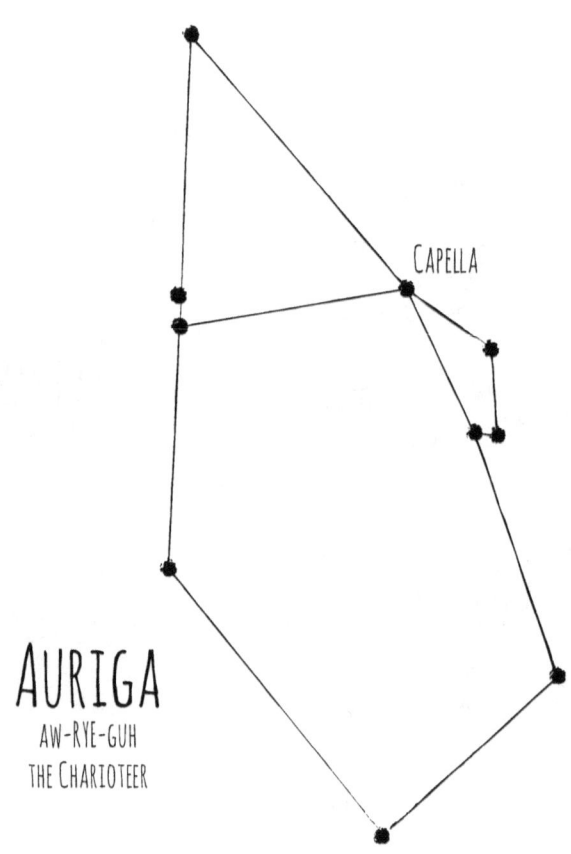

Capella

AURIGA
aw-rye-guh
the Charioteer

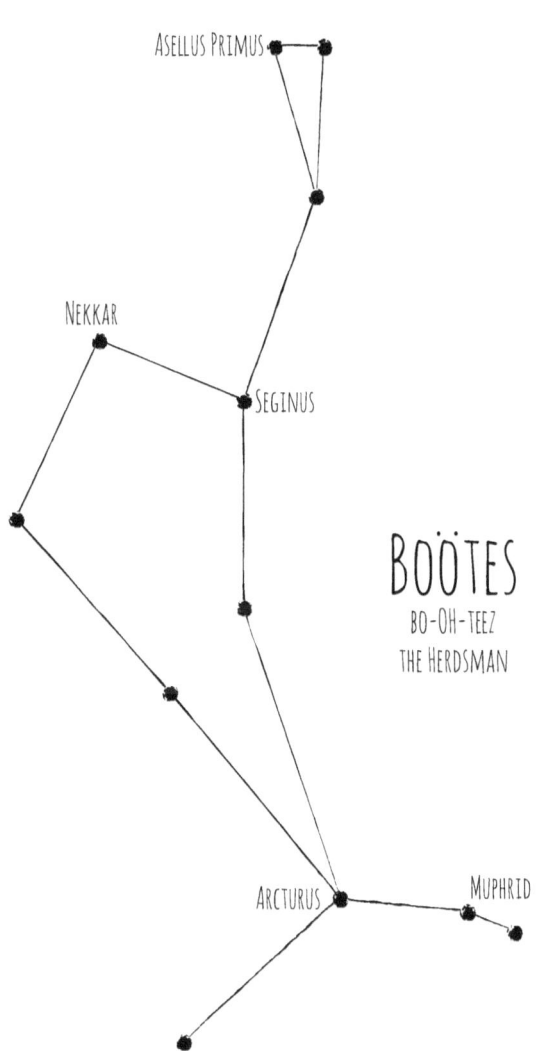

Asellus Primus

Nekkar

Seginus

Boötes

bo-oh-teez
the Herdsman

Arcturus

Muphrid

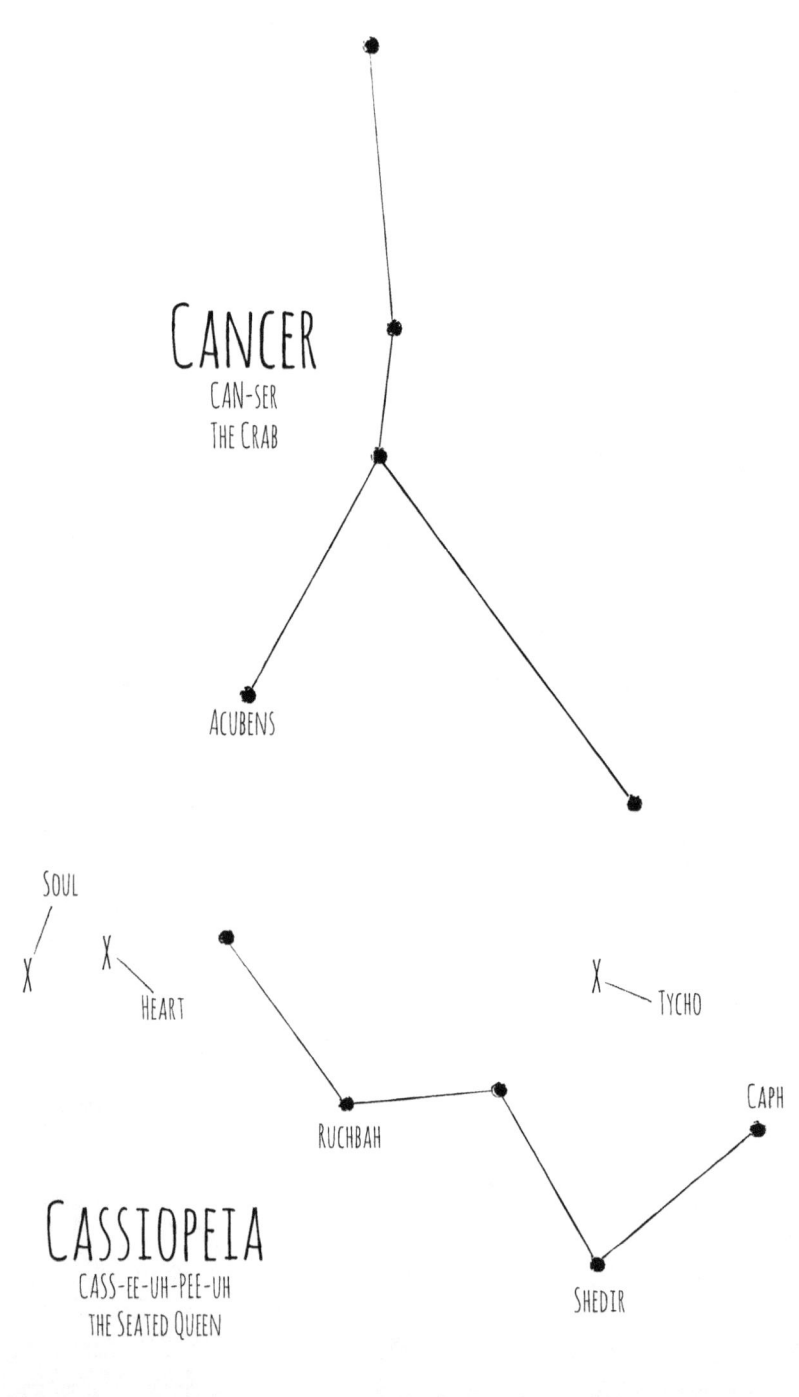

Cancer
CAN-ser
The Crab

Acubens

Soul

Heart

Tycho

Caph

Ruchbah

Shedir

Cassiopeia
CASS-ee-uh-pee-uh
the Seated Queen

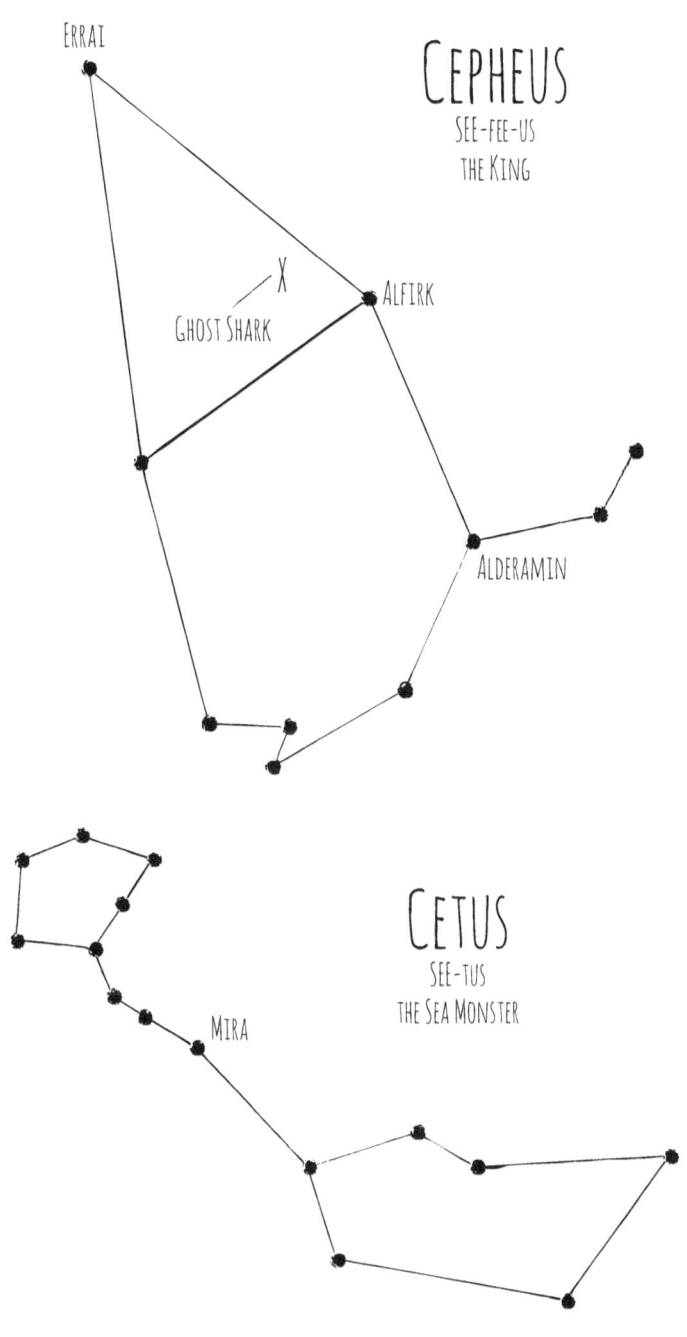

Errai

Cepheus
See-fee-us
the King

X
Ghost Shark

Alfirk

Alderamin

Cetus
See-tus
the Sea Monster

Mira

Coma Berenices
COE-muh BER-uh-NICE-eez
The Bernice's Hair

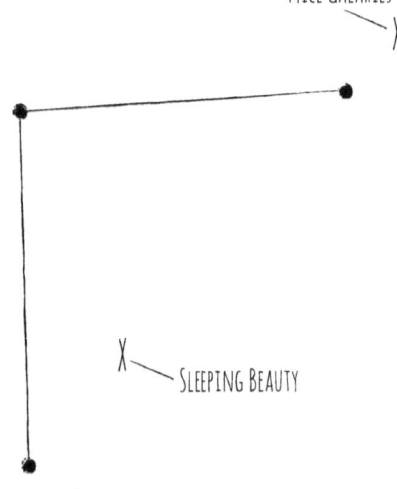

Mice Galaxies

X

X ← Sleeping Beauty

Corvus
COR-vus
the Crow

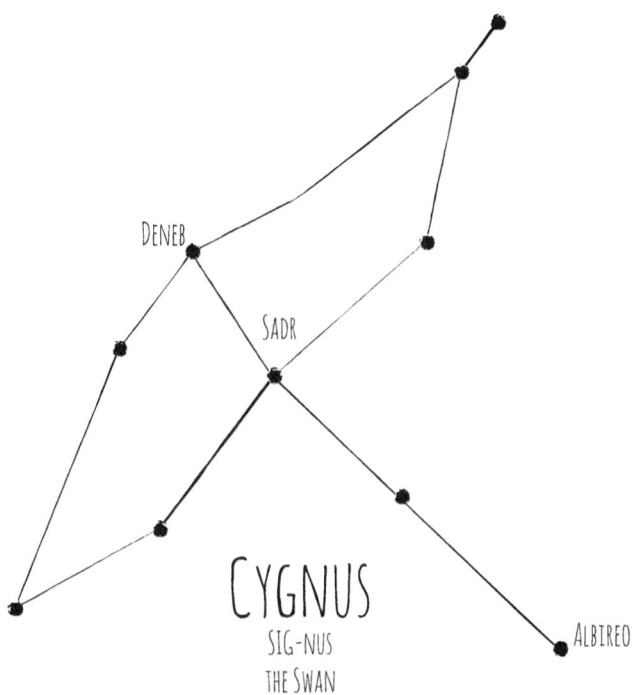

Deneb

Sadr

CYGNUS
SIG-NUS
THE SWAN

ALBIREO

DRACO
DRAY-CO
THE DRAGON

ELTANIN

THUBAN

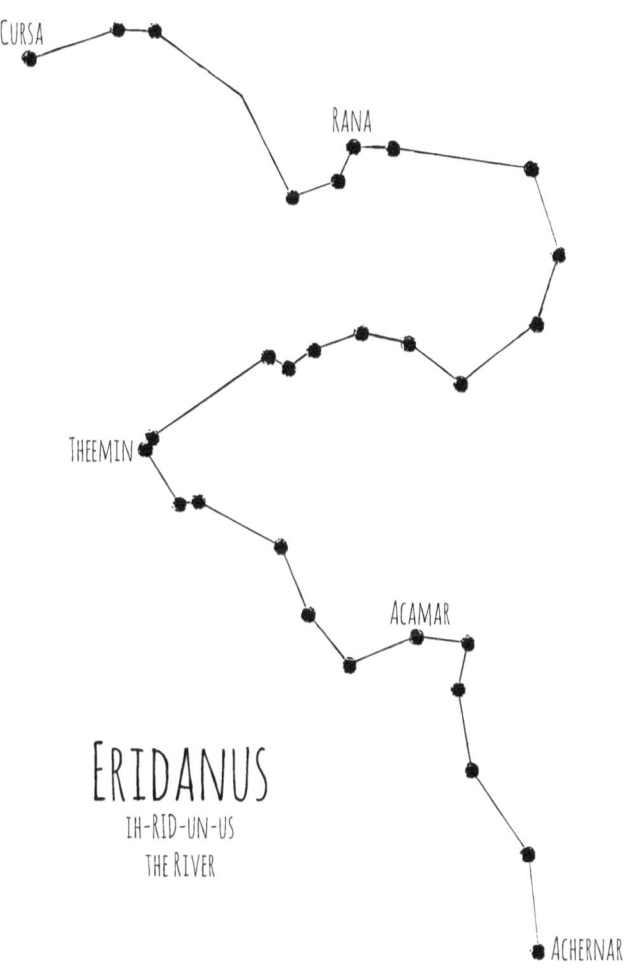

Cursa

Rana

Theemin

Acamar

Achernar

Eridanus

ih-rid-un-us
the River

GEMINI

JEM-UH-NYE
The Twins

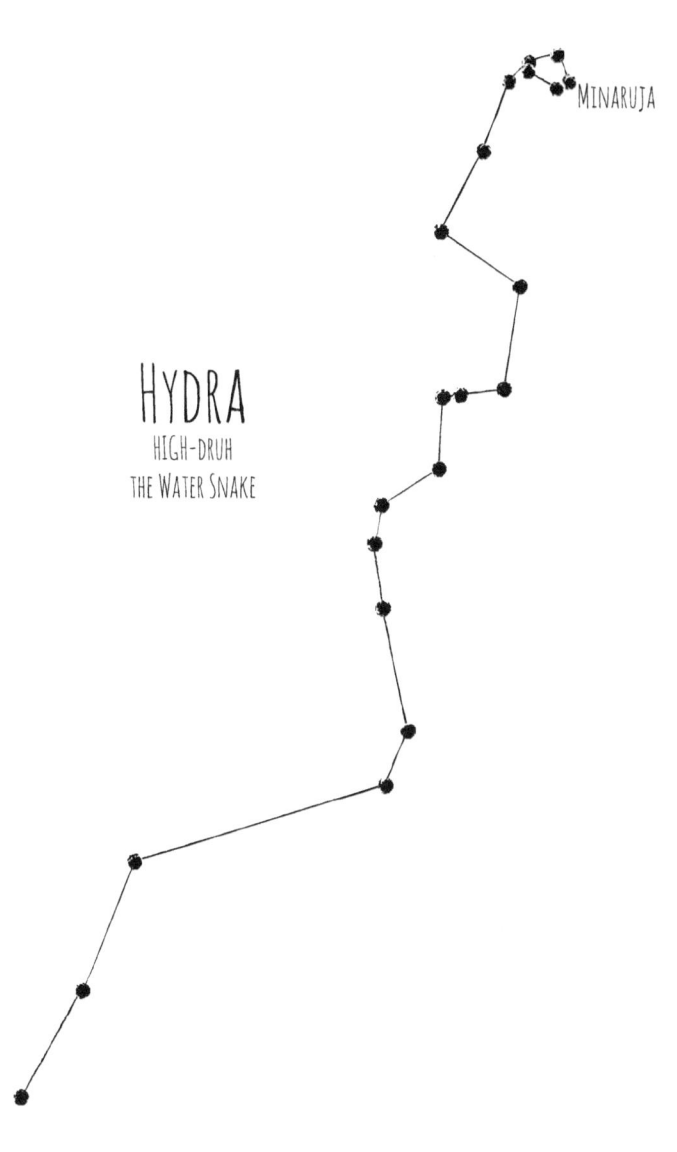

HYDRA
HIGH-DRUH
THE WATER SNAKE

MINARUJA

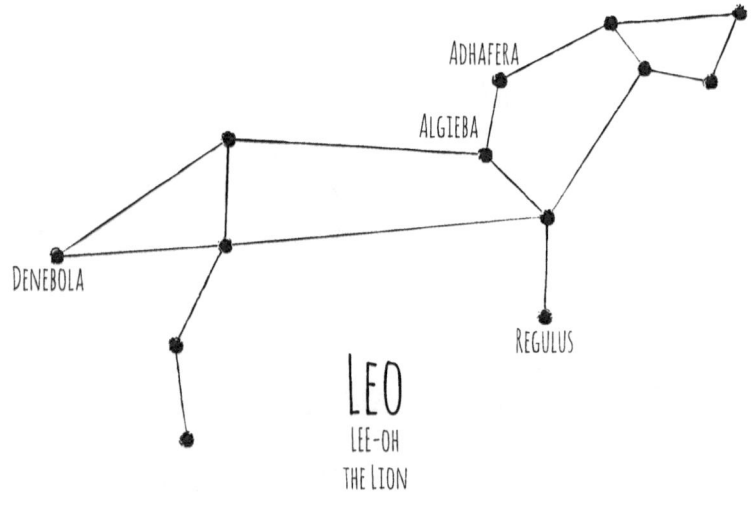

Adhafera

Algieba

Denebola

Regulus

LEO
LEE-OH
THE LION

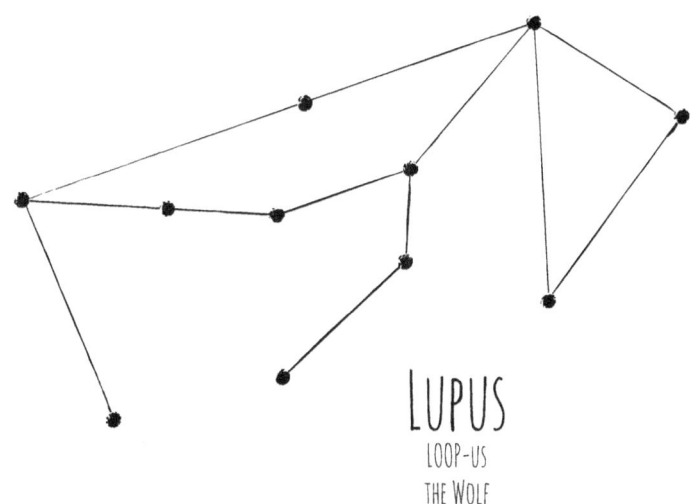

LUPUS
LOOP-us
the Wolf

LYRA
LYE-ruh
the Lyre

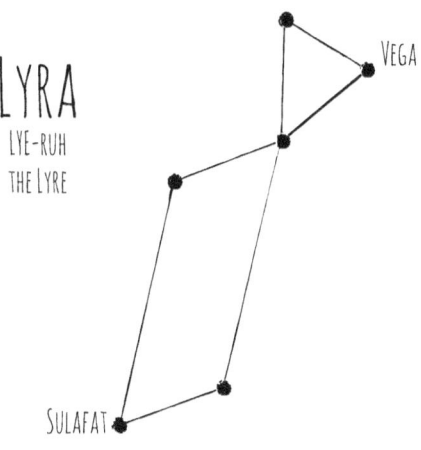

Vega

Sulafat

A lyre is a stringed musical instrument.

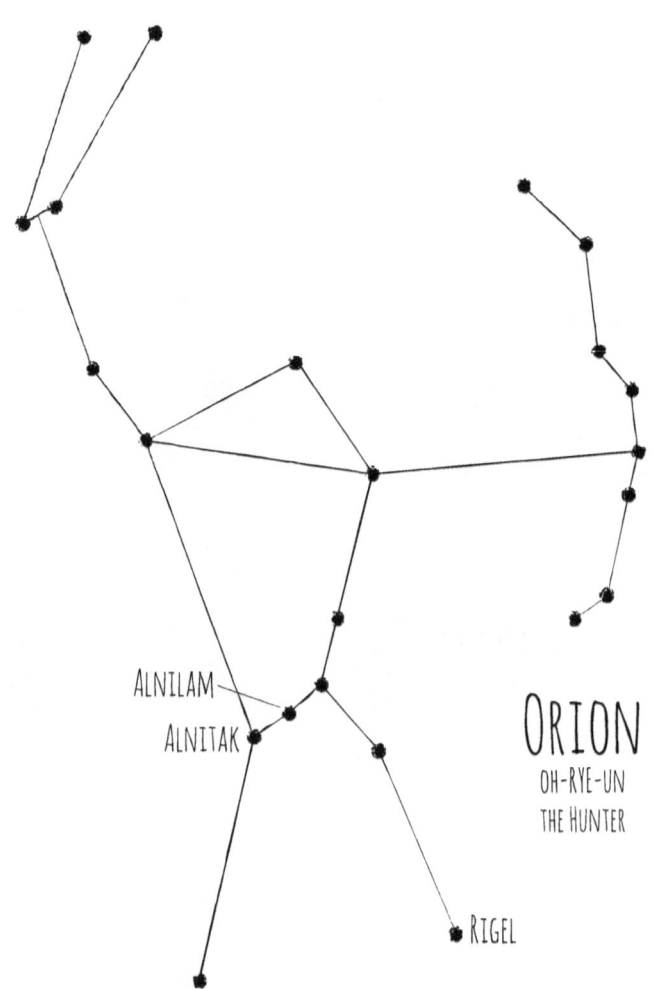

ALNILAM

ALNITAK

ORION
OH-RYE-UN
THE HUNTER

RIGEL

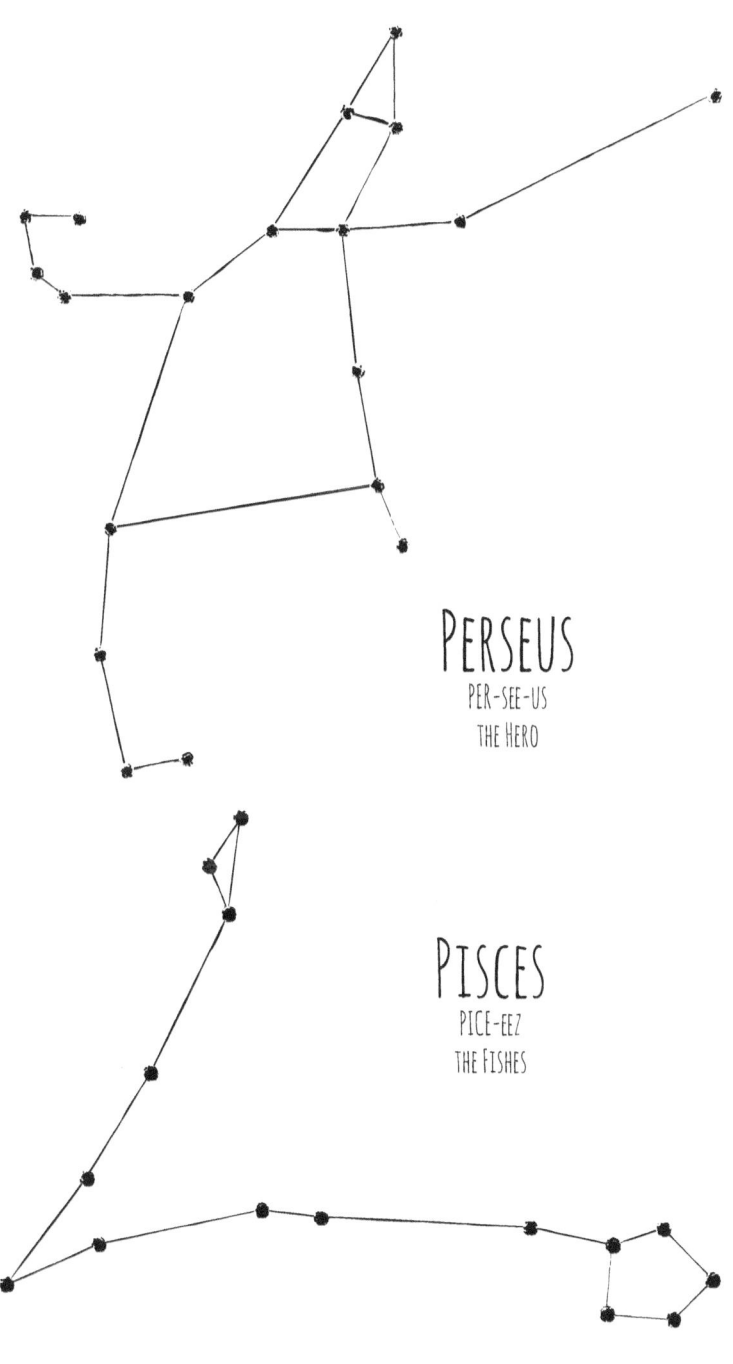

PERSEUS

PER-SEE-US

THE HERO

PISCES

PICE-EEZ

THE FISHES

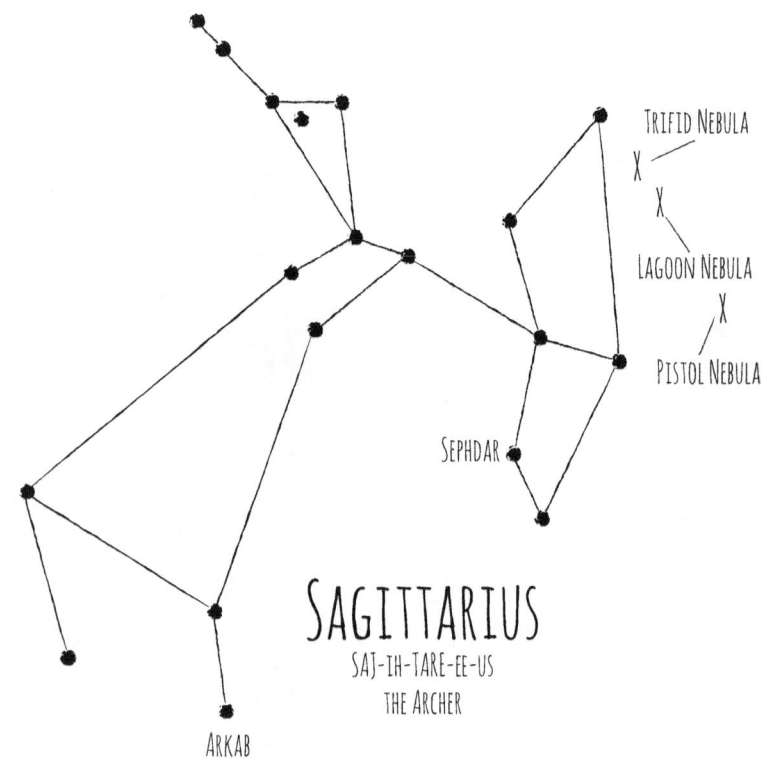

Trifid Nebula

X

X

Lagoon Nebula

X

Pistol Nebula

Sephdar

SAGITTARIUS
SAJ-ih-TARE-ee-us
the Archer

Arkab

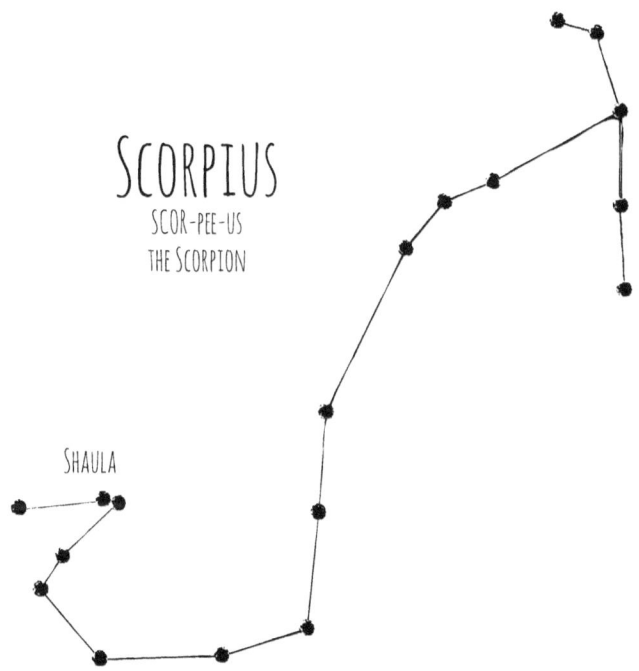

Scorpius

SCOR-PEE-US
THE SCORPION

Shaula

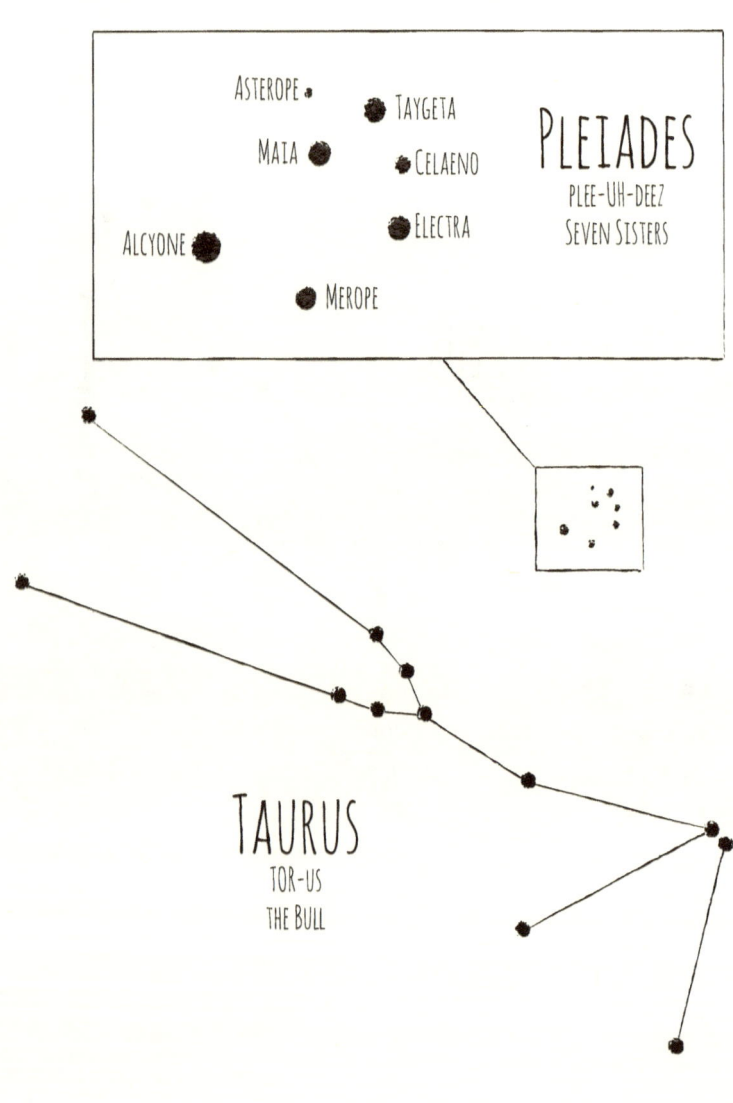

ASTEROPE

TAYGETA

MAIA

CELAENO

ELECTRA

ALCYONE

MEROPE

PLEIADES
plee-uh-deez
SEVEN SISTERS

TAURUS
tor-us
the Bull

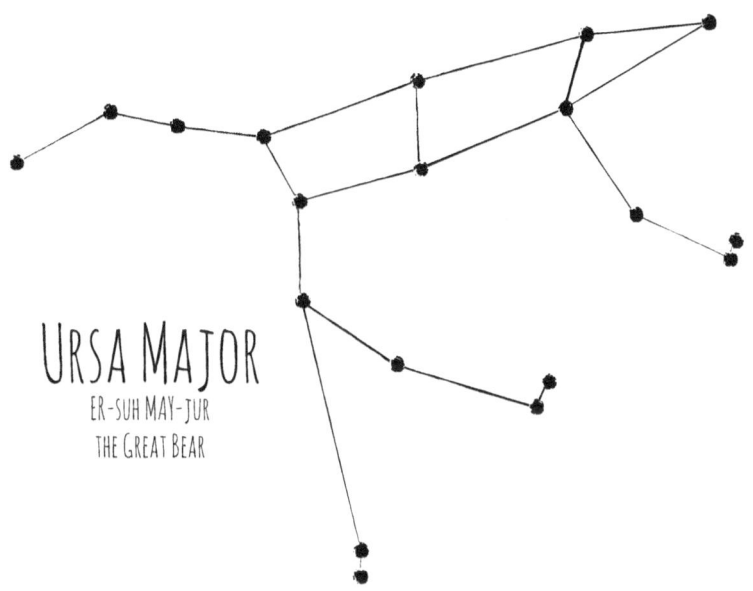

Ursa Major

ER-SUH MAY-JUR
THE GREAT BEAR

LODESTAR
(POLARIS)

URSA MINOR
ER-SUH MY-NER
THE LITTLE BEAR

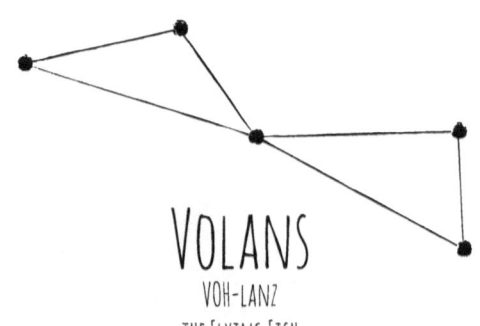

VOLANS
VOH-LANZ
THE FLYING FISH

Haikus of Acknowledgement

Creative Father
Fiery Wind swell within
mold us like Jesus

Irreplaceable
our Woolets and Langhofers
thick blood, lots of love

Ben and Barbara
joining our journey with joy
delight in friendship

Jessica Baron
delightful Science Café
expert reviewer

Walatka's thoughtful
analyzing with logic
didactic angles

Regina Wamba
breathing out beauty
in cover designs

Family Leiter
words floating in moving van
robust group edit

Amy Eye, keen eye
for commas, syntax, and flow
chiseling rough words

Anna, sister dear
superb reader of fiction
splendid in spirit

Marketing Mandy
precisely pressing the press
thankful thoughts of you

Joel and Paul playing
songs of Arcas with lyre
fantasy music

Friends at M.A.S.
star gazers encouraging
vast exploration

Praying, supporting,
together as one body
our dear Riverside

Analytical
great critics writing on web
thank you Reviewers

Perusing pages
boldly entering Arcas
wonderful Readers

B. I. Woolet *(Benji & Ila Woolet)* is the author of the World of Arcas series. Their Arcas adventures began with *The Hunter, the Bear, and the Seventh Sister* and now continue with *Arrows of Darkness*. When the Woolets aren't working, writing, or chasing their four little girls around, they are active in their local community and church. The couple enjoys creating lyrical and literary arts, playing music together, and exploring nature. They are happily married and live in Indiana.

> Connect with the authors!
> www.worldofarcas.com
> www.facebook.com/WorldOfArcas
> Twitter: @worldofarcas

> Find the books on Amazon, Barnes & Noble, iBookstore, and Goodreads.

> Thanks for your support! Please share the World of Arcas with a friend!